EMPIRE OF BONES

BOOK ONE OF THE EMPIRE OF BONES SAGA

BOOK ONE OF THE EMPIRE OF BONES SAGA

EMPIRE
OF BONES

*The Terran
Empire is
dead...*

*Long Live
the Empire!*

TERRY MIXON

BESTSELLING AUTHOR OF *VEIL OF SHADOWS*

Empire of Bones
Copyright © 2014 by Terry Mixon

All rights reserved. No part of this book may be reproduced or transmitted in any form or by any means, electronic or mechanical, including information storage and/or retrieval systems, or dissemination of any electronic version, without the prior written consent of the publisher, except by a reviewer, who may quote brief passages in a review, and except where permitted by law.

This is a work of fiction. All names, characters, places, and incidents are the products of the author's imagination, or are used fictitiously. Any resemblance to actual persons, living or dead, events, or locales is entirely coincidental.

Published by Yowling Cat Press ®
Second Print ISBN: 978-1947376090
Second Edition date: 12/26/2017

First Print ISBN: 978-0692268698
First Print Edition date: 07/25/2014

Cover art - image copyrights as follows:
DepositPhotos/innovari (Luca Oleastri)
NASA and STScI (Hubble)
Footage Firm, Inc
Donna Mixon

Cover design and composition by Donna Mixon

Print edition interior design composition by Terry Mixon and Donna Mixon

Editing services by Red Adept Editing
Reach them at: http://www.redadeptediting.com

Audio edition performed and produced by Veronica Giguere
Reach her at: v@voicesbyveronica.com

TERRY'S BOOKS

You can always find the most up to date listing of Terry's titles on his Amazon Author Page.

The Empire of Bones Saga
Empire of Bones
Veil of Shadows
Command Decisions
Ghosts of Empire
Paying the Price
Reconnaissance in Force
Behind Enemy Lines
The Terran Gambit

The Empire of Bones Saga Volume 1

The Humanity Unlimited Saga
Liberty Station
Freedom Express
Tree of Liberty

The Fractured Republic Saga
Storm Divers

The Scorched Earth Saga
Scorched Earth

The Vigilante Duology with Glynn Stewart
Heart of Vengeance
Oath of Vengeance

Want Terry to email you when he publishes a new book in any format or when one goes on sale?
Go to TerryMixon.com/Mailing-List and sign up.
Those are the only times he'll contact you. No spam.

DEDICATION

This book would not be possible without the love, support, and encouragement of my beautiful wife. Donna, I love you more than life itself.

ACKNOWLEDGEMENTS

Once again, the people who read my books before you see them have saved me. Thanks to Tracy Bodine, Paul E. Cooley, Michael Falkner, Cain Hopwood, Kristopher Neidecker, Bob Noble, Jon Paul Olivier, Felix R. Savage, Christa Wick, and Jason Young for making me look good.

I also want to thank my readers for putting up with me.
You guys are great.

1

Commander Jared Mertz, captain of the Fleet destroyer *Athena*, looked up from his console when his tactical officer spoke. "Contacts bearing two-five-zero by three-three-zero. Gravitic scanners show at least three ships under power and on a slow course toward Orbital One."

He leaned forward in his seat and gave Lieutenant Zia Anderson his full attention. "Put them on the main screen."

The forward display switched from a tedious view of the asteroid they were in a close orbit of to a graphical representation of the immediate area of space. A small blue circle represented his ship. The enemy task force, marked with a red diamond, appeared on a projected course that took it ahead of and below *Athena*'s position. Its current range was just over a million kilometers.

Its slow speed prevented its grav drive signatures from showing up on the gravitic scanners beyond this short range. By his estimation, the task force would need to increase speed by twenty or thirty percent before Orbital One might detect it from deeper in the system.

If *Athena* had been actively scanning with the normal space scanners, the enemy would've detected them much further out and gone dark before the destroyer noticed them. Relying on only the passive and gravitic scanners had been the only way to spot them first.

"Have they seen us?" Jared asked.

The tall redheaded officer shook her head. "I don't think so, Captain. The asteroid we're grappled to seems to have fooled them."

"Keep all active scanners offline, but arm the missile tubes and bring all combat systems to standby. Sound general quarters and send a tight-beam warning to Orbital One."

"Aye, sir."

Lieutenant Pasco Ramirez, *Athena*'s helmsman, examined his console readouts. "Their drives are at minimum, sir. They probably exited the flip point about three hours ago. At their current speed, they'll cross our orbit in about half an hour."

They officially called the incongruity in the space-time fabric that allowed for interstellar travel an Osborne-Levinson Bridge, but no one outside a university used that name. Jared figured it hadn't taken more than fifteen minutes before someone called it a flip point, because that was exactly what happened when the special drives pulled on the weakened area of empty space. The ship ceased to exist in one planetary system and appeared in a different one light-years away.

It had made the existence of the Old Empire possible, and the rebellion that had destroyed it.

"Be ready to bring our drives online at a moment's notice." Jared returned his attention to his tactical officer. "I want to fire two salvos of missiles after they pass us, just before they're out of effective range."

"Sir, we don't have any speed built up," she warned. "They'll have us as soon as they pivot."

The red-team ships would need to turn before they could return fire, because the massive drives a starship required left no room for missile tubes aft.

"I know. With their momentum and course, we might be able to get out of easy firing range before then. If we want to make these war games more than a toss-up, we need to bloody their noses. Keep working on possible scenarios while I chat with Commander Graves."

He opened a channel to operations. *Athena*'s executive officer appeared on Jared's console a few moments later. His second in command already knew what Zia had reported, but Jared summarized the situation and his plan to make the red team pay for its inattention.

Lieutenant Commander Charlie Graves grinned. "It's about time they showed up. I was beginning to think they'd gotten lost."

"I'm sure Admiral Yeats would have something incisive to say about that in the after-action report."

"Wouldn't he?" The lanky officer glanced away from the screen. "Okay, we're starting to get some better data now. It looks like six hostiles, tentatively identified as three destroyers, two light cruisers, and a heavy. We're not supposed to know who's participating in the exercise, but Ensign Enova says she's sure the heavy cruiser is *Spear*. She served her midshipman's cruise on her. The ships match what we'd expect to see of his task force."

Jared allowed the corner of his mouth to twitch upward. "We'll overlook that little violation of the simulation guidelines just this once. Who's in command of *Spear*?"

"Wallace Breckenridge. The ensign says he's a real by-the-book kind of guy. Apparently, he's not the kind that appreciates anyone thinking outside the box."

"Then we'll be giving him quite the unpleasant wakeup call. Let me know if you see anything else as they close range. Bridge out."

The six red diamonds slowly inched toward *Athena* on the screen. The red team would intersect her course about four hundred thousand kilometers away, just inside *Athena*'s most effective targeting range—half a million kilometers.

Time crept by as Jared waited for the enemy to notice their presence or perhaps send a destroyer to check the asteroid out, but they didn't. He let the distance between them open again once they'd passed until the enemy was almost out of optimal missile range.

"Separate from the asteroid, Pasco. Zia, as soon as you have a passive lock, fire. Don't go active until they respond. We might get the second salvo off before they can react."

The screen lit up with four amber sparks representing *Athena*'s missiles as they exited the tubes. They screamed toward the enemy task force, their grav drives at maximum.

"Missiles away," Zia said. "Telemetry indicates target acquisition. Thirty seconds until interception. Tubes reloading."

There wasn't any reaction from the red team for several more seconds, and Jared could imagine some scanner officers gaping as the missiles appeared from nowhere and came howling in from astern. Zia launched a second set of missiles just as the enemy formation changed speed and began turning.

"Full acceleration," Jared snapped. "Evasive maneuvers. Set course for the outer system. Use the asteroid for cover as long as you can." Few of the eight missiles they'd launched would get through the red team's defensive fire, but even one would be enough to leave a mark.

He waited for the enemy task force to return fire, but it didn't. Hadn't the red team been at combat stations? He could almost hear the klaxons blaring and see the men rushing to bring their missiles online.

The enemy destroyers broke formation and began accelerating after them. Their antimissile railguns fired at *Athena*'s first salvo, destroying two of them. Another detonated short of *Spear*, while the fourth lit up the heavy cruiser.

"Hit on the primary target," Zia crowed. "It took him astern. High probability of serious internal damage."

The enemy ships finally brought their weapons online, and a swarm of missiles streamed after *Athena*—four from each destroyer, six from the light cruisers, but only three from the heavy cruiser. Less than half the eight Jared had expected from the large ship.

Still, twenty-seven missiles were much more than a destroyer like *Athena* ever wanted to see chasing her, even at extreme range. "Electronic countermeasures," he said. "Evasion pattern delta."

"I'm working on it," Zia responded curtly, obviously too focused to realize that wasn't precisely the tone an officer should use with her captain.

He grinned in spite of the tense situation. He loved his people.

Athena's second salvo roared in on the enemy. The destroyers had pulled far enough away from their larger brethren that they could no longer provide effective antimissile defenses for them. Their absence became clear when a second missile slammed into *Spear*. The massive cruiser rolled as explosions wracked her internally. It looked like her drives had failed.

Electronic countermeasures lured many of the red team missiles aside. *Athena*'s railguns accounted for some of the rest. The number of missiles that had acquired them at this range surprised Jared. Five got through their defensive fire and roared down on *Athena* like the wrath of God.

The bridge went dark. The only sound Jared could hear was Zia cursing. The consoles reset as the simulation ended and returned to standby mode, still locked out of operational control of the destroyer.

The main screen came to life, showing the curve of the planet Avalon below them. Orbital One sat about ten thousand meters away. The breathtaking view dissolved as Zia put an incoming transmission on the screen.

Admiral Robert Yeats, Commanding Officer of Capital Fleet, shook his head. "While that was a glorious death, Commander, you still lost your ship."

Jared smiled ruefully. "The target was too tempting to pass up, Admiral. I didn't expect their fire to be so accurate at long range."

"Save the heroics for when you don't have a choice. You should've let them pass and been satisfied with warning us they were coming. That *is* what a picket is for, you know."

"Yes, sir."

"The better targeting was one of the enemy advantages for this war

Empire of Bones 5

game. I'm impressed that only five of their missiles got through your defenses. You almost got away with your sneak attack."

"As you say, sir, almost wasn't good enough this time."

The screen split as Captain Breckenridge of *Spear*—probably also the red team commander—and Captain Alice Quinn, the blue team commander, came into the circuit. Breckenridge looked pissed, Quinn bland.

"What kind of bull was that?" Breckenridge demanded. "The sim didn't display *Athena* correctly."

"Actually, it did," Quinn said. "Commander Mertz used an asteroid as cover. Well done, Jared."

"Thank you, ma'am, but I still lost my ship. Not a good day for me or my crew."

The dark-skinned captain nodded. "True, but you took out a heavy cruiser. *Spear*'s fusion plants went critical right after you blew up. That took her out and damaged both light cruisers. That said, while it was an excellent trade-off from a strictly tactical perspective, I'd prefer you came back home alive."

Breckenridge bristled. "*Athena*'s actions were clearly outside the boundaries of—"

"That's enough, Wallace," Yeats said in a tone that brooked no disagreement. "Just accept that you lost this one. Maybe next time you'll be a little more paranoid. That's why we have these war games, to learn what we can before the real shooting starts."

The admiral glanced at his chrono. "We'll have our after-action briefing in one hour on Orbital One. Get something to eat and come ready to tear this operation apart. We have a number of things to discuss. Dismissed. Mertz, please adjourn to your office and stay on the channel."

Jared left Zia in charge of the bridge, took the lift down one deck, and made his way to his office. He wondered what the admiral wanted with him. To chew him out in private? That wasn't the old man's style. He'd tear a limb off you in public and use it to beat you to death if he thought you deserved it.

Once he came back on the channel, the flag officer continued, "Once again, Commander, well done. I'm afraid you won't be joining us for the briefing, though. Send your executive officer to cover for you. You have other plans."

"That sounds ominous, sir."

The admiral smiled. "Not really. Your father has requested the pleasure of your company for dinner. He wants to see you one last time before you ship out on the survey tomorrow."

Jared kept his face blank, but inside he cursed. The very last people he wanted to spend time with were his father and half siblings.

"I see. I will, of course, represent Fleet with honor."

The admiral's brows drew together. "Far be it from me to dictate the actions of a fellow officer in his social life, but when the ruler of the Terran Empire requests our presence, we go.

"Allow me to also stress that while you might have reservations about your relationship with the Imperial Family, it isn't prudent to make an issue of them, even over a secure channel with someone who's known you since you joined Fleet. It's far safer if people think you're happy to be the emperor's son, even if you were born on the wrong side of the sheets."

Yeats leaned forward and spoke more softly. "Fleet is *supposed* to be nonpolitical, but you need to be the most enthusiastic supporter of the Empire and the Imperial Family. People are watching and waiting for you to give them a reason to hold your illegitimate birth against you. You can't give them a lever to use against you, Jared."

Jared sighed a little. "You won't find a more ardent supporter of the Empire or the emperor, sir. It's just hard to be enthusiastic when my half siblings loath me and don't miss a single opportunity to make their objections to my presence painfully clear. The heir couldn't hate me more if I peed in his soup. Rubbing my existence in his face is not doing me or Fleet any favors. One day he'll lead the Empire and I'll be on the beach." *Or dead.*

"The emperor is in excellent health, and the heir wouldn't dare take out a vendetta against a Fleet officer. Don't be so melodramatic."

The admiral hadn't seen how deeply Ethan Bandar hated Jared. No one else had heard the threats the man made when no one else was around. They got worse every time the emperor insisted that Jared come to the Imperial Palace, too.

"I wish I shared your...optimism, sir."

"I'll see you at the final mission briefing tomorrow morning, Commander. Have a good time. Consider that an order." The screen went dark.

Perfect. Jared wished the admiral understood everything he'd had to endure after the Fleet entrance physical had revealed his parentage. He couldn't comprehend why the emperor insisted on torturing him two or three times a year with these "family get-togethers."

Not that any of it mattered, though. He'd go, and he'd do his best not to let his relatives get under his skin.

He summoned Graves to his office. When his friend had taken a seat,

Empire of Bones

he filled him in on his dinner plans. Graves knew how he felt. He'd understand.

Jared took a deep breath and tried to relax his tense back. "I suppose I should be used to the situation. It's been fifteen years since I found out I was his son, but his children complicate things. I'm living proof that their father had an affair, and I'm the reason their mother divorced him. Not a good recipe for making friends."

"I suppose not," his friend said. "I bet we could come up with some mechanical failure requiring your presence."

Jared allowed himself a small smile. "I appreciate the thought, but I don't think that would go over very well the day before we leave on our grand exploration mission. Besides, my news isn't all bad."

Graves gave Jared a suspicious look, probably because of his captain's mock-cheerful tone. "Oh? How's that?"

"I don't have to go to the after action briefing and have Breckenridge burn holes through me with his eyes. You get that honor."

"Today just keeps getting worse," Graves grumbled. "You'd think being blown into atoms would be the ultimate low point, but somehow you found a way to make death appealing. Thanks, Jared."

"What can I say? I'm a beacon of joy. Don't wait up."

2

Princess Kelsey Bandar looked up from her reading as her brother stalked into the library. His thunderous expression gave her just enough warning to mark her place before he exploded.

"He's coming to dinner tonight." The petulant snarl in Ethan's voice dripped with venom.

Those few words told her everything she needed to know about his less-than-temperate behavior. The Bastard was gracing them with his presence tonight. Ethan's use of the word made the mental capitalization mandatory. To be fair, she'd used the word in the same way.

She set her book aside and gave Ethan her complete attention. "I honestly don't understand—why do you let him enrage you like this? You know there's nothing we can do to stop Father from having a relationship with him. I'm not even sure we should try anymore."

Ethan stared at her, shocked. "How can you say that? It's obvious what the scum wants."

She leaned back in her chair. "Is it? I'm not so certain these days. If Jared Mertz was trying to take advantage of his blood, you'd think he'd be a little more aggressive in advancing his career."

"The Bastard forces himself on us time and time again, all Father ever does is cater to him, and now you've become his apologist? The man wants something, and I'm not convinced he won't get it. Father has been muttering and planning something."

She regarded her brother coolly. "In the fifteen years we've known he's been around, I've never heard of him asking for one thing. Not for himself. Not even for Fleet. And God knows Father has a soft spot in his heart for Fleet."

"But... How can you defend him?"

Her brother's anguished face tore at her heart, but she couldn't keep catering to his fixation. "Because Jared Mertz isn't the one that created our family's problem. Father had an affair. Father had a child out of wedlock. Father shamed Mother so badly she divorced him. Jared Mertz is as much a victim of circumstances as we are."

Ethan slapped his palm on the table sharply, making her jump. "No, he is not. I think he knew *exactly* the chain of events joining Fleet would start. He did so knowing that the medical test would show precisely what it did. This is part of a long-range plan to steal our birthright."

That was ridiculous. Kelsey only barely smothered a chuckle. It wouldn't improve her brother's mood one bit. "Take a deep breath. This isn't some deep-seated conspiracy to displace you. Father would never allow that, even if the Imperial Senate did...which it won't. You've let this delusion eat at you too long. You need to get a grip."

Ethan's expression darkened further. "You're being dangerously naive, Kelsey. If one of us needs to wake up, it's you. The Bastard wants the power of the Imperial Throne. Rest assured he won't fool me as easily as he has you. Tell Father I feel ill."

Ethan stalked out of the library even angrier than when he'd arrived.

She rubbed the bridge of her nose tiredly. The normally levelheaded heir to the Imperial Throne had an unhealthy dislike for their half brother. It wasn't reassuring in a man who would one day rule the Empire. The Emperor couldn't afford to have the same kind of petty jealousies as everyone else.

Jared Mertz was a pain in her behind, too, but she had finally gained some hard-won perspective. At worst, he was some kind of power seeker, and her father would eventually see through him. He would never be more than an irritant for her or her brother.

When Jared had appeared in their lives, she'd been just old enough to understand that her family was coming apart because of him. It had taken far longer for her to realize he wasn't responsible for her parents' divorce. That didn't mean she had to like him, but she no longer blindly hated him as Ethan did.

As far as she could see, Father's formal acknowledgment of his bastard son had drastically complicated Jared Mertz's life. It made advancement in Fleet more difficult, because they avoided even the appearance of favoritism. Her discreet checks had revealed his

Empire of Bones

commanders considered him a brilliant officer, and he was long overdue for promotion to captain.

She tried to get back into the book she'd been reading, but her mind refused to focus. The subject of the Empire before the rebellion and resulting Fall usually fascinated her, but she couldn't stop thinking about her half brother…and about herself.

He commanded a Fleet ship now. He'd been twenty-two Terran Standard years old—the same age as she was now—when he'd joined Fleet. He'd known what he'd wanted, and he'd pursued that goal with a single-minded determination even she had to envy. What would she be doing in fifteen years?

With Ethan as the heir, she needed to find a long-term career. Being the spare apparent wasn't very fulfilling. Once her brother married and had children of his own, she wouldn't even be that. She'd be just one more Imperial noblewoman without real purpose in her life. As if there weren't enough of those in the capital.

Fleet wasn't a good fit for her. She'd never been particularly good at obeying orders. None of the social work she'd done had excited her that much, as important as it was. She wanted an all-consuming purpose that she could dedicate her life toward fulfilling. She wanted the things she did to count for something once she was gone.

She sighed. She wouldn't solve that problem tonight. She might as well go see Father. He'd be looking for her soon enough anyway.

Kelsey found Emperor Karl Bandar of the Terran Empire sitting in his private office dressed in the ratty old jacket that he loved. The grey in his beard was almost as plentiful as the chestnut brown. It made her sad to see him age. She wanted him to continue being the vital young man she'd chased around the garden as a girl.

He looked up from his console and smiled. "Kelsey! I was just coming to look for you. We're having company for dinner."

"I heard. Father, you know Ethan doesn't enjoy these dinners."

Her father took off his glasses and set them on his desk. "I know. This is something he needs to adjust to, whether he likes it or not. Jared is his half brother. Yours too, of course. Nothing can change that."

"Yet Jared does none of us any favors by rubbing Ethan's face in it."

Her father looked confused. "Jared? How is he rubbing anyone's face in anything? I've never seen him be anything but polite. Even when others are not," he added pointedly.

"I mean him continually forcing himself on us like this."

"He's not arranging these visits. I am."

She stared at him. "You? I don't understand."

"I've apparently been too vague with my intentions. My apologies. I invite Jared to visit us several times a year so that all of you can come to know one another."

Kelsey sat down in one of the comfortable chairs scattered around the small room. "We've always assumed he was behind them. Ethan is quite certain the man is out to steal the Crown Jewels. Unsurprisingly, Ethan will not be joining us tonight."

The revelation didn't seem to be that big a surprise to her father. "I'll talk with him. Again. I'm sorry for giving you both a false impression. I suspect that Jared doesn't enjoy these gatherings any more than you do. I'd hoped to ease him into the family, but I've probably botched that, too. Perhaps you'd be so kind as to explain it to me: how can I rule dozens of worlds and yet screw up my personal life so badly?"

"I'm going to treat that as a rhetorical question. This...changes things. It's a bit embarrassing."

Her father sighed. "I'm sorry, sweetheart. I specifically invited Jared to dine with us tonight because he'll be leaving on a long-term mission tomorrow. He'll be gone at least a year. Probably two. So you'll have a while for this new information to sink in."

She perked up with genuine curiosity. "Really? What far frontier are you banishing him to? Thule?"

Her father smiled. "That's for marines, and it's not so far away. You should hear the horror stories they tell about the winter training there. You'd think their commanders were all sadists." His expression grew thoughtful. "Well, they *are* marines, so it's a distinct possibility."

"That's your Fleet prejudice talking," she said primly. "Maybe I should join the Imperial Marines to bring some well-needed perspective to this family."

He laughed before he could stop himself. Clapping his hand over his mouth only made his mirth more obvious. "I'm sorry. I shouldn't laugh. The Imperial Marines are a fine group of men and women. I just have difficulty imagining you in their ranks. In spite of your occasionally combative nature, you're a little...petite for a combat role. Besides, you just don't have the requisite killer instinct."

She stood and stared at him haughtily. Unfortunately, her eyes were still at almost the same height as his. "Are you saying that my lowly one point five meters makes me unsuitable for hand-to-hand combat?"

"Yes. I'm afraid that's exactly what I'm saying. I'm positive the smallest woman I've seen in the marines topped you by a head and weighed half again more than you weigh. It might be...embarrassing to the Imperial dignity to have them hold you at arm's length while you swing futilely at them."

Empire of Bones

Kelsey sighed theatrically. "I suppose I need to cancel my order for combat armor and automatic weapons."

"That might be for the best, yes." His eyes twinkled. "Despite my questionable sense of humor, any service would be better for having you, though I really don't think you're suited for the marines."

"Maybe I should date one."

His shocked expression made her laugh. "You should see your face. It's like you've seen a ghost."

He made a gesture for warding off evil. "Don't even joke about that. My heart might fail."

She tilted her head a little to the side. "Why? I thought you said they were fine men."

"They are. Just not the kind of men a father wants his daughter to date. I'll make sure to send any you find attractive to Thule for an extended period. Perhaps a decade will do as an example to the rest."

Kelsey gave him a gimlet eye. "You think you're funny, but you're not." She resumed her seat with a sigh. "I doubt I'm a good candidate for the military at all, honestly. I've tried to get into the social scene, doing good works there, but I'm not satisfied. Thinking about Jared made me realize that he's achieved so much in his chosen field. He commands a ship in the Imperial Fleet. That's huge!"

Her father nodded. "That's a very significant thing indeed. I served in Fleet long enough to gain a tremendous respect for the kind of person who commands a ship in space. The very least of them is a leader of some note. Your half brother is far from the least of them. His commanding officers all respect him. Admiral Yeats told me that if he'd had his way, Jared would be commanding a cruiser task force by now. One day he'll be an admiral. Not because of his connection to our family but in spite of it."

"That won't go over well with Ethan," she mumbled only barely audibly.

She gave him a haughty stare. "Just so you know, that doesn't make me feel any better. I mean, hello, this conversation is about me and my options...or lack thereof."

"You know you can literally do anything. What do you enjoy doing that might translate into some career?"

"I don't know. I'm good at the things you've trained me to do as an Imperial ruler, but that isn't likely. Ethan is depressingly healthy, and I like you too much to have you assassinated."

"Well, that *is* an obstacle to your ascension to the Imperial Throne. Remind me to hire some food tasters at once."

"Right after dinner."

"Ha! Good one! Honestly, there are careers that are perfectly suited for your skills. For example, you trained with that young man from the Department of Imperial Affairs for a while. They handle diplomatic affairs of all kinds inside the Empire. That's something we'll always need."

She nodded slowly. "True. Carlo Vega. He's a senior attaché, and I admit that his work always seemed interesting."

"I'm sure there are other avenues you could pursue. You've been spending a great deal of time in the Imperial Archives, for example. Are you researching something?"

"Aren't your spies following me? I figured they'd already told you what I'm looking into."

"Perhaps I should actually hire some. I'm certain there's a conspiracy going on somewhere that I should know about."

She gave her father a stern look. "Don't try to fool me. Everyone knows you have secret police to spy on everyone."

"Secret police? I had no idea." He smiled. "Seriously, I haven't felt the need to set my spies on you. I'm certain they have far more pressing matters requiring their attention. What have you been researching?"

Kelsey crossed her legs. "If only it were something spies would be interested in. I've just been reading up on the Old Empire. Speculation on what sparked the rebellion that led to the Fall. I wanted to see if I could find anything in the restricted stacks about it."

"Hmmm...The rebellion and the pre-Fall Terran Empire," her father said, his eyes sharpening. "That *is* worthy of study. I seem to recall seeing quite a few new books on the shelves on the subject in the library. What's driving this sudden interest?"

"I read a first-person account of the exploration mission Grandfather sent out. The book has been out for over a decade, but I missed it somehow. Maybe I was a little too young to be interested back then." Or too distracted by her family situation.

"It's a fascinating story," she said. "Imagine exploring the worlds of what used to be the Terran Empire. Finding the ruins of civilization. Searching for lost Terra. That kind of thing could excite anyone. You really should consider sending out another expedition."

He nodded thoughtfully. "That's a good idea. I'll look into it."

"You should. So, what is this mission that's taking my half brother away for so long?"

"Well, that's an interesting story—"

The buzzer on her father's console sounded. He tapped the screen. "Yes?"

Empire of Bones

"I'm sorry to disturb you, Your Majesty. Commander Mertz has arrived at the first checkpoint."

"Send him up as soon as he's in the palace."

Her father stood. "I should go get dressed. I wouldn't want to have you tell me what a disgrace I am for wearing this jacket to dinner again." He pulled her into a hug and kissed her cheek. "Please, do try not to blame Jared for my actions." A smile crept across his lips as he looked into her eyes. "See you in a bit."

Kelsey watched him leave and sighed. As much as she doubted she'd be any more comfortable with her half brother, she'd try for her father's sake. She headed for her room. She had just enough time to make herself presentable.

3

Jared exited his grav car at the secure parking lot just inside the security checkpoint. The Imperial Guardsmen then scanned his person completely. He knew better than to bring anything with him on these visits. That was an invitation to have it confiscated. These people made the security sweeps at Orbital One seem negligent. He sent his holiday gifts weeks in advance rather than bringing them himself.

As the silent man in pressed whites ran a wand over him, Jared wondered what became of the gifts he gave his half siblings. They probably threw them out. Prince Ethan most likely burned his.

The Imperial Family sent a combined gift, almost certainly picked out by his father. Usually something useful to a serving officer, though expensive.

When he was a child, his mother had regaled him with stories about when she worked in the Imperial Palace. He'd hung on every word and dreamed of what he'd ever do if he met the emperor.

Of course, he'd had no idea just how well she'd known the ruler of the Empire.

He'd graduated the regional Fleet academy and was taking his final acceptance physical here on Avalon. It was significantly more thorough than anything he'd gone through before, but he hadn't been concerned. At least until they took another tissue sample for "further DNA testing."

He'd sat waiting for the results in a small medical room for so long that he'd begun to suspect he had some subtle genetic flaw. Looked at in the proper light, he supposed he did.

In the end, the doctor was not who came in to tell him the results. The emperor himself did.

Of course, he'd known who the emperor was. Even asteroid miners who'd been born in the depths of space knew what the emperor looked like. Jared had watched every State of the Empire speech since he'd decided to become a Fleet officer.

That had been the least of the shocks on that cursed day. Finding out he was an Imperial bastard had set his world off course. For his own part, the news was so far out of his realm of experience that he rejected it. Someone had to have made a horrible mistake.

Only they hadn't.

The next few months had been a special kind of hell. Why the man had decided he needed to tell anyone else was beyond Jared's comprehension. One couldn't turn on a vid without seeing something. The only thing anyone talked about was the disintegration of the Imperial couple and the bastard child who caused it.

Worst of all, everyone around him knew. He could feel them staring at his back, whispering about him when they thought he wasn't listening...blaming him.

Then there was the small minority of people that thought they could benefit from cozying up to him. Those unfortunate few were sadly mistaken in their estimation of his influence. Imperial blood brought him no power. He tirelessly avoided the appearance of ever trying to exert any sort of influence while also going out of his way to preserve the appearance of loyalty to the Imperial House, no matter how he might feel inside.

He struggled with the effects of that day even now. The guard finished scanning him, his expression blank. Jared had met this particular man a dozen times over the years, but he'd heard scarcely a handful of words from him. Did he despise Jared? Did he fear that Jared would take some action against his master? Perhaps he was just being unapproachably professional.

Jared would probably never know. It hurt to be isolated this way from everyone around him. To have everything he did dissected to reveal any suspected hidden motives. He could never be certain what people really thought about him.

"If you'll come with me, sir, I'll escort you to the palace," the man said. Much the same as he had during the last half dozen visits.

A heavily armored grav car took them to the palace proper. The grounds were huge and beautiful, as always. That was the one thing he

Empire of Bones

really did envy his half siblings for, their easy access to such lush and lavish parks at a moment's notice.

The car entered an underground parking garage, and his keeper handed him off to different guards, who treated him with the same sterile attention. They scanned him again. Of course.

He raised his arms as one guard ran a scanner over every part of his body. A second stood close by, her hand resting on her belt beside her holstered weapon. Once the man was certain Jared wasn't about to explode, he checked Jared's ID and took another ocular scan.

Only then did they allow him to pass, but never without an armed escort, of course. Everyone seemed to have a weapon but him.

Jared stopped at the elevator and examined his dress uniform in the mirror. He made one last check that the gold rank insignia on his black jacket and shined boots were free of smudges. His black beret with his ship's insignia completed his uniform. The red striping along the black pants legs gave just the right flair, in his opinion. Not that anyone had consulted him during the last uniform redesign. He hadn't even been born then.

They rode up to the residence level in silence. The guards took him through enough halls that he was almost certain he'd never be able to find his way back out on his own. As far as he could tell, they never brought him in the same way twice. While it probably wasn't true, the special care they took to turn him around made it all feel...personal.

Then again, perhaps they only rearranged the artwork. The collection of paintings and statues was never the same. A significant number of them were on loan from the Imperial Museum, pre-Fall works from the homes of the wealthy here on Avalon and recovered from the worlds they'd rediscovered since they returned to space. It probably didn't hold a candle to what had been in the Imperial Palace on Terra, but it was enough to interest even someone not into art, such as himself.

Eventually, they stopped at the doors to the Imperial Family's private rooms. The guards stayed outside and allowed Jared to proceed alone. They probably thought that wasn't the best idea, but the emperor insisted that Jared be treated as family.

Jared had no idea what the guards thought of the emperor summoning his bastard son to dinner. There was no telling.

The emperor's legitimate children felt no need to restrain their emotions. Crown Prince Ethan's distaste and loathing were obvious enough to earn rebukes from his father. The heir didn't let that stop him though.

Ethan's twin sister viewed him with similar distaste, but Jared thought that stemmed almost exclusively because Jared was the physical proof of her father's infidelity. She wasn't blatantly hostile. She seemed to prefer a cold, distant demeanor. Only the emperor made any effort to make him feel welcome. Of course, he was the one who insisted that Jared come calling, so that only seemed right.

When Jared entered the enormous living room, the emperor arose from his comfortable chair in front of the fireplace to greet him. "Jared, it's so good to see you again. Come, sit with me."

Jared suppressed the urge to bow. Even after fifteen years, that wasn't easy. Innate respect for the Crown sat deeply in his bones. That was true for most of the Imperial population. He extended his hand instead.

Even the idea of shaking the Imperial hand was mind numbing. It seemed disrespectful. He silently thanked God that the man didn't insist on a hug.

The small table between the two chairs held a decanter of amber liquid and two glasses. One already had two fingers of drink in it. Jared's father sat back down and poured some into the second glass.

Getting into the mental space where the emperor became his father was difficult. Jared took the proffered drink and sat. The whisky was smooth and warm. It was probably older than he was.

The emperor wore casual clothes. His salt-and-pepper hair and fine wrinkles showed that age was taking its toll. He eyed Jared's uniform with amusement.

"You know you don't need to wear that. Not that I have anything against Fleet. My time there is one of my fondest memories, though I'm sure my superiors didn't see it that way at the time."

"Admiral Yeats disagrees. If I wore anything else, it would be as if I showed up naked."

That brought a laugh from the older man. "I see. Well, far be it from me to cause you any more problems than I already have. We'll start dinner in a few minutes, but I wanted to take a moment to congratulate you on your new assignment. It's well deserved."

Jared sipped his drink. "I'm excited. Fleet picking me to probe beyond our borders is an honor."

"I was about your age when the last expedition took place. I'd already left the Fleet by then. I made it to lieutenant and felt that was an accomplishment. I badgered my father to send me along, but he wouldn't hear of it. The Crown Prince needed to be here on Avalon."

He raised his glass to Jared. "Being chosen for this assignment is quite an achievement. The Terran Empire is meticulous about who they appoint to command an interstellar vessel, much less who they send out

Empire of Bones

to possibly contact other systems. Though I'm sure you already know this, allow me to state for the record that I pulled no strings. You earned this honor on your own merits. Well done, Commander."

"Thank you, sir."

The two of them sat sipping their drinks and talking about recent events for the next ten minutes. Even after all these years, Jared still wasn't sure what the emperor hoped to see happen. The gulf between them was too wide. Perhaps the man just wanted to connect with his illegitimate son. That wouldn't be easy for anyone, but it was probably more difficult for the emperor.

He rose when the emperor did and followed him into the dining room. They'd just walked in when Princess Kelsey came in the other door. She wore a pale blue dress made of some light material that showcased her elfin figure. The men sat once she'd seated herself. Jared made no move to hold her chair for her. He'd learned the hard way that she didn't appreciate the gesture from him.

The princess was dainty. A full head and a half shorter than him, she couldn't have weighed more than forty-five kilograms. Long curly blonde hair framed a heart-shaped face with bright blue eyes. Some nobleman would be happy to have her. Jared wished the poor bastard the best of luck.

She shook out her napkin. "Ethan is feeling ill tonight and begs our guest's indulgence for his absence."

A polite fiction, Jared knew, but infinitely preferable to the hostile sniping disguised as conversation the prince favored. "Of course, Princess. I hope he recovers swiftly. Please send him my regards."

Their father didn't look very pleased, but he didn't make an issue out of it. "Kelsey, to answer your earlier question, Jared has been appointed to command an exploratory expedition beyond the borders of the Empire. He'll be leaving tomorrow. We won't publically announce it until after they've departed."

Her expression brightened. "That's wonderful! Congratulations. I've been reading about the last expedition. It all sounds very dangerous and exciting. Will you be looking for Terra?"

He smiled, pleased at her enthusiasm. "I'm sure everyone would be happy if we found it, but that isn't our mission. We'll be locating unexplored flip points and seeing what's on the other side of them. The odds are very good we'll find something similar to the primitive systems we've already discovered."

She looked disappointed. "You don't think you'll find anything else?"

"Perhaps there will be some intact ruins from before the Fall. That's what the science community hopes anyway. A true treasure would be chancing on some undamaged computers, ones the rebels hadn't fried. Finding Terra or any other major world isn't very likely considering Avalon was on the edge of the Old Empire. This part of space didn't contain one of the core systems they spoke of in the old stories."

"Wouldn't that be something to see?" The emperor mused. "I've seen the few existing images and videos of Imperial City on Terra. The buildings seemed to touch the skies. I've always thought the Terran Empire should have Terra as one of her planets again."

The emperor shook his head. "I suppose I should just be pleased that our ancestor was able to flee here and that the few rebel ships that followed him didn't eradicate all life before they were destroyed. We lost so much."

Jared had seen the crater left after the destruction of the former capital of Avalon and its spaceport. He understood completely.

The servers came in with dinner. The palace chefs had cooked the fish to perfection. It smelled delicious. Jared sipped the wine the man poured for him with approval.

Jared continued the conversation after taking a bite of his crisp salad. "I've been looking over the records since I received my orders. The worlds we rediscovered didn't seem high tech before the Fall. They were mostly agricultural planets and mining systems where the asteroid belts made mineral recovery easy. Things would've been very different in the core systems of the Old Empire."

The pictures of Imperial City told that tale effectively enough. Terra must've had tens of billions of people. Those not killed in the war would have starved. Oh, certainly, humans were hard to exterminate completely, but the death toll must've been staggering. He could see from their faces that the other two had some idea of what he was implying.

His father nodded. "We were lucky. Society dropped back to prespaceflight technology, but now we're expanding again. We're still the same Terran Empire, our history and rule unbroken. Thanks to Lucien and Fleet's sacrifice."

Princess Kelsey ate quietly for a while before coming back to the subject. "We've explored quite a ways, haven't we? How far away do you think the core systems of the Old Empire are?"

Jared shrugged. "No one really knows. Frankly, we're not even certain we're exploring in the right direction. Avalon was a resort world with tall mountains for skiing and wilderness for the well to do. One far away from the rest of civilization. When the rebels took out our capital and spaceport with a kinetic strike, it wiped away any computer that had

Empire of Bones

that information. The global EMP strike did the same for the rest of the planet.

"That seems to have been the pattern on all the worlds we've rediscovered. All orbitals and spaceports destroyed. The rebels seem to have used EMP weapons to fry any electronics left on the surface. A few very general maps survived, mostly in the few abandoned and overlooked asteroid mining facilities, but none of them showed our sector of space. That's where our only remaining images of Terra come from."

He took a bite of his fish, letting the taste fill his mouth. "We might be exploring along the edges of the Old Empire. We know it was huge. We've colonized dozens of systems. We've probed the flip points two or three hops beyond our borders, which means we've some knowledge of over a hundred other systems."

"Why don't we go faster? We've had flip drives again for almost a hundred years."

Her father answered the question. "Because flip drives require very rare exotic elements to construct. Combined with the expense of building ships, that limits Fleet's size. With the mines we found on Grathan a few years ago, the supply of those elements is no longer an issue. However, the cost to extract and ship them still is. Fleet is expanding now, which frees up a few ships to explore. I've decided to have four of the older destroyers assigned to this exploration duty on a permanent basis."

He nodded his head toward Jared. "No disrespect to your ship, of course."

"None taken, sir. *Athena* is a magnificent ship, even if she isn't the newest in Fleet anymore. Her crew is the best."

"Of course. The worlds we've settled had populations ranging from primitive hunter-gatherers to preindustrial," the emperor said. "Incorporating them into society and raising their standard of living is a huge strain on our economy. We have an obligation to help any civilization we find. That creates a great strain on the Empire's finances. However, we are working to streamline the process. We've been working with the universities over the last decade to train young scientists to accompany these expeditions, too. That doesn't happen overnight."

The young woman nodded. "I suppose that makes sense. How far will you go?"

"However far we can get in nine months," Jared said. "We'll explore well enough to bring a good record back. If we find something interesting, that return date is subject to my discretion, so if we're late, it doesn't automatically mean disaster."

"Is trouble likely?"

"We didn't lose any ships during the previous expedition, but that might have been luck. We really have no way of knowing."

"I wish I could go."

"Everyone on this mission has a job to do, ma'am. Do you have any skills that would make it a good idea to bump one of them?" He certainly hoped not.

Princess Kelsey shook her head. "I wish I did. Unfortunately, the life of a princess isn't very useful in providing real-world experience."

After they finished their meal, they returned to the living room and talked late into the night. He knew he'd have to hustle in the morning in order to catch the early shuttle to Orbital One, but he was loath to disrupt the first real pleasant moment he'd had with his half sister.

Eventually, however, he had to leave. He rose to his feet. "As much as I have enjoyed our visit, I'm afraid I need to call it an evening. The mission briefing is early tomorrow…this morning. Thank you both for the exquisite meal…and for the pleasant conversation."

His father stood and shook his hand. "I look forward to hearing what you find. Know that the Empire and I are proud of you, and we're behind you completely."

"I pray you find everything you hope and more, Jared," Princess Kelsey said. "Be careful out there. I also look forward to hearing about all your adventures when you return."

A different pair of guards waited for him when he left the Imperial residence. They led him back to the lift and escorted him to the underground garage. They stopped at the security checkpoint and let him walk to the grav car alone.

He thought that was odd until he saw who was standing beside the vehicle. Crown Prince Ethan.

"Your Highness," Jared said in a tone free of inflection as he nodded his head forward. "I hope I didn't keep you waiting long."

"Save your feeble attempts at humor, Bastard. I hope you had a good time tonight, because it won't be happening again."

A chill ran up Jared's spine. "Is that so?"

The prince stepped into his personal space. "For your sake, it had better be. This is the one and only warning I'm going to give you. I will not allow you to continue scheming against my family and me. Stay away, or I will make certain you never trouble me and mine again. Am I clear?"

"You act as though I have a choice. If you want to see the last of me, speak to your father. When the emperor summons you, you come."

Empire of Bones

Prince Ethan's expression contorted into a snarl. "You think you're clever? Very well. We'll do this the hard way."

Jared felt an uneasy sinking feeling in the pit of his stomach as he watched the prince stalk away. Just what he needed—more Imperial intrigue. At least he'd have a few years' reprieve before seeing his brother again. Perhaps the boy's rancor would cool during Jared's absence... before he did something they'd both most certainly regret.

4

Kelsey went back to the library after dinner. It was very late, but all the talk about the Old Empire had made her want to go back over what she'd been reading again. She went directly to the paper books. Many of the modern works were in electronic form, but she preferred paper where possible. The smell and feel of real books filled some need inside her that a tablet didn't.

An incredible and irreplaceable amount of history from before the Fall had been lost during the orbital bombardment. While the only population center hit was Wash Gorge, the city surrounding the spaceport and planetary operations center, that didn't mean that the rest of the planet had escaped. EMP weapons had burned out every piece of electronics on the face of the planet.

Military equipment was hardened to survive that kind of thing, but the battle in orbit destroyed all that. When they as a people finally returned to space, nothing useful remained. The major wreckage had burned up on reentry over the centuries or wandered far into the depths between the planets.

Thankfully, the kinetic weapon that killed everyone in the capital city hadn't left any radiation. They were able to rebuild in the fertile valley. Avalon had been a very popular vacation destination before the Fall. Even with the total destruction of the only major city on the planet, almost a hundred thousand people had survived.

The last emperor of the Old Empire had even sent his son fleeing before the last of the Imperial Fleet went to engage the rebels in a do-or-die last-ditch effort to save the Empire from total destruction.

It certainly seemed that do or die turned out to be the latter, since no Fleet vessels ever followed Lucien to Avalon. Of course, no rebel vessels came either, thank God. Perhaps they'd exterminated one another. Kelsey certainly hoped the rebels were long gone.

The boy-emperor's escort had stuffed him into a life pod as soon as their ship made orbit. A wise decision, since the rebels destroyed their ship before Lucien's pod even made it to the atmosphere. The escorting Fleet units fought bravely, but they couldn't stop the attack on the planet.

Even though it was impossible to know for certain, the prevailing theory was that they fought to mutual extinction with the rebels. All anyone knew for sure was that any detailed knowledge of the rebels and their aims was lost in the chaos and death.

One thing they did know was that some Fleet units had defected and fought savagely against their brothers. The aims of the rebels remained a subject of intense debate in the various history departments to this day.

She opened her favorite book on the subject to one of the few surviving pictures of Lucien, taken a few months after his arrival. The boy-emperor looked filthy and had a heavy sling full of grain over his shoulder. He also looked like a man determined to save every one of his subjects if it killed him.

His example of working just as hard as every one of his subjects set the tone for his descendants. All sought out public service. All gave much of their time to improving the lives of the people they ruled. Yes, the people were no longer struggling to survive the winters, but the same desire to serve filled her.

Kelsey envied her half brother. He was living her dream and boldly going into the Old Empire. She knew he'd find the answers she craved. Perhaps that would make up for the chaos her family had made of his life.

The library door opened and her father came in. "There you are. I went to your room to talk, but you'd vanished. I was afraid you'd snuck off to stow away on the expedition."

She perked up a little. "Do you think I could hide out until they made it into the Old Empire? I could pack enough food to stay in some crawlspace and sneak out for showers."

He laughed and sat down beside her. "I'm afraid not. I'd worry terribly about where you'd gotten off to and send word to every corner of the Empire to search for you. The fact you just expressed an interest in the expedition means I'd send word to Jared. He's a good man. He'd

Empire of Bones

29

turn his ships upside down to be sure you hadn't slipped aboard. He knows them much better than you do."

"Pity. Seriously, though, what could I do to prepare for a future mission? I know the competition to go must be intense. I'm not sure I'm good enough to make that final cut, no matter how hard I work. Sometimes your best just isn't good enough."

"You are rather behind in your technical education if you wanted to be a leading scientific candidate on a future mission," he admitted. "The people who made the cut this time worked hard for a decade or more in their chosen fields of study. You'd probably have to expend a similar amount of time going forward to be where they are now."

She slumped in her chair. "That's what I was afraid you'd say. I'm afraid being an empress in training isn't very useful on a mission of exploration."

"True. That's more Jared's job. Perhaps you should look over the personnel manifest to see what kind of specialties they might need for future expeditions. I know I have it somewhere in my personal files."

He retrieved a tablet from the table and authenticated himself on the system. Then he dug around the palace computers for a few minutes. "Here we go. This file has the full list of people and their specialties. Well, except for a few last-minute decisions by the university heads."

Kelsey gave him a curious look. "Last-minute decisions? I'd have expected they knew who was going months or years ago. What do they have to do with making the final selections anyway? Shouldn't Fleet do that?"

"The four premiere Imperial universities are funding the conversion and outfitting of the freighters housing the science labs. They're also training almost two hundred specialists in any number of scientific fields per mission. Shouldn't they narrow it down to the best-qualified ones?"

"That's not the question I asked, Father. It seems to me that the only reason the final choices haven't already been made must be due to politics or money."

He raised an eyebrow and smiled a little. "That's a bit cynical but probably true. There's a lot of prestige on the line. I'm sure a few last-minute endowments have been made to alter a few choices, though I'm confident that no one incapable of doing the work would make the final list."

"Perhaps I should make a large contribution from my trust fund to one of universities. That puts both money and political interest on the line."

"Let's say you did. What role would you play in the expedition?"

She scanned the file slowly. The roster covered every possible scientific field: geology, biology, archeology, history, physics, and almost everything else she could name…and more than a few she couldn't. Most of the people listed had multiple areas of study under their belts.

Curious, she had the tablet sort the data by discipline. Indeed, every field had a number of people. From an exploratory angle, they seemed to have all the bases covered.

So, following that logic, what might they be missing? One thing she'd learned early in her Imperial training was that big problems didn't usually come from contingencies you put in place. The things that often bit you on the backside were the ones you'd never considered in the first place. What had they planned for and what had they missed?

"Do you have the full mission parameters?" she asked.

He again took over the tablet long enough to give her the information. She noticed he wasn't reading over her shoulder. He was watching her.

She'd seen him do this before. He was seeing how she reacted to a problem and how she approached solving it. Did that mean there was a weakness in the mission planning, or was he just using this as a teaching moment? She'd find out soon enough.

It took half an hour to read the full mission brief. She knew some of it was in all likelihood classified, but she had the highest-level clearances imaginable. The spare apparent needed to have the same skill set and access to details as the heir. Her father undoubtedly knew some secrets she didn't, but he never skimped on sharing classified information with her.

She almost asked for the crew manifest for Jared's destroyer, *Athena*, but she saw her father already had opened it as well. He'd anticipated her thought process. Of course. An emperor had best be thinking a few moves ahead of everyone else.

Kelsey leaned back and stared at the ceiling once she finished reading. All the information was buzzing through her head. She knew it would coalesce into an understandable bundle with a little more time, but already there was something nibbling at her consciousness. Something was missing.

Was it a missing skill or an unconsidered possibility? It seemed as if they'd planned based on the events of the previous exploration. So, what hadn't happened on that mission?

They hadn't found extensive ruins before, but this mission was well equipped in case they did. They hadn't found advanced civilizations either. She pondered that. The orders said they would avoid interacting with any human populations. Well and good, if they were as primitive as those found thus far.

Empire of Bones

But what if they found a more advanced people? The mission orders didn't address that possibility. They just instructed Jared to avoid contact. Escape and evasion might prove impossible with a space-capable civilization. What would they do then?

Make contact. Negotiate. Set up diplomatic relations.

"Father, there are no trained, experienced diplomats on any of these manifests. What if they need to interact with an advanced society that becomes aware of their presence?"

"Let me see." He took the tablet and scanned the files. "Fleet has the military side of operations in hand. The science ship has the scientific side. It looks like there may be a gap in the mission statement. I'd suppose that Jared will act as the face of the Empire."

She narrowed her eyes. "No offense to my half brother, but is he trained as a negotiator? I'll grant that he has a lot of patience, but he's a military officer. If trouble comes up, he'll use the tools he knows. In this case, weapons."

Her father looked less than convinced. "Come now. I'm certain he'd never open hostilities without significant provocation."

"Probably not, but shouldn't someone trained in diplomacy ride along in case something delicate needs to be addressed? They should have someone onboard who can explain delicate things, like why his ship might be sneaking around in someone else's territory. It hasn't happened thus far, but the possibility increases with every mission."

Her father leaned back and contemplated her for a minute. "What are you suggesting? That I should send you to cover that position?"

Kelsey shook her head. "No. The Department of Imperial Affairs has people that settle disagreements between the worlds of the Empire every day. Carlo Vega, or someone like him, would be perfect. I'd say send two experienced negotiators per mission."

Her father stared off into the distance for a few minutes before nodding. "I think you may be right. I'll go back to my office and make some calls. I'll need to act fast if I want to make this happen. I don't want to delay the missions."

He stood and stretched. "You've served the Empire well tonight, Kelsey. This oversight could have had very drastic consequences. Well done. Now, it's late. You'd best get some sleep. One never knows what unexpected events will land on one's lap first thing in the morning."

5

The next morning disabused Jared of the notion that things would go more smoothly just because he'd had a good evening. He woke late, missed the first shuttle, and ended up docking at the far side of Orbital One. He normally enjoyed walking through the station's bustling corridors, but Admiral Yeats wasn't fond of tardy officers.

The yard technicians in their bright-blue jumpsuits seemed to be everywhere. He'd never seen so many of them clogging the corridors before. He finally made it to the conference room ten minutes late.

The room held several dozen people, about evenly split between Fleet officers and civilians. The civilians would be the senior scientific team leaders. Everyone turned to stare at Jared as he took the empty seat beside Graves. Charlie's expression gave nothing away, but there was a deep twinkle in his eye. He'd be teasing Jared about this for months.

Admiral Yeats fixed Jared with an unfriendly stare designed to melt junior officers. "So good of you to join us, Commander. Would you like me to start over?"

"No, sir." He felt a flush creeping up his neck. "I apologize for my tardiness."

The admiral gave him another beat of silence before returning to his notes. "As I was saying, the four converted freighters housing the science teams have completed their refits and are ready to go. The science team leaders have checked the labs and addressed all deficiencies. The four destroyers and their accompanying science vessels will depart as soon as all personnel have reported aboard."

He made a gesture to the conference room door. "I'm certain you've all noticed the people swarming around Orbital One. The shipyard technicians are leaving the ships and departing for Avalon to take some well-deserved rest. Enough will remain on hand to address any last-minute issues, of course.

"The chips in front of you contain the full rosters of your expeditions. The expedition commanders are already familiar with the senior science people, but there were some eleventh-hour substitutions that these lists accurately document."

Admiral Yeats tapped the recessed console in front of him, and the lights dimmed. The Imperial star map with connecting lines denoting matched flip points appeared on the wall screen. Green dots represented the core systems, blue marked the rest of the Empire, and yellow noted the explored but unaligned systems.

The map looked like a toy designed by a lunatic. Flip lines shot out for a hundred light years, then came back in fifty, only to shoot out another direction. It all seemed perfectly random. One system only ten light years away from Avalon took four flips to get there, traveling over three hundred light years. Most known systems had two flip points, but a few had only one and several had three.

Red dots represented star systems that no one had ever visited. Most wouldn't have flip points at all. That much had come down through their oral history. The vast majority of worlds would never see human visitation.

The admiral highlighted four systems with unexplored flip points on the periphery of the Empire. "While there are literally dozens of possible paths, the experts have selected these four systems for attention at this time. Each has habitable though unoccupied planets. In a pinch, you could survive there if trouble strikes.

"With the distances involved, it will take your ships about a month to get to your kickoff points. We don't expect you back for eighteen months. I'm aware that might be conservative if you find something interesting, but rest assured we'll come looking for you if you don't make it back in three years. You'll be leaving probes in every system you explore, starting with your kickoff points. Keep them updated with your most recent situation reports as you move on and recover them on the way back. We'll use them to follow you if need be. Fleet doesn't abandon its own."

He swept the room with his gaze. "I don't expect you to run into trouble you can't handle, but if you do, I expect you to be prudent.

Empire of Bones   35

Retreat if there is danger beyond your ability to handle it. The Empire needs to know what you find. If things really go into the toilet, the science ship will retreat while the destroyer provides cover. Understood?"

Once they had all muttered their understanding, he turned off the screen. "The Terran Empire is proud of each of you. You're our best and brightest. I have no doubt you'll make us proud. Good luck. Dismissed. Commander Mertz, a moment."

Charlie leaned over as he rose to his feet. "I'll get the marines to organize a rescue party if you're not back to the ship in half an hour."

"Thanks," Jared muttered.

Once everyone else had left the room, the admiral took a seat beside him at the table. "Would you care to explain your tardiness?"

"I have no excuses, sir."

Yeats's expression cracked a little, allowing a small smile through. "You sound just like your father when you say that. It's a bit uncanny. I'm not looking for an excuse, just an explanation."

Jared took a deep breath. "Dinner went much better than I anticipated and I stayed very late. I missed the first shuttle, and the departing shipyard crew delayed me. I'm sorry, sir."

The admiral's smile widened. "That's excellent news. I officially retract my disapproval. Hell, you could've missed this briefing and I'd still be happy to hear things are improving on that front. Might I ask what happened to make things better?"

"Princess Kelsey expressed an interest in the expedition. She wanted to hear everything I could tell her. I wouldn't be surprised if she started working on an angle to help with future expeditions."

"I hope she does. An Imperial patron would be helpful in a number of ways. She could help shepherd an increased budget through the tight-fisted old men in the Imperial Senate. Of course, a major find by any of the teams will spark a full-blown follow-up and have incalculable benefit for Fleet."

Admiral Yeats rose, and Jared stood. He clapped his hand on Jared's shoulder. "I wish you the very best of luck, Commander. Go bring home the bacon, and bring your people back with it."

"Yes, sir."

He followed the admiral out of the briefing room and fought the crowds toward the upper levels of the orbital. *Athena*'s cutter waited there. The rest of the crew was already aboard ship, so he was the only passenger.

The trip was brief. He took a moment to admire *Athena*'s lines through the port. *Athena* was only a destroyer, so she looked like a toy beside *Best Deal*, the converted freighter housing the science teams.

Freighters needed to be large to carry as much cargo as possible between systems. It stretched 3,500 meters and looked like a block 450 meters wide and tall. It displaced millions of tons and could only crawl along under that tremendous load, even with upgraded drives.

The labs only took up a small amount of that vast space. They'd left the remaining cargo areas as is to carry any recovered artifacts. Six cargo shuttles seemed like overkill to Jared, but the ship normally carried them as well as two civilian personnel cutters. Jared had to admit they might come in handy.

The freighter normally flew with thirty officers and three hundred and seventy crew, but that took a full load of cargo into account. The captain of *Best Deal* had released two hundred of his crew slots to the science teams. That made the remaining crew grumble, but if push came to shove, they could compel the scientists into manual labor. Although Jared was sure doing so would cause innumerable complaints.

Athena might look like a minnow beside *Best Deal*, but she was a deadly one. She was a mere six hundred meters in length. Her hull was one hundred and twenty meters across and eighty tall. Her crew complement was much larger than the size difference would suggest, with twenty-one Fleet officers and two hundred and twenty-nine crew. The ship also had a detachment of thirty marines to provide armed personnel.

She also had twice the speed of the massive freighter. This meant that she could make the journey to the target star system in a little over two weeks if traveling alone.

Thankfully, the flip points in a system were usually just outside the system's habitable zone. If they were further out, the trip would take even longer.

The placement had something to do with the mass of the host stars, but that didn't seem to dictate the number of flip points in a system. It made cosmologists a little crazy because no one really knew why only some stars had them. If someone ever figured out that mystery, he or she would win the Lucien Prize for sure.

The cutter maneuvered adroitly to the forward docking port assigned it and mated with hardly a bump. Jared waited for the light over the lock to go green and entered his ship. *Athena* had three personnel cutters and two marine combat pinnaces. The marine small craft berthed at the aft of the ship near marine country. Up front, the cutters took up three of the four docks. The fourth was for visiting vehicles.

The closest lift took him to the bridge in a matter of minutes. It wasn't in the nose of the ship, as the entertainment vids liked to portray,

Empire of Bones

but in the ship's center. Command and control needed to be one of the most protected areas of the ship—not because the commander was more important but because loss of control meant probable death in combat.

Not that he'd ever been in real combat. No living Fleet officer had.

Helm and tactical took up the front of the bridge. His console was in the center of the compartment, and three unattended consoles faced to the rear and side of the oval chamber. Extra crew could staff those positions if something happened to the main consoles, but they typically housed observers.

It was a much tighter fit than in the vids, too. Barely seven meters long and five wide. A heavy cruiser's bridge was about twice that size.

Graves stood as Jared entered. "You made it back alive, I see. I was just about to send the marines."

Jared smiled and took the seat his executive officer had just vacated. "It was a close thing, let me tell you. What's our status?"

"All personnel are present. The last load of supplies came on board five minutes ago. *Best Deal* is running behind. Of course. Things seem a little disorganized over there. Captain Keller said they would be ready in ten minutes."

That likely meant fifteen or twenty minutes. Anything that had to do with the civilian scientists seemed to be prone to delays.

Jared shook his head with a smile. "There's no use pushing for them to go faster. That would slow them down even more. I can't wait to see the first emergency drill over there."

Charlie rolled his eyes. "No kidding. People running in every direction and some not bothering to go to emergency stations at all. Too busy with real work to be playing sailor. It'll be a real laugh."

"I wouldn't start chuckling just yet. I'm sending you over to set it up and grade the results. Then you'll work with Captain Keller to get a training plan in place to see they get better. If things go to hell, I don't want them killing themselves."

"Thanks," Charlie muttered.

Lieutenant Anderson turned toward them. "Captain, there is a cutter requesting permission to dock. It says they have a couple of late-arriving crewmen."

Jared arched an eyebrow. "I thought you said everyone was aboard, Charlie. Did you misplace someone?"

Graves looked puzzled. "Everyone *is* accounted for."

"Zia, who are the crewmen?"

She spoke into her headset. "They say they have the diplomatic representatives on board."

Jared brought up the crew manifest on his console. No diplomatic representatives. According to his orders, he'd be representing the Empire if need be. "Permission to dock is granted. I'll go down myself and find out what's going on. Charlie, you have the bridge."

"Aye, sir."

Jared took the lift back down to the forward docking bay. He heard the muffled clank of the cutter docking just as he arrived. A bit of cold mist puffed out of the lock as the interior and exterior hatches slid open. A crewman in a dark grey flight suit stepped out and saluted him, right fist to chest. He'd just returned it when two other people followed the man out.

Jared didn't know the gentleman in the lead, but he looked like a diplomat. Tall, his dark hair shaded with distinguished gray, and impeccably dressed. However, the young woman behind him was all too familiar.

"Princess Kelsey," Jared growled. "What are you doing here?"

6

Kelsey made certain to keep Carlo Vega between Jared and herself. The diplomat didn't react to her half brother's expression as he held out his hand. "Captain Mertz. So kind of you to meet us. I'm Ambassador Carlo Vega from the Department of Imperial Affairs. I'll be your diplomatic attaché on this voyage of discovery."

He stepped to the side, exposing Kelsey. "I believe you know my assistant, Kelsey Bandar. For the duration of our assignment, she will not be acting in her Imperial capacity. Rather, she will operate solely as deputy ambassador."

Jared's face clouded even further. "This isn't a casual trip through the park, Ambassador Vega. It has the potential to be very dangerous. I cannot be responsible for a member of the Imperial Family under these conditions, no matter how they choose to style themselves."

A mulish expression settled across her face, although she tried to fight it. "I apologize for the surprise, but this matter is settled. I'm staying."

"The devil it is. I cannot be responsible for your safety in this environment, Your Highness. You're leaving, even if I have to strap you into that cutter myself," Jared assured her. He looked like he'd do it, too. She'd never seen him so angry.

Vega's bland expression didn't flicker at their exchange. "I'm afraid this assignment isn't open to debate, Captain. These orders come directly from His Imperial Majesty. All four expeditions are receiving experienced diplomats and young people with extensive negotiating experience to train in this role for future missions."

As two crewmen wheeled a cart full of luggage from the cutter and began unloading it on the deck, Jared swore creatively. Kelsey made note of some of the catchier phrases for personal use later.

"This is madness," her half brother finally managed. "What if she's injured or killed? She's second in line to the Imperial Throne!"

Vega smiled. "I believe her father was a Fleet officer when he was heir to that very throne. He understands the dangers inherent to her making this voyage. No fault will attach to you or Fleet if such a tragedy were to happen."

"I am well aware of the risks as well," Kelsey said. "I'm fulfilling my duty to the Empire just like you are, Jared."

He pinched the bridge of his nose, possibly counting to ten. "Fine. I'll see that we assign appropriate quarters to you. But I want to make a few things very clear."

He stepped into Kelsey's personal space and stared down at her. It took a great deal of willpower not to step back. "This is my ship. I am the commander of this mission. You may be an Imperial princess, but on my ship, you will obey my orders. I will not tolerate disobedience or disrespect of any kind. You are subject to the same rules and expectations as the rest of my crew. Do you understand me, Deputy Ambassador Bandar?"

She opened her mouth to say something, but Vega cut her off. "Yes, Captain. We understand completely. I accept full responsibility for educating Deputy Ambassador Bandar on the behavior required of her."

Not bothering to hide the doubt on his face, Jared stepped back. "See that you do, Ambassador. How many guards has she brought with her?"

"None. When I said she wasn't acting as an Imperial princess, I wasn't kidding. Before you offer, she will not need any marines to act in that capacity. We trust this environment to be free of that kind of threat."

Jared shook his head. "More madness. Very well then, I'll send some people to get you settled in. Report to the executive officer once you've stowed your belongings."

He turned on his heel and stormed to the lift without any parting pleasantries. That was probably for the best.

Kelsey had never seen that side of her half brother before. Gone was the polite officer that came to visit a few times a year. Missing was the man who'd accepted her cold anger and indignant disdain without a

Empire of Bones   41

word in his own defense. The intimidating man she'd just seen was no less a ruler than her father inside this, his domain.

Vega turned to her as the crewmen from the cutter brought out the last of their luggage. "I trust you see how serious Captain Mertz is. He'll be looking for any reason to drop you off in a life pod and let someone else pick you up, so you'd best keep that sharp tongue of yours under firm control, Kelsey."

"I have no intention of getting crossways with my half brother, Carlo. I'll behave."

"That is your first mistake. Listen to me very carefully. Forget that man is related to you. We are no longer in your domain. Captain Mertz is now God and his executive officer is his prophet. Familiarity is your enemy. If you want to make this assignment work, you need to treat him as a total stranger. Be formal. As far as you are concerned, his first name is now Captain. If it's a really good day, perhaps 'sir' will work."

"And if he says run, I ask how fast?"

"No. You keep your mouth closed and run as fast as you possibly can. Consider this your first challenge as a diplomat of the Empire. If you avoid getting locked up, you'll be doing pretty well."

She pondered that while they waited. The crewman waved at them and shut the hatch to the cutter. A loud clank announced its departure. A departure that trapped her on a ship with an angry man that didn't want her anywhere close. She'd best listen to Carlo's advice and take this very seriously.

They only waited a few minutes before the lift opened again and three men came out. Their uniforms were subtly different from one another. The man in front had the same blue tunic over black pants that Jared…Captain Mertz had worn.

The other two men had black tunics over black pants. They also had red stripes on their sleeves where the man in front of them had two wide red bars on the shoulders separated by a thin red line. She'd probably best spend some time learning what those meant.

The men in back bowed. The man in the blue tunic did not.

Kelsey couldn't help noticing he was more than passingly handsome with his cropped blond hair and blue eyes. A hint of deviltry sparkled in his smile. He held his hand out to Vega. "Welcome aboard, Ambassador. I'm Lieutenant Commander Charlie Graves, *Athena*'s executive officer."

Vega took his hand and smiled as he shook it. "Thank you, Commander. It's a pleasure to be here. I'm very sorry for the last-minute disruption. I assure you I had my very own version of it a few hours ago when the Secretary of Imperial affairs woke me up. This is my assistant, Deputy Ambassador Kelsey Bandar."

The officer's expression told Kelsey he knew exactly who she was, but no hint of it made its way to his voice. "Deputy Ambassador Bandar. A pleasure."

"For me as well, Commander Graves."

"Ratings Welch and Soto will see that your gear is stowed. I'm afraid the cabins don't have enough space for everything you've brought, but all your bags will be readily accessible if you need something from them. Come this way, please."

He led them back into the lift, leaving the two ratings to handle the baggage. "We're putting you into separate cabins. They were two-person cabins, but I think it best for senior personnel to have some privacy to do their work."

Vega nodded. "Excellent, Commander. I like Miss Bandar quite a lot, but not that much. She might snore."

Kelsey laughed when Carlo winked at her. "If I might ask, where are the displaced officers going?"

"We have some missile tubes offline for repairs. They're almost big enough for one person each, if they hold their arms over their heads."

Kelsey felt herself gape before she remembered that hint of wickedness she'd seen in his eyes. She snapped her mouth closed and shook her head. "You had me for a moment. I'm going to need to keep an eye on you."

He grinned, making himself look even more roguish. "I couldn't resist. We're adding extra bunks in one of the small conference rooms. They'll need to go into marine country to use the head, but they'll have some extra space to make up for the inconvenience."

"Why didn't you put us there?" Vega asked.

"Because you'd need to go into marine country to use the head."

"I'm sure the marines aren't so bad," she objected.

"Of course not, but they are a little rough around the edges. I shudder to think about the diplomatic crisis one of their late-night poker games would cause."

The lift opened onto a tight corridor with several crew members hurrying along on some duty or another. She followed Graves's example and pressed her back to the wall when they passed. She wondered why the officer was giving precedence to the others for a moment but decided it was not the right time or place to ask the question. There was probably a logical explanation.

Graves stopped at a hatch marked 6P432. "This is your cabin, Ambassador Vega. Deputy Ambassador Bandar is two down and on the other side of the corridor. Memorize your room numbers so someone

Empire of Bones

can get you home when you get lost. Everyone does when they first come aboard, and so will you."

"Or they'll put us into a missile tube," she muttered, imagining the pranks that could happen to new people on a ship.

The executive officer laughed. "That particular prank isn't appropriate for civilians. You're not going to end up in marine country either. Not unless you intentionally go there. The crew will find...subtler ways to welcome you aboard."

He pressed his thumb on the lock, and the hatch slid open. "I have authority to enter every cabin but won't do so unless there's a reason. In this case, I need to be inside to add your access to the room. I could do it remotely, but I don't have your biometric data. Please press your thumb to the lock, Ambassador."

Vega did so and looked inside the cabin curiously. "Very interesting."

Graves did something inside the door and stepped back outside. "Ratings Soto and Welch will see that you have access to your belongings and help you stow away what you will need in your cabin. While the compensators keep the grav drives from tossing things around during normal maneuvers, we secure everything just in case. They will also see to your safety briefings. Deputy Ambassador Bandar?"

He had her press her thumb to the lock beside her hatch and gave her identical instructions. Her cabin was 6P435. Vega still stood inside the open hatch to his cabin, so the officer looked at both of them when he spoke again.

"Don't wander around until you get your orientation. This ship can be a dangerous place to the uninitiated. Not because of the people, but some equipment can be lethal to the untrained. If you inadvertently found yourself in engineering, you might touch something that could kill you before your body hits the floor. Everything dangerous is marked as such, but you don't know how to recognize that yet. Stay put. Understood?"

His voice held a hint of command. Not like Captain Mertz. More subdued but crystal clear.

"Yes, sir," she said.

He smiled. "I don't need a 'sir' from either of you. Just pay attention while you learn your way around the ship. Feel free to examine your cabins while you wait. Now, if you'll excuse me, we're about to break orbit, and I should be at my station."

Graves returned the way they'd come with a purposeful stride.

Vega gave her a pointed look and went inside his cabin. The hatch slid shut.

Taking the not-so-subtle hint, she stepped into her new home. The hatch slid closed as soon as she stepped away from it. One quick glance told her a fact that should've been obvious before she came aboard. Space was at a premium. Her closet at the palace was larger than this two-person cabin.

Life was full of unexpected challenges.

The layout was quite Spartan. Two bunks folded out from the wall, one above the other. The far wall had a compact desk that looked like it folded up when not needed. The wall opposite the bunk had two wardrobes built into it.

Even with two, she wouldn't have much space at all for clothes. If she stretched out her arms, she could easily touch the bunk and the wardrobe at the same time. Three strides took her from the foot of the bunks to the desk.

She sighed. Well, if her father had lived this way, so could she. The thought brightened her mood. She'd be able to share some stories with him that would bring them closer. Besides, this was an *adventure*—the adventure of her lifetime. She didn't need to think about what she didn't have. She needed to think about what she was getting.

Kelsey sat down at the desk with a smile. She keyed in her thumbprint and started sorting through the publicly available files on the network while she waited for her luggage to arrive.

Let the adventure begin.

7

Jared spent the next three weeks reviewing personnel files for the scientific staff and consulting with the senior scientists over the communications channels. They'd need to have another face-to-face meeting soon, but Jared thought that would have more impact if he waited until they were ready to jump into the unknown. The delay gave him time to review the scientists' backgrounds.

He already knew his crew, including the marines, in detail. Adding familiarity with several hundred scientists and almost that many merchant officers and sailors took time, but he could at least begin the process. He needed the distraction to take his mind off his unwelcome guest, even if only for a little while.

He hadn't gone out of his way to ignore Princess Kelsey...or rather Deputy Ambassador Bandar, but he hadn't sought her out, either. He'd focused his attention on her boss instead. Ambassador Vega was a levelheaded man and went out of his way to work with Jared and his officers. He fit in so well that it was hard to believe that he hadn't been aboard for months.

Any time Jared encountered Kelsey was a different matter. She was always distantly polite, almost like a silent rebuke for his reaction to her presence. His overreaction, rather. She hadn't stepped over the line once. She hadn't really come close. Somewhat to his disappointment.

Now that they'd passed through the fourth flip point and were travelling in unclaimed territory, he needed to address their problematic relationship and call a truce.

He ran into his first obstacle when he went to find her. Since she had no assigned station, she could be almost anywhere on the ship. Well, not engineering, the bridge, operations, or the missile tubes. He decided against paging her because that would make it seem as though he'd summoned her. Rather than get her back up, he'd just have to play "find the princess."

Jared started leaving word for people to call him if she showed up, but he hadn't found her in any of the places he thought most likely. He considered searching the maintenance shafts, but he wasn't sure how she could've gotten into them. It was as if she'd vanished.

Time to form a search and rescue party, and no one was better for the task than the marines. He made his way to marine country and stopped dead just inside the large hatch blazoned with their unit flash.

Deputy Ambassador Kelsey Bandar, second in line to the Imperial Throne of the Terran Empire, sat at a table with four burly men and a wiry woman dressed in battlefield trousers and black T-shirts. Cards and chips covered the tabletop. More than half the chips sat in front of the Imperial scion.

The princess had dressed down in a plain blouse and slacks, and she'd pulled her unruly blonde hair back into a loose ponytail. She took a sip of what looked like beer and tossed some cards out face down. The dealer slid her some replacements with a look of wary respect.

When some of the watchers spotted him, Jared held up a hand to stop them from announcing his presence. The sight of the Imperial princess gambling with some of the roughest, toughest men and women in space boggled his mind.

There was no one he'd rather have at his back than a squad of marines, but he'd never in his wildest dreams let his sister—if he'd had one growing up—gamble with them. She'd come home scratching herself and swearing. If she didn't come home pregnant.

Lieutenant Timothy Reese, the detachment commander, slid around the compartment until he stood beside Jared. "Captain. I've been keeping an eye on things, but I'm starting to think I never needed to worry. She's bonded with them like their little sister."

The odd parallel to Jared's thoughts made him glance sharply at the marine officer. Reese grinned. "Their sister, not someone else's."

Jared shook his head. "Are they letting her win? That's a first. I thought the Imperial Marine motto was to never give a sucker a break."

"That's pretty close to the unofficial motto. When it comes to cards, they don't cut anybody any slack. She doesn't need any help, though. She's beating the proverbial pants off all of them, despite their best efforts. I've been watching to make sure she wasn't cheating.

Empire of Bones

Though I have no idea what I'd do if I found out an heir to the Imperial Throne was cheating card sharks like my people. Probably applaud."

Jared tried to imagine where she could've learned to play poker at this level and failed. It seemed wildly out of character for her. He made a mental note to ask about it one day.

Kelsey picked that moment to stretch, and she must've caught a glimpse of him out of the corner of her eye. She spun her chair toward him and stood. "Captain Mertz. I didn't see you come in."

"My apologies for interrupting your game, Deputy Ambassador. Might I have a moment of your time?"

She counted out her chips, gathered the Imperial credits the dealer paid her, and bowed to her fellow players. "I'll come back and get the rest later."

"You wish," the burliest of them said with a grin. "We'll get ours back next time."

"How's that working out for you so far?"

Everyone at the table laughed. Obviously no hard feelings there. Any intimidation they may have felt at her Imperial stature wasn't apparent now.

Kelsey joined him at the door. "Thanks again for making me welcome, Lieutenant Reese."

The young officer smiled. "Anytime, Kelsey. Consider marine country your second home. Come down in a couple of days and we'll give you a tour of the firing range. The assault rifles might be a bit much for you, but we have some kickass pistols."

The young noblewoman grinned. "I'll hold you to that."

Jared raised an eyebrow at the marine but said nothing as he followed Kelsey out.

She turned to him in the corridor. "What can I do for you, Captain?"

"You can help me figure out how we can work together going forward. I realize neither one of us is overly fond of the other, but we need to get past that. At best, we'll be together almost two years. At worst, three or more."

She nodded slowly up at him. "We have a lot of history to get over, but you're right. This mission isn't the time or place for allowing our feud to continue."

He nodded. "Allow me to start off by apologizing for not having sought you out before now."

"No apology needed. I'm certain you've been very busy. I may not know precisely what a Fleet captain does, but taking on a second ship full of scientists and coordinating a mission of this magnitude must occupy a lot of your time."

A wry smile crossed her lips. "I'm sure that an official stowaway wasn't the most anticipated part of your day either. I don't blame you for being angry with me. It wasn't my idea to come, but I didn't object when the opportunity presented itself."

"Have you gotten a tour of the ship?"

The princess nodded. "Only the common areas. It's fascinating."

"Then let's tour some of the restricted areas. Starting with engineering. Perhaps you can explain what you mean while we walk." He started them toward engineering. "Who else had a hand in your being here? Your father, I assume."

"Our father," she corrected him. "I know that hasn't exactly been a pleasant truth for either of us, but it's a fact we need to accept."

He sighed. "It seems like we could manage to forget that for the time being." He closed his eyes and sighed even deeper. "Fine. Our father."

She explained her late-night discussion with the emperor. "Then he woke me early the next morning and hustled me onto a shuttle. I didn't know where I was going or why until Carlo explained it to me."

Against his will, he found himself nodding. "You do know how to take the fun out of a good mad, don't you?"

"I'm sure I'll do something to legitimately piss you off soon enough."

He chuckled. "I am sorry that our circumstances have put us at odds. I've often considered what my life would be like if I hadn't joined Fleet. If I'd stayed at home and done anything else, everyone's lives would be so much simpler." He gave her a serious look. "I truly regret what this has done to your family."

She sighed. "Me, too. Yet there isn't one thing we can do to change the past. All we can do is make a better tomorrow."

"That sounds like a slogan. Here we are. Stay beside me and don't touch anything without asking."

He pressed his thumb to the pad beside the double doors and stepped inside when they slid open. The area just inside engineering opened up quite a bit. The ceiling was three stories tall, and the room spread the full width of the ship. Massive machines with attached consoles filled most of it, and a subtle humming seemed to make his teeth vibrate a little. There was also a hint of electricity in the air.

"Dennis."

Dennis Baxter turned and gave him a high sign. He said something to the people clustered around him and strode over. "Captain. What can I do for you?"

"This is Deputy Ambassador Kelsey Bandar. Kelsey, this is *Athena's*

Empire of Bones

chief engineer, Lieutenant Commander Dennis Baxter. Dennis, I'd appreciate it if you gave her the grand tour."

Baxter's eyes widened. "I'd heard you were aboard, Princess. Welcome."

She took his hand and shook it. "Thank you. Please, call me Kelsey. Or Ambassador. I'm not acting in an Imperial capacity, and we're all going to be together for some time. Treat me just like you would anyone else."

"As you wish. Call me Dennis. Come on over, and I'll give you the highlights."

He led the two of them to the center of the huge compartment. "Toward the aft are the ship's grav and flip drives. The fusion power plants are under our feet. These consoles here, here, and here monitor everything to be sure we're in good shape. Andrew, give the lady your seat."

One of the men rose and stepped to the side of his console. Baxter gestured for Kelsey to sit.

She sat gingerly, making a show of keeping her hands as far away from the console as she could while looking at the bewildering layout of graphic displays. A large screen directly in front of the seat showed some kind of complex flowchart.

Jared only had a general idea of what he was looking at. Fleet kept its officers focused on their primary fields of study. He'd come up the tactical track, so weapons systems were more his speed. He'd heard of some officers that jumped tracks, but they were the exception rather than the rule. Besides, engineering officers didn't have the combat skills the command track required.

Baxter leaned over Kelsey's shoulder. "Let's take a look at the inside of the port fusion plant. Press that big green button right there." He pointed to one right in front of her.

She pressed it, and every light on the console flashed red just as Baxter said, "Not that one!"

Kelsey threw herself out of the chair, terror etched across her face. Until Baxter's chuckles gave him away. Her eyes narrowed, and she hit the chief engineer in the arm as hard as she could. "How could you! That's mean!"

Then she whirled on Jared. "Did you know what he was doing?" she demanded.

He held up his hands in a gesture of innocence. "I had no idea what that button did. I did fail to mention that Dennis is something of a practical joker, though. You did tell him to treat you just like everyone else."

The princess crossed her arms over her chest and glared at them both for a moment before she smiled a little. "Okay. That was pretty good."

"I couldn't help myself," Baxter said. "All you did was lock the console. In any case, we were running a diagnostic routine, so it's offline. There was never any danger."

"You're still going to pay for that. Now, let's get a real tour."

Jared followed them as Baxter led her deeper into the bowels of engineering. She was a lot different than he'd imagined. Their interaction had always been uncomfortable and stiff. To see her with a sense of humor and such a natural ability to bond with total strangers had him reevaluating everything he thought he knew. Perhaps she was more suited to the role of diplomat than he'd realized.

Baxter took her deeper into engineering. "These are the flip drives. More precisely, the Osborne-Levinson Bridge initiators. No one calls them that. When we dump the capacitors into them, they trigger the gravitational fault in the flip point in such a way that it reverses polarity and takes us to the other side. It's all over before we can even measure the event."

She looked at the massive machine and shook her head. "Just the concept of going light years in the blink of an eye boggles my mind. How do you get your head around something like that?"

He shrugged. "I'm an engineer. I can understand the practical results without knowing all the theory behind it. That's for the scientists over on *Best Deal*. When they start droning on, I flip myself to the other side of the room."

Kelsey laughed. "Have you talked with them about it? I think that would be a fascinating conversation."

"I have. They wanted to change the parameters of what our probes look for, so they had to explain it to me. I immediately went for alcohol once they were gone."

She laughed again. "I'm looking forward to meeting them."

Jared inserted himself there. "We'll have a few combined meetings to plan out things once we reach the kickoff system. I know they love to find someone willing to listen to them explain things, so you'll have plenty to hear."

He turned to Baxter. "What kind of changes did they make to the scanning parameters?"

"They wanted me to increase the sensitivity threshold. There are apparently some competing theories about how weak a flip point can be, and they wanted to be sure that they didn't miss something. I warned

Empire of Bones

them they'd probably get false positives, but they thought that would be acceptable. In any case, I can always change the settings back."

The next stop on the tour was at the grav drives. Baxter rested his hand against one. "These are just like the gravs on every car you've ridden in, just a lot more powerful. Since we use more power and make them very large, they provide much more thrust. Enough to make the trip between flip points in a matter of days."

"I've heard that, and we're making good time, but what about that acceleration? Shouldn't it mash us into jelly?"

"Absolutely not. I'd look terrible in a sandwich. Grav drives work by altering the gravitational gradient of the space-time around a ship. Think of it like falling. You don't feel acceleration as you fall. A failed drive would leave you going exactly the same speed you were already going."

The communicator on Jared's belt beeped. It reminded him that he should issue the diplomatic team some of their own. That would've made tracking Kelsey down significantly simpler. He brought it to his lips. "Mertz."

"Lieutenant Anderson, Captain. We need you up on the bridge right away."

He felt his gut tighten. "Is something wrong?"

"*Best Deal* just signaled their test probes located a flip point."

He whistled. "That's pretty good range to find it from this far away."

"I'm sorry, sir. I should've been clearer. They found a previously undetected flip point between here and the target point."

He shared a look of surprise with Kelsey and Baxter. "I'll be right there."

8

Kelsey followed Jared to the bridge. He was so intent that he seemed to have forgotten she was with him. She wasn't about to remind him. She wanted to know what was going on.

He strode out of the lift and directly to the console in the center of the oval-shaped compartment. The curved front wall held the largest vid screen she'd ever seen. Two large consoles sat in front of them. Two unoccupied consoles behind him faced the rear wall, while a third sat on the far side of the room.

Commander Graves surrendered his seat to Jared. "Doctor Cartwright seems pretty sure that the flip point he detected is real."

"Put the system up on the screen."

The view of the star field vanished, replaced by a graphic of the system. Kelsey found it easy to read. The star and planets were obvious. The small blue circles represented the ships. That meant the green circle behind them and the one in front of them had to be the flip points.

An amber circle appeared between the ships and the most distant flip point. To her eye, the new flip point looked like it was about a quarter of the way toward the flip point they'd been heading toward.

Graves pointed at the screen. "The area in question is almost directly ahead of us and about eighteen hours away at our current speed."

Jared studied something on his console. "What exactly did Cartwright say?"

"The discussion became unintelligible when he tried to explain in more detail."

"Zia, get the good doctor on the screen for me." He looked over and seemed to notice Kelsey for the first time. "Oh. Everyone, this is Deputy Ambassador Bandar. Kelsey, you know Commander Graves." Graves smiled and bowed his head in acknowledgment.

Jared pointed toward the man and woman seated in front of him. "Lieutenant Pasco Ramirez, my helm officer. Lieutenant Zia Anderson, my tactical officer." Both turned and nodded briefly toward her before returning their attention to their consoles.

"Take a seat at one of the unused consoles, please," Jared said. "They're locked, but I'd appreciate it if you kept your hands off the controls anyway."

As if she'd touch another button after that stunt in engineering. "Yes, Captain. It's a pleasure to meet you all." She sat down and clipped the belt around her lap before folding her hands on top of it.

Lieutenant Anderson turned in her seat. "I have Doctor Cartwright, sir."

"On screen."

The representation of the system vanished, and a grandfatherly looking man with fringes of white hair around his bald skull and the most outrageous mustache Kelsey had ever seen appeared. It came off to the sides of his mouth in little points. He looked quite jovial and very, very excited.

"Captain Mertz! Isn't it wonderful?"

Jared smiled politely, but he didn't come out and agree. "We'll see, Doctor. Why don't you give me a general overview? Please consider my relative lack of knowledge about flip points in general. How did you find it when the other scouts coming this way didn't?"

"We have the most sensitive flip scanners since the Fall. Possibly even before. Also, after their initial examination of this system, I doubt anyone has come back to check it again. After all, we had no reason to suspect such a weak flip point existed until recently."

"Elaborate on that. In simple terms, please."

Cartwright reached up and absently twisted his mustache. "Very little is known about pre-Fall technology, but early explorers found bits and pieces drifting in space when we finally climbed out of Avalon's gravity well again. Most of the battle debris was long gone, either burned up in the atmosphere or thrown into various corners of our solar system. One of the things we found was an Osborne-Levinson Bridge scanner from one of the combatants."

The older man turned as though he expected there to be a whiteboard behind him and looked frustrated that there wasn't one. He crossed his arms across his chest. "During the intervening years, we

Empire of Bones

determined its function and replicated it. Once we got into space, we refined that technology even further.

"A young theoretical cosmologist at our university recently reviewed our prevailing understanding about flip points and developed a competing theory which allowed for the possibility of a weaker flip point."

Jared nodded. "You updated the probes with that in mind? Got it. Do you think the Old Empire knew about these weak flip points?"

The scientist shrugged. "We have no way to know for sure. Does it matter if they did?"

"I suppose not. What does this theory say about these weaker flip points? Are they safe to use? Do they go shorter distances?"

"The theory is too untested for those details to be more than educated guesses. We should be able to calculate how strong the flip points are, at least with enough certainty to guess at their safety. My personal feeling is that they lead to closer systems, but we won't know until we send a probe through."

Jared nodded. "Get your people working on refining the data for this particular flip point. We need to have a better understanding before I decide if it's safe to attempt using it."

The scientist nodded sharply. "I have people working on that right now, Captain. I should have some observations by the time we get there. At the very least, I should have much more refined scan data. I suggest we meet tomorrow morning to discuss this in person."

"That sounds like a plan, Doctor. We'll see you on *Best Deal* at 0900."

The older man nodded. "We'll be ready, Captain."

The transmission ended abruptly. Kelsey redirected her attention to Jared. "Are you planning on using it?"

He turned in his seat. "Perhaps. Its unusual nature means I'll at least send a probe through to take some readings. If the other side looks interesting and it seems safe, I'll consider exploring it."

He rose to his feet. "Charlie, get second shift to take over for the evening. We need to get a good night's sleep if we expect to have any chance of understanding what the good doctor tells us."

"Aye, sir."

Jared turned to Kelsey. "Would you care to join me for dinner in the officers' mess?"

She unbuckled her restraint and stood. "I'd like that. Today's been a long, productive day, and I'm famished."

The officers' mess couldn't hold more than two dozen people, and even so, it was only a quarter full. A crewman in a white apron came over to their table. "Captain, Ambassador." He set out water for them. "The mess is serving some excellent fish tonight. I'd recommend it."

She nodded, and Jared followed her example. Once the man was gone, she looked over at her half brother. "Is the food here different from what the enlisted eat? I've been eating there."

"No. Some ships have entirely different menus, but I've always believed that officers and enlisted should eat the same food. Most ships in Fleet are that way. The only reason we have separate messes is so the crew doesn't feel like the officers are watching them when they're off duty. In fact, *Athena*'s officers eat in the crew's mess once a week and on special occasions."

He took a sip of his water and smiled. "I have to admit that you've surprised the hell out of me today. You've always been so reserved. I had no idea you could play cards with the marines on their own terms."

"They were a little leery at first, but I think I've won them over. The Imperial Guards at the palace taught me well. They recruit from inside the Imperial Marines, you know. Frankly, I really enjoy being around people that don't bow and scrape. They tell me what they really think. I like that they treat me as if I belonged and shouldn't be up on a pedestal."

"That should've been true in any case. I see that I've done you another injustice. I apologize for doubting that you had what it takes to be here."

His admission made her preen a little inside. However, his honesty deserved a frank response from her. "I'll confess that I haven't warmed to you very much over the years. I blamed you for what happened to my parents for the longest time. Once I became old enough to understand that wasn't true, it made me feel guilty but didn't change how I treated you. For that, I apologize.

"You're much more complex than I gave you credit for. Seeing you working here is like watching a different man—a leader. Someone who commands respect and demands obedience. A lot like my father. Our father. It's a pity Ethan doesn't get to see this side of you."

Jared looked a little embarrassed. "I've never felt comfortable in the palace. I honestly don't think I ever will. Pardon my frankness, but I doubt seeing another side of me would improve my relationship with your brother."

"Until recently, my brother and I thought you initiated the visits. He thought you were trying to…"

"Curry favor? If so, I'm particularly inept at it. Your brother hates me, and you can barely tolerate me."

"Perhaps that's because we really didn't know one another. I suspect

Empire of Bones

that played a role in our father's thought process when he sent me on this mission with you. He hopes we get past our differences. As do I. This trip could be a chance to start over for both of us. I'm not saying that things *will* change, but we have an excellent opportunity to start fresh."

He smiled a little. "I'd like that." He took a bite of his dinner as soon as the man deposited the plates in front of them. "Mmm. Very nice. So, while you've been exploring the ship, what has Ambassador Vega been doing?"

"Pretty much the same things as me. I see him in the mess hall, mostly. He also spends a lot of time in his cabin. I'd imagine he has a ton of background information to study. Information that I'm already familiar with."

Jared took a drink of his water. "I probably should get together with him before the meeting tomorrow and bring him up to speed. I know I wouldn't want to be blindsided first thing in the morning."

"Good idea. I ate with him at lunch. He had some indigestion and said he'd rest for the afternoon. He's probably feeling better. Let's finish, and we can go talk to him together."

They ate the rest of the meal and chatted about the ship and crew. Kelsey quickly discovered that talking about his people was a sure way to get Jared into an enthusiastic conversation. He really cared about them.

That made the rest of the meal fly by, and they finished before she knew it. Jared stood and led the way back down to her deck. She hoped she eventually learned the ship's layout. It seemed like she got lost almost every day, even after all this time.

Jared stopped outside of Vega's hatch and knocked. When no one answered, he tried again. "He's probably in the mess or wandering around. Remind me to get both of you communicators so that people can contact you."

He brought his communicator to his lips. "Bridge, this is Mertz. Page Ambassador Vega and route his call back to me."

"Aye, sir."

A louder version of the voice came from the concealed speakers overhead. "Ambassador Vega, please call the bridge on the nearest communications unit."

After about thirty seconds, the call repeated. Then the voice came back over the communicator. "I'm sorry, sir. Ambassador Vega isn't responding."

Jared frowned. "Thank you. Mertz out."

He put the communicator back onto his belt. "I suppose we'd best check to be sure everything is okay." He touched his thumb to the lock, and the hatch slid open. "Ambassador? This is Captain Mertz. May I come in?"

Jared stepped inside and cursed. She followed him inside and immediately saw Carlo Vega sprawled on the floor. Jared knelt by his side and felt for a pulse on his neck before pulling his communicator again. "Medical emergency. Medical team to Ambassador Vega's quarters. Chief medical officer to Ambassador Vega's quarters."

She edged closer. Vega's eyes were open and didn't seem focused. "Is he still breathing?"

Jared shook his head. "No. The medics have to check him, but he's gone. It looks like he's been dead for a while."

Kelsey covered her mouth with her hand and stepped aside as the medical team rushed in. They got right to work, but she could tell by the looks on their faces that Jared was right. Carlo Vega was dead.

9

J ared waited for the medics to make the final call, but he knew Carlo Vega was beyond resuscitation. The man's skin was cold to the touch. Medical science was capable of doing some amazing things, but bringing the dead back to life wasn't one of them.

Doctor Stone arrived less than thirty seconds after the crash team. She knelt at the man's side and examined him before shaking her head. "He's gone. Take him to the morgue, and I'll perform an autopsy."

The slender, dark-haired woman stood and walked over to him. "Captain, I'll get started tonight, and I should have some preliminary results on your desk by morning. I'm not seeing any indications of injuries. Do you know if he had any medical conditions?"

"No. As far as I know, Ambassador Vega was healthy."

Stone grabbed a tablet from the medical cart. "I saw him around but thought he came over from the freighter. I have copies of their medical files, but nothing for the ambassador."

Jared sighed. "They boarded at the last minute. I should've verified that they turned over their files and scheduled them for a checkup first thing."

"They? There's someone else running around the ship that I don't know about?"

He nodded toward Kelsey. The young noblewoman stood with a sick expression on her face, silently watching the team move Vega to a stretcher. "My half sister accompanied Ambassador Vega as his deputy. I'm surprised you hadn't heard."

Doctor Stone closed her eyes for a few seconds. She didn't open them when she spoke again. "You're telling me we have a member of the Imperial Family on board and I don't have her files? I haven't examined her. What if she dropped dead? Not to trivialize Ambassador Vega's death, but that would be a disaster. Captain, forgive me for any impertinence, but what the hell were you thinking?"

Jared bowed his head in acknowledgment. "I obviously wasn't."

"I need her in the medical center right now. Ambassador Vega can wait until tomorrow."

"Of course, Doctor. Let me introduce you." He walked over to the princess. "Kelsey, this is Lieutenant Commander Lily Stone, our chief medical officer. Doctor, Deputy Ambassador Kelsey Bandar."

Kelsey took the doctor's proffered hand. "I wish we hadn't met under these circumstances, Doctor. I'm not here in an Imperial capacity, so please just call me Kelsey. Or ambassador, I suppose."

"Call me Lily, then. I'm very sorry for your loss. Did you know Ambassador Vega well? Did he have any medical conditions that you know of?"

Kelsey shook her head. "I've worked with him some and he trained me in diplomacy, but we never discussed any medical information. I had lunch with him today, and he said he had indigestion. I should've come back here with him."

Lily put her hand on Kelsey's shoulder. "People have indigestion every day. While I'll consider it when I start looking for answers, the heartburn might have nothing to do with his death. Don't blame yourself for things you can't reasonably expect to control."

"That's not going to be easy."

"No, it isn't. I didn't have any medical records for either of you. Did you have a copy of yours?"

Kelsey shook her head. "I barely had time to pack a few bags. I'd imagine he had as little warning as I did. Medical records were the very last thing on my mind."

"Then I need you to come to the medical center with me. We need to do a full medical exam."

The princess chuckled without any real humor behind it. "I assure you, I get the very best of medical care. I'm as healthy as a horse, even if I can't prove it."

"I'd wager that Ambassador Vega would've told me something very similar. Everyone on this ship is required to go through a medical checkup when they come on board. It's on me that I didn't examine Ambassador Vega. I'm not going to repeat that error." The doctor's voice had no give to it. Her words were a polite order that Jared knew she'd see enforced.

"Go with her, Kelsey. Arguing with a doctor is like running headfirst into a bulkhead: pointless and very painful."

Kelsey nodded. "Of course. Captain, I need to find out if Ambassador Vega had any files that I need. It looks like I'm going to be stepping up in a big way, and I need to know what the Department of Imperial Affairs sent along. What instructions they might have given him. We've spoken a lot, but we both imagined we'd have more time to train me."

Jared nodded. "I'll have a couple of people come down here and find everything they can. Look at me, Kelsey. Nothing in this job is as big as what you've trained for already. If you can sit on the Imperial Throne, you can handle this mission."

She smiled a little. "Thank you, Captain. I suppose you're right. Doctor?"

Doctor Stone led the princess out, and the medical team followed with Ambassador Vega. Jared hoped to hell he was right about her, because if things went south on this mission, she'd be in the hot seat, and all their lives might depend on her diplomatic skills.

He called for some technicians to screen everything Vega had for files, including the bags he'd had stored. He instructed them to transfer everything they found to Kelsey's computer. Then he went back to his cabin. He had enough time to do some paperwork, and then he'd get a good night's sleep. Tomorrow might be a very long day.

* * *

SLEEPING TURNED out to be more difficult than Jared had hoped. He lay awake for a couple of hours before he finally drifted off. His dreams weren't quite nightmares, but Carlo Vega kept following him everywhere he went. Waking up early was welcome.

His cabin was generous by Fleet standards. It actually had a large private head, a kitchenette, and a small work area. He normally used his office near the bridge to handle paperwork, but he made some coffee and sat at his station to review his inbox. No autopsy report, but that wasn't a surprise. Lily would've spent the evening going through Kelsey's examination results. She'd probably run labs late into the night.

Vaguely dissatisfied, he worked on various reports until he had to get ready for the flight to *Best Deal*. He took a sonic shower and dressed for the day. He ate a quick breakfast in the officers' mess, and when Kelsey failed to put in an appearance, he ordered her something to go. She needed fuel to get through the day, too.

She answered his knock looking disheveled. She'd obviously slept in and probably had an even worse night than he had. "What?"

Jared held out the bag of food and a cup of coffee. "You need to get ready. Our cutter leaves in a little more than half an hour. I'll be waiting for you in the forward docking bay."

Kelsey took the food and closed the door without another word. He smiled. Not a morning person. He imagined she'd been a joy when her father woke her up and stuffed her into the cutter.

He went to the docking bay and helped the pilot with his preflight of the cutter. The man probably didn't appreciate the interference, but he wisely said nothing. Sometimes being the captain had tangible benefits. The other officers coming over for the briefing started arriving ten minutes before departure time.

Kelsey hurried in with less than sixty seconds to spare. "Sorry. I got lost."

"We're going to have to send you around with the damage control teams to learn the ship's layout."

From her expression, she didn't get that he was joking.

"Just kidding. You'll figure it out. Come up front, and you can sit in the flight engineer's seat. We don't need one for such a short trip."

Jared locked her console and made sure that she was strapped in before sliding into the pilot's chair. The assigned pilot took the copilot's seat. He slid a headset on and made sure he was on the control frequency. "*Athena*, this is *Athena Three*. Ready for departure."

"Roger, *Athena Three*," Zia said. "You are cleared for immediate departure. Have a good flight, Captain."

"Thanks, Zia. *Athena Three* out."

He undocked and dropped the cutter out of its slip. The screens cleared and displayed the star field. It was beautiful, as always. *Best Deal* showed clearly on his scanners. It was less than five minutes away. The acceleration he applied put *Athena* behind them and made *Best Deal* grow quickly on the screens.

"*Best Deal*, this is *Athena Three* on approach. Request docking instructions."

"*Athena Three*, you are cleared for docking port two. You are the only flight inbound at this time, so you may proceed directly to the dock."

"Thanks, *Best Deal. Athena Three* out."

He quickly mated the cutter to the docking port. The indicators turned green, and he locked the controls. Then he lit the "disembark" light in the cabin. "Ensign Kruger, you have the boat."

Empire of Bones

"Aye, sir. We'll be ready to depart whenever you are. Have a good meeting."

Jared unstrapped and waited for Kelsey to precede him out of the cutter. Several merchant crewmen waited for them in the docking chamber. One of them saluted Jared. "Captain Mertz? This way, sir."

Jared returned the salute and followed the man with Kelsey at his side. The rest of his officers followed them into the bowels of the ship. For once, he had no idea where they were going. He'd been here before, but the ship was still under renovation then.

They went down several corridors in turn and took two separate lifts. Eventually they entered a huge conference room. It looked like it could seat a hundred people, and it was almost full.

They'd reserved half the seats at the long conference table in the center of the compartment for his officers. A quick count confirmed there was one for Kelsey.

Anton Keller, the grizzled merchant captain of *Best Deal*, sat at one end of the table. The seat opposite him sat empty, reserved for Jared. Dr. Zephram Cartwright sat midway along the side facing the large screen at the head of the room. The elderly scientist looked as though he'd been up all night, but he seemed pleased.

Captain Keller stood, and the scientists followed his example after a beat. It wasn't in their culture, and Jared wasn't offended at the unintentional discourtesy. He couldn't expect scientists and merchants to know how Fleet demonstrated respect to commanding officers.

Jared sat. "Gentlemen, thank you for meeting with me so soon. I'm sure you've all been very busy and still have much work to do, so let's get this under way. Allow me to introduce Ambassador Kelsey Bandar. She joined *Athena* at the last minute, so you may not have been aware of her presence."

Keller bowed his head. "Welcome aboard, Ambassador."

Once everyone had taken their seats, Jared gave the chief scientist his full attention. "I think we should get right to the matter, Doctor. What do we have here?"

"Thank you, Captain Mertz." Cartwright slid his finger along a control on the table in front of him, and the lights dimmed. The screen on the wall—larger than the one on *Athena*'s bridge—blinked to life with a representation of local space. The diagram clearly showed *Athena* and *Best Deal* in relation to the newly found flip point nearby.

"What we have here is definitely a flip point. Close-range scans leave no room for doubt. It has a significantly weaker gravitic field and is notably smaller as well. This flip point is scarcely ten kilometers across."

That *was* small, less than one quarter of the normal size. "Do you think it's an anomaly, or might there be more of these scattered around?" Jared asked.

"I spent quite a bit of time reading the papers that have proposed this kind of occurrence last night. I believe that there may be more of these, though I doubt they are nearly as common as standard flip points."

He switched the screen to a series of graphs. "Without getting into the fine details, the flip point appears to be stable enough to use. How far it goes was a lively subject of debate over coffee this morning. I'm willing to wager that it likely leads to a system quite close by. Perhaps less than a dozen light years away."

Kelsey leaned forward. "Do you think it's safe to use, Doctor?"

The scientist shrugged. "That's one of the reasons I'm advocating that we send a probe through. Until we get the readings from the other side, we have no way of knowing."

Jared nodded. They had more than enough probes and could build more if needed. "I'll want to go over what you've discovered and recorded on your scanners, but I'm good with sending a probe now. When can you have it ready?"

Keller spoke up. "I took the liberty of having one prepared. We can launch it at your order."

"Excellent. I like when people are ready to execute a plan. You have a 'go' for the probe."

The merchant captain touched his controls. "Launch the probe."

An amber spark representing the probe appeared on the screen and accelerated away from *Best Deal*. It made its way into the nearby flip point in less than a minute and braked to a stop. Moments later, it vanished.

"Flip successful," Keller said. "It's programmed to scan for half an hour and then flip back."

Jared nodded. "Good. While it's doing its job, let's have a more detailed introduction of the senior scientists and my crew. I'd intended to do this when we were a little further along, but it looks like we might possibly be at a new kickoff point if things look interesting over there."

Kelsey frowned at him. "You intend to go through it? That seems relatively risky. No one has ever used one of these weak flip points before."

"Frankly, it would take something really interesting on the other side to convince me, but I'm not rejecting it out of hand. I'll make the decision when we go over the probe's recordings."

They spent the next half hour introducing themselves to one another and giving a short summary of individual backgrounds. The Fleet

Empire of Bones

officers were thankfully brief, but the scientists rambled. It was interesting, though. These were some very talented minds present.

They were listening to a distinguished older woman speak when the console chimed. The probe had returned. Keller tapped on his controls. "Pardon me, Doctor Nelson. Downloading the scanner readings now. I'll throw the map up on the screen."

Jared watched closely as a representation of the target star system appeared. With only half an hour to scan, the details were preliminary and very general. The star was a standard yellow star. No planets were marked, but they were hard to see without long and detailed data processing.

One thing stood out. The flip point on the other end was even smaller than this end. It only covered about seven kilometers. Doctor Cartwright grunted. "Interesting. I didn't expect the other end to be so small. The theory didn't really hint at that."

Jared connected the small console inset into the table to the feed as it came in, scanning for anything interesting. While it loaded, he glanced at the scientist. "Now that you've seen the other side, do you think it's safe?"

"It should be. The probe made it there and back. Though I wouldn't recommend it if there isn't a pressing reason."

An icon appeared on Jared's screen, flashing in lurid scarlet. He blinked in shock for a moment and looked at the scientist. "It looks like we have our reason. I want to know everything you can divine about that flip point, and I want it fast."

Kelsey leaned over and stared at his console. "What is that?"

He looked back at the flashing icon. "It's a Fleet distress beacon. But not one of ours."

Her gaze whipped up to his face. "You mean that's from the Old Empire?"

Jared nodded. "I've seen drawings of one in old reports. There were a lot of them in the skies during and after the rebel attack on Avalon. I have no idea what the data coming in with it is, but it definitely means something is over there, and we have to go after it."

10

Kelsey thought about what the distress beacon might mean all the way back to *Athena*. The implications were huge. It was the biggest discovery since the Fall. That probably meant they would briefly explore what they'd found and head right back home. The news was exciting and terrible all at once.

She sighed. Well, it was good for the Empire, even if it meant she probably wouldn't be coming back out with them. That might be for the best. Without Carlo Vega, she was filling some very big shoes.

The cutter docked, and she politely separated from Jared and the rest. She needed time to think. He'd call her before they made any major moves.

Her thoughts occupied so much of her attention as she walked that she didn't notice that Doctor Stone had stepped up beside her until the woman spoke.

"Welcome back, Kelsey. Do you have time to come down to my office?"

She gave the dark-haired Fleet officer a sideways look. "That sounds ominous."

The doctor smiled. "You're in perfectly good health. However, there are some things we need to talk about in private."

"Carlo?"

"Him, too."

Kelsey shrugged and followed the other woman back down to the medical center. The smell of disinfectant made her shudder. She was all too familiar with the closet-sized office just off the main treatment room after last night. She sat and was surprised when Stone ignored her desk and took the seat beside her after she closed the hatch.

"As I said, your test results came back clean," the doctor said. "You're healthy and look like you'll be that way for many years."

"Good! So why do we need to talk?"

"Captain Mertz is your half brother, correct?"

Kelsey nodded. "He is."

"I don't know how to explain this, but I took a genetic scan of you last night, and it doesn't match him at all."

Kelsey frowned. "That's impossible. They matched his scan to my father."

Stone nodded. "Yes, they did…at Orbital One, where they have all the medical records of all Fleet members past and present. I don't have the emperor's medical information in my database, but the notation in Captain Mertz's file says it is a conclusive and verified match. The emperor is his father."

"I don't understand."

The doctor reached out and took Kelsey's hand in hers. "If he's a match with your father, then you aren't."

"What?" She pulled away abruptly. "That's insane. Of course I am. How could I not be related to my father?"

Doctor Stone leaned back, her eyes full of sympathy. "I know this must be a horrible shock. It's not standard practice to do a paternity verification with married couples. Even with the Imperial Family. Unless a court intervenes and requires one."

Kelsey stared at the other woman blankly, unsure of what to say.

"I'm sorry to tell you this, Kelsey, but if Captain Mertz's test was correct and he is your father's son, then there is no conceivable way you can be the emperor's biological daughter. There is simply no room for inaccuracy in the test, but I ran it three times to be sure."

That just wasn't possible. Kelsey shook her head. "I don't know where the mistake is, but something isn't right. If you didn't make it, someone else did with Jared."

"I'm pretty sure they checked everything many times to be sure with him, as well. Your father acknowledged his paternity despite the impending destruction of his marriage. He wouldn't have done that unless he was absolutely certain."

They sat in silence while Kelsey's thoughts ran around in tight circles. If the doctor was correct, then her life was a lie, and so was her twin brother's. The heir to the Imperial Throne.

Oh, crap.

Empire of Bones   69

She covered her face with her hands. "This can't be happening."

"If he isn't my father, who is?"

"That's a question I'm definitely not qualified to answer. All I can say with any certainty is that it wasn't the emperor. I'm not blind to the array of political implications this information creates, but I'm not worried about that right now. I'm worried about you. None of this changes who you are one bit."

Kelsey shot to her feet and stared pacing the office. "Oh, but it does. Oh, God, does it." She started waving her hands around with each thought. "It throws the entire Imperial succession into chaos. My brother and I are just as much bastards as Jared is. More so since we have no Imperial blood. At least he has the emperor as a father."

"You're wrong," Doctor Stone said firmly. "A father is much more than a genetic donor. Your father raised you. He loves you. Many fathers have adopted children. They are still very much fathers to them. Jared may share his genetics, but he is not the man's son by any stretch of the imagination."

"What am I going to do?" Kelsey moaned. "When the Imperial Senate gets wind of this, it could tear the Empire apart."

"Then don't tell them."

Kelsey stopped in her tracks. "If only it were that easy. No. Someone will talk. Someone always talks. Then we have a much larger problem on our hands."

The Fleet officer looked up at Kelsey serenely. "I'm not telling anyone other than you. They'll only know if you say something."

"You haven't told Jared already?"

Stone shook her head. "This is private medical data. I have it locked down under my seal. I'm only obligated to tell you."

"But they told the emperor that Jared was his son. How could you keep silent when I'm not?"

"That doctor violated his oath when he did that. I will not violate mine." The doctor's voice was as unyielding as *Athena*'s hull. "You were already aware of Jared's parentage, so I broke no rules in comparing the two of you and informing you of my findings. The captain has no need to know about this test. If you choose to tell him, that's your business, but a secret doesn't stay secret for long when you tell more people."

Kelsey sank back into her chair. "Truly? You'd keep this just between us? Never tell anyone...ever?"

Doctor Stone rose to her feet and strode to the desk. She tapped the screen a few times. "There. I've erased the test results and deleted your sample from the medical database. No one will ever know unless you decide they must. I'd personally advise against it for all the very good reasons you've mentioned.

"At the very least, take the time we're away from home to consider your options. There's always time to tell your father later. Once you say something, though, you can't unsay it."

Kelsey rubbed her temples. "The irony makes my head ache. I've been an insufferable bitch to Jared for almost my entire life because my father cheated on my mother. Now I find out my mother did the exact same thing. She didn't know about Father's infidelity at the time, so it wasn't even a case of revenge. That's rich.

"I've had a hard time forgiving my father for what he did. Now I have to start over with my mother. She had to have wondered if we were his. What woman wouldn't connect the dots with the timing? Her outrage at his indiscretion really burns me up. She made such a spectacle of playing the injured spouse. God, that's infuriating!" Kelsey was so angry that she felt her eyes tearing up.

The doctor again took Kelsey's hand into hers. "I'm so sorry to have been the messenger of this bad news."

Kelsey wiped at her tears and squeezed the woman's hand. "It's not your fault. No one on this ship is responsible. I have plenty of time to contemplate what to do about it later. What can you tell me about Carlo?"

Stone released Kelsey's hand. "That's more complex. The precise cause of death was an acute myocardial infarction. Even if he'd been standing in the medical center, I probably wouldn't have been able to save his life. There was nothing you could've done."

"What about the indigestion? Was that a symptom?"

"It often is, but in his case it wasn't because of the heart attack. The complexity came into play when I started looking for the cause of the heart attack. It turns out he somehow suffered an overdose of a chemical agent. One he shouldn't have had contact with under any circumstances I can imagine. I don't even believe there is any of this substance on this ship."

Kelsey shook her head. "Hold up. Are you saying he was poisoned?"

"Possibly." The doctor softened her tone, "Who might have wanted him dead?"

A wave of nausea washed over Kelsey. "I have no idea. He got along with everyone we met. Can you tell when it happened?"

"I'm still working on that angle. It's possible he consumed the poison at breakfast. Did you eat with him that morning?"

She shook her head. "I was up late, so he went without me. I'm not a morning person. I think he was over on *Best Deal* for a briefing with Jared."

Stone nodded. "I'll ask the captain when I update him on this in a few minutes. There's going to be a full investigation. If this was murder, we'll get to the bottom of it."

They talked a little longer, but Kelsey eventually excused herself. She needed to mull over everything she'd just learned.

She retreated to an out-of-the-way spot she'd discovered—the navigator's cubby. The small chamber was little more than a seat and console within a concave bubble. The view was extraordinary, and it never seemed occupied. It probably existed in case there was some kind of major systems failure.

She strapped herself into the seat and raised it into an extended position, giving her a near-360-degree view. The sea of stars washed over her, dim until her eyes adjusted to the faint light. The view never failed to make her feel insignificant. Particularly so today.

The news about Carlo stunned her, but she kept thinking about her parentage. Was keeping silent the right decision? No one had found out in over twenty years. Given her family's position, the odds were very good they wouldn't ever find out.

Yet did she have the right to keep that information from Ethan? He tended to be something of an ass at times, but he was her brother.

It would wreck him. He'd tied his whole identity to his position as Imperial heir. To say he wouldn't take the news well was a profound understatement.

For her, it wasn't that important. She never expected to inherit the Throne. That was someone else's job. She cared much more about her family bonds than her social status.

Did this change everything for her?

Perhaps not. Her father and mother loved her, and she loved them, even if she was furious with Mother right now. The doctor was right. If she ended up separated from an Imperial title, it wouldn't change who she was. Father wouldn't toss her out the door. Based on how he treated Jared, the news wouldn't alter his behavior one bit.

However, the Imperial Senate would strip Ethan of his position. She had no idea who they'd replace him with. Neither did they, she was sure. Although they might all refer to one another as good friends and colleagues, the fractures in the Senate were deeply divisive. A vote to remove the confirmed heir would take a two-thirds majority. So would approving another heir.

They might agree on removing a bastard from the succession, especially if he wasn't the emperor's. They'd never agree to a replacement that wasn't the child of the emperor. The conservative senators would staunchly favor one of their own, as would the social liberals. Since each had more than a third of the membership in the Senate, there would be no compromise. Goodness knew how long that stalemate would last.

Even if they did settle their grievances, they would probably install a senator as the heir. A disastrous precedent. A coup in everything but name. She'd spent her life learning that the needs of the Empire were more important than her own.

No good could come of letting the truth out. She had to keep the knowledge to herself. She couldn't allow her father to know. He'd feel obliged to make the knowledge public. Just look at what he'd done with Jared.

Ethan would act out in some way if he found out. She knew it. He was entirely too impulsive and ruled by his emotions when he felt threatened or slighted. So she could never tell him, either.

Jared would probably keep the knowledge to himself, but she couldn't be certain of that. He had his own version of honor, and he hated being the Imperial Bastard. No, she could only trust herself…and Doctor Stone…to keep the secret.

"Ambassador Bandar, please report to the bridge."

The voice from the console startled her. She touched the now glowing icon to acknowledge the page with an acceptance signal. The man who'd called would see that she'd responded.

The call likely meant that Jared was ready to fill her in on his plans. Or he'd talked to Stone about Carlo Vega. She'd find out soon enough.

11

Jared had just finished giving his orders to Ramirez and was watching the ship begin moving toward the flip point as Kelsey walked onto the bridge. He gestured for her to join him at his console. He looked furious.

"Doctor Stone just left. She told me you know what she found."

Kelsey's expression darkened. "About Carlo. Yes. It's horrible. Who would do such a thing?"

"We don't know. Yet. You can rest assured that we won't stop looking until we do. A destroyer doesn't need a security department like Orbital One, but we have some qualified people. Since he ate breakfast with me on *Best Deal*, it may take quite a while to determine exactly what happened."

Though Jared had a few ideas. He suspected the situation was more complex than it appeared. Since Kelsey hadn't been spending time with him, she didn't know one critical piece of information. Vega had brought a gift for Jared from the Imperial Family: candies from a specialty house. Unfortunately, Jared secretly hated coconut.

Or perhaps fortunately. At least for him.

He'd taken advantage of Kelsey's absence to tell Vega to enjoy them with his compliments. He'd watched the man have one that morning. Now Jared suspected someone had poisoned at least one of the treats and that Jared had been the intended target.

Stone hadn't been able to tell if the poison had been in any specific food, and Jared had no proof that Crown Prince Ethan wanted him dead.

Allowing his suspicions into the record would have any number of negative consequences. Kelsey wouldn't believe her brother was a killer. No loyal Imperial citizen would imagine the heir to the Throne as a murderer. Especially with nothing but the word of the Imperial Bastard.

Jared would let the investigation go forward and let it come to its own conclusions. He'd searched for any remaining candies, but Vega must've eaten them all. Based on how they were packaged, the fatal dose would've probably been in the last few pieces. No evidence left to link the poison to the true killer that way.

Maybe his people would find a surprise on *Best Deal*. Someone who secretly hated Vega. Not likely, but possible. That would be the best possible outcome. Otherwise, Jared would be watching his back for the rest of his life once they made it back home.

He pushed the thoughts out of his head. He had more pressing things to deal with. "In the meantime, we're going through the flip point. The plan is to take *Athena* across and send word back via probe. They're based on standard data drones and still have the communication and data storage equipment installed."

Communication drones routinely flipped back and forth at the major flip points throughout the Empire, accepting data transmissions and sending them on at the other side. They couldn't do many flips without maintenance and recharging, so the Empire didn't use them in less traveled areas. Though that might change if they found anything half as interesting as he imagined they might on this trip.

"I've got a cutter standing by to take you over to *Best Deal*," he continued. "They'll follow once *Athena* is safely over."

Kelsey shook her head. "I'm assigned here, and I'll go across with you."

Her answer set him back for a moment. She'd been so cooperative the other day that he'd forgotten how willful she could be. This was more like the Kelsey he knew.

"That's not open to negotiation, Kelsey."

"Ambassador Bandar in this case, Captain. I've reviewed Ambassador Vega's orders. The ambassador goes wherever this ship does. Those orders fall to me now. I'm sorry if I seem obstinate."

He considered arguing, but he was honest enough to admit that she was probably within her rights. "Let's hope we don't regret that decision." He raised his voice. "Zia, have the cutter pilot stand down. She won't be needed after all."

"Yes, sir," she responded. "We're inside the flip point."

Empire of Bones 75

"Helm, bring us to a stop in the center."

Lieutenant Ramirez touched his console. "All stop, Captain. Flip drive standing by."

"Ambassador," Jared said formally. "We are prepared to flip. Please strap in to one of the observation seats."

Kelsey did so without any fuss. She sat facing the screen with her hands folded on her lap when she finished securing her belt.

Jared opened the shipwide channel. "All hands, this is the captain. We're about to flip to an unexplored system through an untested flip point. Secure your sections and report to operations when you're ready."

"Where is Commander Graves?" Kelsey asked.

"His battle station is in the operations center. On a destroyer, that means a three-man backup control room. If something disastrous happens to us, he'll assume command. Otherwise he's responsible for supporting us while we control the ship."

On a larger ship, they'd have a dedicated staff to interpret the scanner readings and help keep the captain informed about the tactical situation, but a destroyer really didn't need that level of support. Admittedly, it would have been helpful in this case.

Perhaps a light cruiser would be a better choice for future missions. The improved command and control systems would be a plus, and more missile tubes never hurt.

"Bridge, this is operations," Graves said over the communications link. "All departments report ready to flip."

"Thanks, Charlie." Jared nodded to Ramirez. "Give us a thirty-second warning and flip the ship."

"Aye, sir."

The flip warning sounded from the overheads. The countdown went by silently until Ramirez spoke again. "Flipping the ship."

A normal flip was over in less time than a person could detect, though it didn't feel instantaneous. It disrupted people's equilibrium for a few moments, which was why everyone strapped in before a flip. Once that effect passed, everything was back to normal before the helm officer announced they had made it.

This flip was anything but normal.

According to Jared's inner ear, some giant hand picked up the ship and spun it like a top. As the ship reeled, he felt glad he'd strapped in. He would've fallen out of his seat if he hadn't. The sensation persisted, and he almost lost his lunch. Someone did, although he couldn't tell whom. The sound of them retching and the smell almost pushed him into joining them.

He forced himself to focus on his console. They'd completed the flip and were floating in a new system. Obviously. If they hadn't made it all the way, he probably wouldn't be feeling so terrible. The ship's status was still green, so the mechanical parts of the ship had made it just fine.

"Flip complete," Ramirez gasped. "Holy God. I feel like someone kicked me in the…well, you know."

Jared most certainly did. The nausea was actually very similar to that event, though the disorientation wasn't. He pushed the feelings to the back of his mind and focused on his job. "Operations, I want a status on every person onboard."

"Aye, Captain." Graves sounded just as bad as Jared felt.

A glance over at Kelsey revealed that it had been her he'd heard retching. She sat bent over and holding her gut.

He unbuckled his restraint and staggered to his feet. He managed to make it to her side without falling over. "You okay?"

She looked up, her eyes not really focused. "That sucked."

He chuckled ruefully. "Indeed. Chin up. It'll wear off."

Jared found some rags in the emergency repairs cubby and cleaned up the vomit. He could've called someone to take care of it, but his people had more important things to do. The rags went into the disposal bin. The life support system quickly whisked the sour odor away.

He held himself upright against the bulkhead and verified everyone else seemed to be recovering. He made it back over to his chair without mishap and sighed gratefully as he strapped himself back in.

"Bridge, this is operations," Graves said. "All hands are accounted for. A few will be going to the medical center when someone can help them, but everyone is conscious and responsive."

"That's good, Charlie. Get to work nailing things down about our new location."

He killed the circuit. "Zia, what can you tell me about the flip point?"

She studied her console. "It looks like it did in the probe scans. Obviously the trip through was a lot rougher than we normally see. It's closer in to the system primary than usual, too. About the orbit of Avalon. The star looks a little dimmer and smaller than Avalon's, so the habitable zone is probably smaller. I don't have any more information on possible planets, but our location seems to be clear of debris."

"What about that distress beacon?"

"I'm picking it up loud and clear. I have a direction, but I'm unsure how far away it is. We'd need to move perpendicular to it for a little ways so I can triangulate. I can tell you that it's outside our orbit, so it's not a habitable world."

Empire of Bones

"Let's wait until everyone can move around first. Now that we're safely here, let's recover."

It took about ten minutes for the worst of the dizziness to fade. Kelsey seemed to be recuperating a little more slowly, but she had far less experience with flips than his crew did.

"What happened?" she finally asked him.

"That smaller flip point must mean it's a more difficult ride, apparently. We won't know for sure until the science teams get here. Zia, load a probe with all our scanner data and append a warning that it's a bad transition. We don't want them worrying for too long. Send it once you're done."

"Aye, sir."

"Bridge, this is operations."

"Mertz here. What have you got?"

"We're still working on the system data, but I have a rough estimate on our location relative to known space. You know how Doctor Cartwright bet it would be a short-range hop?"

"Is it?"

Graves chuckled. "I hope you took him up on that bet, because we're at least five hundred light years away from where we started."

Jared felt his eyes widen. "That's preposterous. The longest known flip is less than two hundred."

"Not anymore."

They were farther away from known space than the current Empire was across. That counted the previously explored but unclaimed space.

"Thanks, Charlie. Let us know when you have anything else for us."

"Right. Operations out."

"Pasco, take us on a perpendicular course from the distress beacon. I want to know how far away it is."

Ten minutes passed as they shifted position. Doctor Stone reported in that a dozen people had come with exceptionally bad nausea. It looked like Kelsey wasn't the worst hit. Stone expected them all to recover shortly.

Once he finished talking to the doctor, Zia called out to him. "I have a rough range to the distress beacon, Captain. It's about three hours away at moderate acceleration. I don't see anything at that location, so it's probably small. Nothing showing on the gravitic scanners."

"We'll go after it once *Best Deal* arrives and is ready to travel. After all this time, a few hours more won't matter."

He brought them back close to the flip point, and they waited.

Without warning, the empty space inside it wasn't empty anymore.

Best Deal popped into existence half a dozen kilometers away. Zia reported it looked good from the outside, so Jared had her hail them.

Their response time was long enough to worry him, but Captain Keller finally answered. "Wow. That is the worst thing I've ever felt."

Jared chuckled in sympathy. "Agreed. Get a status on your people and get back to me. We have a team standing by if you need medical assistance."

In the end, it took almost two hours to get the freighter ready to move under her own power again. Luckily, they also had no serious issues with the crew. Everyone made the flip in one piece.

Jared was about to order them to set course for the distress beacon, but a priority call from Doctor Cartwright made him pause.

"Captain," the scientist said, "we may have a problem." The older man looked like he'd taken a ride in a centrifuge. His skin was almost grey, and the hair he had left was sticking straight out.

"What kind of problem, Doctor?"

"A detailed scan of the flip point shows instability. The gravitic field almost looks like a slowly spinning vortex. A whirlpool."

"That's not normal?"

The older man shook his head. "Absolutely not. I've never seen anything like it before. The motion was too subtle for the probe to pick up. I'd have sounded the alarm if I'd had any inkling about it."

Jared felt his gut tighten. "An alarm about what?"

Cartwright shrugged. "I'm not exactly certain, but anything this different from the norm is worth noting. I suspect that the rotating gravitic field is what caused such intense disorientation. While concerning, that isn't my biggest worry. The field is weak. Even the other end of this flip point has a normal strength field, though it is smaller. Not so here. This end is only half the strength I would've expected."

"What might that mean, Doctor?"

"I don't know," he said a bit crossly. "Perhaps nothing. The flip back might be worse than the one to get here. Perhaps the flip back won't work at all."

Jared's heart froze. "Not at all? The probes made it back without any issue."

"The probes are tremendously smaller than our ships. I'm only hypothesizing, and that is the worst case."

"What would be the results of a failed flip? Would the ship go part way and break up? Be destroyed on the spot?"

"Doubtful. The most likely outcome is that the ship doesn't go anywhere at all. The gravitic field could be too weak to open for a ship

Empire of Bones 79

from this end at all. If so, then you'd hit the button and a lot of nothing would happen."

That was better than blowing up. "Thank you, Doctor. We'll figure this out shortly, so keep your scanners on the flip point. I want to know as much as possible when the time comes."

He closed the connection and called Graves. "I want all nonessential personnel shifted over to *Best Deal*. Transfer any critical supplies as well. We're going to make the transition back over to be sure we can go home."

Jared turned his attention to Kelsey. "You're going over to *Best Deal* with every single person I can do without. I'll log your objection, but if this ship doesn't come out the other side, I want you here with the rest finding another way home. They'll need you a lot more than I will."

He expected her to argue, but she nodded. "Of course, Captain. No objection."

In the end, they shifted more than three quarters of the crew over to *Best Deal*. The skeleton crew left on board was just enough to operate the ship. The marines objected to him ordering them off the ship, but this wasn't one of those situations where they could do much good. He manned the bridge alone.

Jared moved the ship back to the center of the flip point and signaled *Best Deal* that they were transitioning. He took a deep breath and activated the flip drive. The graphs showed the drive peaking, but nothing else happened. *Best Deal* still sat right there on his scanners.

They were trapped.

12

Kelsey waited on *Best Deal* until everyone else had returned to *Athena*, taking the last flight back. The loss of their way home had hit everyone hard. She still couldn't get her head around it. Too many shocks to her system, she supposed.

She listened to the scientists hashing out theories while she waited for her departure time, but except for using bigger words, they were saying the same thing as the Fleet officers. They didn't know what had happened. Not really.

Sure, they knew the flip point was defective, but not why. They'd be tearing apart the science behind everything for years without ever knowing what made these things tick, she suspected. The bottom line was that they were stuck until they found another flip point leading back to known space.

She pointed that out to them. The Old Empire had gotten here somehow. If it didn't use the defective flip point, then there had to be at least one more in this system.

That sent the scientists scurrying to the scanners. They shot probes in every direction, including toward the distress beacon.

The crew of *Athena* was busy when she finally got back, so she retreated to her seat on the bridge and sat quietly. After a while, they seemed to forget she was there. That was just fine by her. She had plenty to think about. Particularly Carlo Vega's death.

She had no idea why some unnamed person had killed her mentor, but his death didn't seem like an accident. What could motivate someone to murder him, though?

She'd asked some questions while she was on *Best Deal* but gathered no new answers. She wasn't exactly an investigator. Someone else would need to track down the person or persons behind the attack.

Lieutenant Anderson eventually reported the probe going toward the distress beacon had picked up a ship. Jared sat up a little straighter. "What can you tell me about it?"

"Just that it's a ship. We're too far away to get any more details."

"Ramirez, confer with *Best Deal* and have her follow us at her best speed. Bump us up to full speed."

"Aye, sir."

When they finally had a visual, the tiny speck on the screen could've been a smudge for all Kelsey could tell. Light was a little dim this far from the primary. She watched it with intense interest as the probe drew closer.

To think, they were about to see a ship of the Terran Empire at its heyday. It was obviously in one piece and had some kind of power. The thought of what they could learn staggered her.

The dot slowly resolved itself into a tumbling shape. It looked a little like a toy spaceship.

Lieutenant Anderson spoke up. "We're close enough to get some relative size data, Captain. That ship is significantly larger than *Athena* is. It's larger than the biggest ship in our fleet, though not by a tremendous amount. Perhaps one class larger than a heavy cruiser."

"Interesting," Jared said. "A battlecruiser?"

The ship on the screen grew slowly larger until Kelsey could see the hull clearly. It was spinning as well as turning end over end, but it appeared intact. The value of the find was immeasurable. Even though the interior was in all likelihood wrecked, they could still learn so much just by studying what remained.

"The probe is in station-keeping mode," Anderson reported. "I'm recording the exterior visual as it turns. I should have a complete picture in a minute."

"Any sign of battle damage?" Jared asked.

"There's something back in the engineering section. Not a rupture, though. I'm putting it on screen."

The view of the spinning derelict vanished, replaced by a still of the hull. A long gash had split the hull open. It looked like something had melted the metal.

"That's beam damage," Jared said.

"Beam damage?" Kelsey asked.

He turned his attention to her. "The records mention them. The Old Empire had missiles similar to the ones we do, but they also had beam weapons. That's something Fleet has been experimenting with for years. Unsuccessfully, so far."

"Surface scan complete," Anderson said. "There are several other areas with similar damage. Nothing on the scale of the breach in engineering, though."

Kelsey shook her head. "Something like that could've cut this ship into blocks. Why isn't it worse?"

Jared tipped his head toward the screen. "That ship had energy screens, if the old stories were correct. An enemy would have to be damned close or have done a lot of damage to the screens to get to the hull. It's possible the crew surrendered and then abandoned the ship. With that kind of damage, I'd expect something like that. They probably activated the distress beacon so it could be located later. Then they never came back."

"Do you think it's a renegade Fleet ship?"

He shrugged. "We may never know. It's kind of moot at this point."

"Captain, I have a name for the derelict," Anderson said. The image on the screen changed to show the bow of the ship. The large white letters spelled out her name. *Courageous*.

"I bet they were," Jared muttered. "How long until we reach the wreck? Are you picking up a power source for the distress beacon?"

The woman checked her screen. "We're about thirty minutes out. The probe is picking up indications of an operating fusion plant in the stern of the ship. It's running at low levels and seems to be fluctuating in output."

"Is it dangerous?"

"I'm not certain. That's more a question for an engineer, sir."

He nodded and rose to his feet. "Call the department heads to the conference room. Ambassador, would you care to join me?"

* * *

THE CONFERENCE ROOM on *Athena* was a lot smaller than the one on *Best Deal*. Kelsey took the seat next to Jared and tried to stop her brain from racing in circles. A relic of the fabled Empire of old, smashed and ruined, but still far more advanced than they were. She ached to explore its secrets.

Jared rapped the table with his knuckles, quieting the chatter. "Let's get started. The fusion unit over there is the biggest concern. Dennis, what can you tell me?"

Lieutenant Commander Baxter looked a lot more serious than when Kelsey had seen him last. She'd never guess at his questionable sense of humor if she'd met him now.

"The fusion plant is on the verge of failure. I'm astonished it lasted so long, frankly. The technology behind it must've played a role, but it was probably also at a very low output setting. Otherwise it would've crashed before now."

Jared nodded. "What do you mean by crash? Would it explode?"

"Ordinarily, I'd say no. Ours, for example, would trigger a safety interlock and shut down if they became unstable. However, the fluctuations we're seeing tell me that any safety system has already failed. We need to kill that power unit as soon as possible. I want to get a team over there without any delay. We might have weeks or months, but we might only have hours."

"How much warning would we have before it fails?"

Baxter shrugged. "Who knows? Probably time enough to get out of there. Possibly not. Personally, I'm willing to take the risk. I already have a team of volunteers standing by."

Kelsey couldn't fathom why people could be ready to risk death that way, but she also didn't understand why firefighters ran into burning buildings when there weren't people inside. From his expression, Jared did understand the urge, though.

The captain turned his attention to the tactical officer. "Zia, anything to add to our scanner take?"

"Quite a bit, Captain. The life pods are all still in place, and so are the ship's boats. Another ship must've done whatever evacuation they could manage. The interior is frozen. Life support is not online. Other than the power readings from the fusion plant and the distress beacon, everything else seems to be offline."

"We'd go in wearing suits anyway, but that's good information. Thanks. Lieutenant Reese, we'll want volunteers from the marines to help provide security and some muscle if we need it."

The marine officer nodded. "I have two squads ready to go in armored vacuum suits."

"Do you have anything to help us get inside? I'm certain that the hatches are locked, and we don't have the keys, even if we had power for their systems."

"We can cut through a hatch with boarding cutters. It won't be pretty, but it'll be quick."

Lieutenant Commander Graves gave Jared a look. "You've said 'we' several times, Captain. You aren't planning to go over there, are you? Not before we make sure it isn't going to blow up."

Empire of Bones

Jared nodded. "Actually, I am. I've made a study of all the material we have on pre-Fall Fleet ships. It might not be much, but I might be able to make a difference. Besides, you heard Dennis. We'll probably know before it goes critical."

"I heard him say 'probably,'" Kelsey said. "You can't risk yourself like that. You're the mission commander."

He turned his attention her way. "Actually, I can. My orders regarding the recovery of pre-Fall technology are crystal clear. I'm to do everything within my power to do so, even at moderate risk. The ship can get along without me, and my personal knowledge might be critical to recovering this ship. In any case, I'm the one that makes that call."

Graves didn't look particularly happy at that response, but he nodded. Grudgingly. "We'll keep a close eye on the situation from out here. If I make the call to evacuate the wreck, will you override me?"

"Probably not," Jared responded. "I don't want to die for a piece of junk any more than the next guy. If you say run, I'm not waiting to ask how fast."

Kelsey didn't like this one bit. Her elation at the find evaporated. She might not know him that well, but part of her quailed at the idea of her half brother taking such an awful risk. Even if he wasn't her blood, she didn't want to lose him.

"What about the scientists?" she asked. "Could some of them help with defusing the power plant?"

The engineer shrugged. "Possibly, but most likely not. They're theory, not hardware. I'll have them available if I have a problem. Like not knowing whether to cut the red or blue wire."

Kelsey gave him a quelling glare. "That isn't funny."

He grinned for a moment before his expression faded back to seriousness. "No, it's not. We need to get a move on, Captain. We might regret chatting an extra few minutes later."

Jared stood. "Bring the ship to alert status and back off to a safe distance. We'll depart as soon as the teams are in the marine pinnaces. Dismissed."

Kelsey wanted to follow him and say something, but she had no idea what. Be careful? Duh. She'd just have to trust him to do his job and come back safely.

Instead, she followed Graves back up to the bridge and commandeered one of the empty consoles. She'd watch every step of their mission on the big screen.

Graves stepped beside her console. "Let me enable the visual controls for you. Then you can pause, rewind, and zoom what we see on your console if you feel like it. The suits all have helmet cams."

"Thank you. May I call you Charlie?"

He smiled. "I'd like it if you did."

"Charlie, has he lost his mind?"

He chuckled. "I sometimes wonder. No. He wouldn't be going if he didn't think he had a reason to and a good possibility of coming back. He wouldn't risk his crew for nothing."

She took a deep breath. "Okay."

"*Athena*, this is *Marine Two*. Both pinnaces are ready to depart."

Graves walked back to the command console and opened the channel. "God speed, *Marine Two*. Come back safe."

"Roger that. *Marine Two* out."

The main screen picked up the two pinnaces shortly after that as they made their run to the wreck. The marine craft were significantly larger than the passenger cutters. Marines were armed and their ships armored. Perhaps if the ship blew up while they fled, that would give them an extra chance of surviving.

Kelsey sat back in her seat and tried to loosen her tense muscles. This was going to be a long, stressful day.

13

Rather than displace the marine pilot, Jared sat in the back with the rest of the marines and engineering techs in *Marine Two*. They'd be docking on the forward half of the derelict while Baxter went aft. If their way was blocked, Jared's team might make it to the fusion plant faster.

He had the small screen in his vacuum suit tuned to the visual from the external cameras. The wicked spin on *Courageous* made matching course a challenge. One miscalculation and the wreck would swat them like a bug.

The pilot eased close to the derelict and then lined up with the tumble. Thankfully, the rotation wasn't too bad or they might not have been able to match with it at all. The pinnace corrected for the spin and made contact with the other hull hard enough to rattle his teeth.

"We're locked down, Captain," the pilot said on the mission frequency. "We're about a dozen meters from what looks like an emergency hatch. You'll need to use magnetic boots and tethers. The centrifugal force is powerful."

"Roger. Be ready to haul ass if we come running back."

"Aye, sir."

Lieutenant Reese stood and began hooking the men together with tough lines. "If someone comes loose, I want everyone to grab the hull with your hand clamps. We'll always have half of us holding onto the ship, just in case."

They all checked one another's suits again. Only then did the marine officer pump the atmosphere out and open the assault ramp.

The stars spun crazily over the steady horizon of the derelict's hull. It made Jared a little sick to his stomach, so he focused his eyes on the back of the man in front of him. That settled him down. The floodlights on the pinnace brightly illuminated *Courageous*'s hull.

They made their way slowly onto the Old Empire ship and toward the emergency hatch. The team moved at a snail's pace. A man broke loose halfway to the hatch, but they pulled him back down.

When everyone stopped moving, they hunkered down and activated their hand clamps. A bright red line surrounded the large hatch, and rescue instructions were painted right on the hull. It looked very similar to the ones on *Athena*.

Jared didn't expect it to work, but he twisted the emergency handle as instructed. The hatch slowly pulled into the ship, revealing a large airlock with dim red emergency lighting.

"That's useful," Jared said. "It must be internally powered. Quite a tribute to its designers."

He switched to the mission frequency. "Team One, we've opened the external hatch. We're going in."

"Roger that," Baxter said. "No joy back here. We're cutting ours open."

Jared pulled himself into the airlock and wedged his arm through a handhold. The airlock had bags and boxes full of equipment, and probably rescue supplies. The interior hatch wouldn't open while the outside one was open, so the team had to split up. The half that followed Jared inside held on tight as he closed the hatch. He held his breath, but the inner door opened as easily as the exterior.

The corridor beyond was in total darkness. Any emergency lighting had failed. He advanced inside far enough to plant his feet against the wall and turned his helmet lamp on. They'd need to be very careful of the centrifugal force inside, too. One inattentive moment could maim or kill.

Once the second team made it inside, Jared sighed in relief. "Okay, let's start working our way back toward engineering."

Movement inside was almost as slow as outside, if less nerve-wracking. Baxter reported that they were inside a few minutes later.

"We're seeing some damage," the engineer said, "but I think we'll make it to engineering without too much trouble. Why don't you head for the bridge? You might be able to bring some controls online from there."

"Agreed," Jared said. "Let us know when you get there."

Empire of Bones   89

A hatch ahead of them was open. With the wicked spin, the wall it occupied was more of a floor. He looked inside and recognized a personnel cabin. It looked normal, though the spin had thrown everything against the outside bulkhead.

He started to edge past it, but something caught his eye. There was a body in the detritus. "Hold up. We have a body. I'm going inside."

It occurred to him as he lowered himself down the steep slope that the person below was centuries beyond his ability to help, but the impulse to go had been instinctual. A minute wouldn't hurt them, and the video might be helpful to the scientists.

He managed to get inside without injuring himself and moved the debris until he could see a woman's face. At least he felt certain it was a woman. All the moisture in her body had evaporated in the vacuum, leaving her remains mummified and frozen solid.

She wore a uniform very similar to the ones hanging in his closet. She was Fleet. A glance at her arm showed her to be a senior petty officer. He moved the junk around until he could see all of her. There were no obvious injuries.

He climbed back up to the corridor. "Let's press on to the bridge."

Jared found an internal diagram near the first lift they encountered. It indicated they needed to climb five decks from the next lift forward.

"Captain," Baxter said. "We're in main engineering. That shot damaged the flip drive but didn't destroy it. It missed almost all the major equipment. I'm somewhat surprised they weren't able to make repairs. We have some bodies in Fleet uniforms. It looks like the damage exposed them to space."

"We found a body, too. We're almost to the bridge lift. Find the fusion plant and get it shut down."

"Aye, sir."

They had to pry the doors apart when they reached the lift. Luckily, the platform wasn't between them and the bridge. The particular nature of the spin made getting there an easy walk.

The lift doors at the bridge level were hard to open from the shaft, but they finally gave up the ghost. Jared stepped out onto the bridge and froze. It was significantly bigger than *Athena*'s bridge, but that wasn't its most striking feature. Each seat held a dead Fleet officer.

"Baxter, we have bodies on the bridge. Something is very wrong."

"Sounds like. We're at the fusion plant. I'll call you when I figure it out."

Jared turned to his men. "Fan out in pairs. Explore the nearby areas. Be careful." He singled out one of the men to wait with him.

He climbed to what he thought was the captain's console and studied the man strapped in there. His body was in a very similar condition to the woman they'd found earlier. His uniform indicated he was a full captain, though there wasn't a name tag. He wore an odd-looking headset. There were no microphones, and it didn't cover his ears. He couldn't determine its purpose. There was no obvious sign of injury that Jared could see.

A trip around the bridge told him none of these people had battle wounds, yet they'd all died at their stations. The damage to the ship wasn't bad enough to kill them here. Or that woman. Something else had caused their deaths. All wore the strange headsets.

Maybe he could bring the captain's console to life and find something. Fleet built all the critical systems on *Athena* with small power units to operate with if the main systems went offline. Surely the Old Empire worried about battle damage taking out the main power grid, too.

Dust coated the console. He brushed it away with his gloved hand. It was a flat panel, very sleek and futuristic. The irony of thinking that about a 500-year-old wreck made him snort a little.

He felt around the sides and under the rim for an emergency power switch. He found it on the right side up front where no one could unintentionally hit it, but it was still within easy reach by the captain.

The consoled flickered when Jared flipped the recessed switch. He didn't think it would come on at all, but it slowly brightened. The layout of the virtual controls was unfamiliar to him, though he thought he could figure them out.

This was a ship's status screen. The pattern of the red and amber dots formed a ship. Almost all the dots were red, so he picked one of the few amber ones toward the aft of the ship. The display expanded at a touch and showed what he guessed was engineering. The dot remained amber, but some text appeared beside it.

It was the fusion plant. The safety interlocks were disabled. It said so right there. The output was fluctuating, and there was a lurid warning about the danger of explosion.

He opened a channel to the chief engineer. "Dennis, I have the captain's console up and running. I have a reading on the fusion plant. It says someone overrode the safety interlocks. It has a warning about the output fluctuations."

"That's more than I'm getting here," the engineer grumbled. "The controls seem fried. At least the displays are. Perhaps that's why they overrode the interlocks. This plant shouldn't be operating without the local controls."

"Are you going to be able to shut it down from there?"

Empire of Bones

"Probably not. I'm accessing the video from your helmet cam. That looks bad. I want to shut the plant down right now. You're going to have to drive for me."

Jared felt his stomach flutter. This was all too similar to his nightmare of having to do something in engineering. It never ended well. He took a deep breath. "Talk me through it."

"Seriously? As if I know their control systems any better than you do. Tap the amber icon for the fusion plant."

A tap opened a menu of options. Powering it off wasn't one of them.

"There at the bottom," Baxter continued. "Tap where it says safety interlocks."

A touch brought up the option to enable the safety interlocks. "What will that make it do?"

"If I'm right, it'll cause the fusion plant to shut down."

Jared considered that. "What if you're wrong?"

"If that's a clever way of asking if it'll explode, I think not. At worst, it should leave things in the same configuration. It shouldn't make it go critical."

Jared expected Graves to chime in there, but he didn't, so he mastered his apprehension and tapped the button. The icon for the fusion plant turned red.

"It went red!"

"Relax. If it were going to explode, you'd never have noticed the color change. The plant shut down exactly like it was designed to do."

Jared let out the breath he hadn't realized he was holding. The danger was past.

"Good work," he said. "Now, make sure there are no other surprises in engineering that might cause us problems. Mertz out."

He had to experiment before he figured out how to expand the status back out. Then he went hunting for a reason for the bridge crew to be dead. It took ten minutes, but he finally found the answer in an input log for the console.

Someone had vented the atmosphere to space from this console. He double-checked to be sure, but it appeared *Courageous*'s captain had killed his own people. What Jared couldn't understand was why.

Reese signaled him. "Captain, you need to come down to the deck where we entered the lift and come forward half a dozen hatches."

"What do you have? Patch it through to me."

"Sir, I really think you need to come see this in person."

If his marine commander said he needed to come in person, Jared was smart enough to trust him. He and his companion made their way carefully back down, and Jared saw several men standing outside one hatch looking in. He made his way up to them and looked inside himself.

It was a mess hall. It held hundreds of dead bodies. Centrifugal motion had piled them in the corner, but he couldn't mistake what this was—a graveyard.

He felt the gorge rising in his throat but managed to master the urge to throw up. The crew of *Courageous* hadn't escaped after all. This ship was a tomb.

14

Kelsey stood in the docking bay on *Best Deal* wearing her very best dress. The heels she wore were killing her feet, but sitting wasn't an option. She felt drained. Thankfully, it was almost over. The last three days had been hell.

A Fleet crewman blew a piercing blast on his whistle, the tune all too familiar to her at this point. Jared and the other Fleet officers, dressed in their resplendent black-and-red dress uniforms, came to attention as the hatch slid open.

The marine honor guard brought their weapons in front of them as their comrades brought the last of the crew from *Courageous* aboard. The men held the sealed boxes high, slow stepping as if the very gravity of the situation held them tightly to the deck.

Seeing so many dead, both the horrible images from the dead Fleet vessel and the coffins passing her one at a time, felt unreal. Nothing she'd ever done before had prepared her for the impact of Fleet welcoming home their dead.

Jared held his salute until the last of the coffins had passed. A number of storage compartments would hold the dead until they returned to Avalon. Fleet never buried anyone in space. Fleet didn't abandon their own.

She put her hand on Jared's shoulder. "Come on. We both need a meal and a stiff drink. I hear the brains have a really nice bar."

He raised an eyebrow tiredly. "They have a bar? How did I miss hearing about it? Better yet, how come you know about it?"

"The marines. They know every bar within a light year."

"Of course they do. Sure."

It didn't take them long to find the place. Someone had outfitted one of the smaller cargo compartments with tables and chairs. The smell of food coming from somewhere made her hungry. A number of crates made up the bar itself. She waved down the server, who looked more like a physicist than anything else.

"Can we get beer and something from the mess?" she asked. "Sandwiches would be fine."

"Of course, Ambassador, Captain. I think we can do significantly better than that. I've been watching the ceremony on the vid feed, and you deserve it. Do you have any preferences?"

Jared shook his head. "Anything would be fine. Thank you..."

"Doctor Brad Parker, Imperial Institute of Science. I'm the planetary sciences team leader."

She'd been so close. Not. "I'll take whatever you get for him, Doctor. Thank you."

"My pleasure. Be right back with some beer." He headed off through the crowd toward the bar.

Kelsey turned her attention back to Jared while surreptitiously kicking off her shoes. "Not to be morbid, but are you sure you've found everyone?"

He nodded. "Search teams covered every part of that ship three times. All five hundred and eighty-five of them are now safely back in the hands of their brothers and sisters. Their time alone is over. Fleet and marine personnel will stand guard outside their temporary tomb until we can see them properly interred. Then the permanent honor guard will keep watch over them."

"Why does that tradition exist? I'm not putting it down, but I don't understand the thought behind it."

"The single surviving Fleet officer that made it to Avalon's surface asked for it from the people that found him. He said it was tradition. He inducted his rescuers before he died, and they kept watch over him.

"We've followed that tradition ever since. The Imperial Cemetery at the Spire serves for the interment of all the Fleet dead from day one. Even when we didn't have ships."

She started to say something, but the scientist brought them their beer, so she waited for him to leave before continuing. "That doesn't need any explanation. Honor speaks for itself."

He raised his glass in salute. "As an institution, we stand on the shoulders of those who came before us. They're watching over us, and we don't dare fail them."

Empire of Bones

"Father has said similar things. I've always thought that was incredibly romantic."

"Thank you for being there with me. With us. We all appreciate the honor you've shown our sacred dead. It will not be forgotten."

As tired as she was, Kelsey sat up straighter. "Today, I wasn't Ambassador Kelsey Bandar. I was Princess Kelsey of the House of Bandar, daughter of your emperor and liege. Though he is many light years away, he stood among you today with the Terran Empire behind him. Remember that."

Jared bowed his head. "We are grateful."

She sighed and surreptitiously rubbed her aching feet. "I've been watching things on *Courageous* over the vid. What kind of shape is she really in?"

"Not bad at all, considering her age and the battle damage. She's structurally sound, even though she doesn't have power. Baxter even said he might be able to repair her, if he had the time and knowhow. Now that we've used the pinnaces to stop her tumble, we can get people on and off her without any difficulty.

"Baxter is working on some kind of standby power that can be strung in through the hole in her engineering compartment to power the main grid. That should allow us to see how much of the computer and ship's systems are fit enough to power up. He promised to have something ready by tomorrow."

She took a sip of her beer. "I'm impressed that you stopped that tumble. I never thought that would even be possible."

"It doesn't matter that the pinnaces are small. Every bit of thrust from their grav drives worked to slow her bit by bit. One could even stop the spin at Orbital One with enough time. To every action there is a reaction."

"What do we do now? Both with the ship and getting home?"

Doctor Parker chose that moment to return with two salads and a platter of sizzling meat mixed with vegetables. The scent made her mouth water.

"Here you are," the scientist said. "On the house. Of course, everything here is always on the house, but you get the idea."

She smiled at him. "Thank you, Doctor Parker."

Jared added his thanks and waited for the man to leave before continuing. "We're stocked for a five-year mission, though the last two of that is preserved rations. A freighter has a lot of space, even after the conversion to a science ship, so we don't need to worry about running out of supplies just yet. I expect we'll find plenty of habitable worlds as we try to find our way home."

"How will we do that? We can't even guess where a flip point will take us. Without being able to follow the path we used to get here, I'm at a loss how we get back." She tried to keep from sounding depressed at the idea of not going home, but she knew it colored her tone.

Jared smiled. "You have to have faith. We'll get there eventually. *Courageous* came from the same Empire we did. No matter how daunting the journey, we can make it home."

"How do we know it didn't come here through that damned flip point? It might have been trapped here."

"Then where is the ship that crippled her?"

"Destroyed. Drifting in space. Fell into the star."

"Aren't you a pessimist?" he asked, taking a bite of his salad. "While our probes haven't searched every kilometer of this system, I'm confident that we'll find that the enemy had fled the field. Probably through the flip point we detected partway around the ecliptic."

Kelsey froze with her fork partway to her mouth. "You found another flip point? Why haven't I heard this before?"

"Eat before you chew on me. The salad is much tastier than my dress uniform." He infuriatingly waited for her to take a bite. She had to admit it was good. She was famished.

He continued as she started putting the food away. "One of the men came up and whispered it to me just before that last pinnace docked. It's a full-sized, absolutely normal flip point."

"That's wonderful news! I'll drink to that!" She lifted her beer and took a healthy drink.

"I've been thinking about what we can do, and I've come up with several things. First, we'll finish exploring *Courageous*. We can recover a lot of *Courageous*'s equipment and store it in *Best Deal*'s holds. Then we prep a probe with every bit of data we have and send it back to the system on the other side of the flip point. A search party will eventually come this way, and then they'll know about the weak flip point."

"Could we get one to go back and contact the Empire?"

"That's a lot less likely. Baxter is going to tear one of the probes apart and try to build enough redundancy into it to make that happen. If it works, we're still looking at a couple of months to get a ship out here."

He tried some of the meat. "This is good. Even though they can't come after us, they can send supplies through if we can't get out of this sector. Living in ships would suck, but we can do it. I still don't believe we'll need to. I suspect we're closer to Terra than we ever were before."

Kelsey raised an eyebrow. "Why would you think that?"

"A hunch. Someone chased *Courageous* here and killed her. Hopefully we'll find out more as we explore the ship, but I'm willing to bet the rebels did it."

"The rebels chased Emperor Lucien to Avalon," she pointed out.

"Yes, but none of them came back. They had more pressing business elsewhere. Since they were here chasing a Fleet unit, I'll bet that means we're deeper into the Old Empire. Admittedly, I could be wrong, but I prefer to be optimistic."

They ate silently for a while. The food was better than good, Kelsey decided. Not that she could eat everything. She let Jared finish her food before she ordered a second beer.

"Nothing I've ever read said why the rebels did what they did," she said at last. "Who were they, and why were they so vicious? They'd used a kinetic strike on a city that couldn't shoot back. That attack killed over a million people. Now *Courageous*. They were crippled and left to die. That's not just a minor difference of opinion."

"Perhaps they weren't left to die. Perhaps they ran out of options. *Courageous* is a long way from the flip point in a slow orbit. A ship at rest isn't detectable at that kind of range. This system has two very large asteroid belts in addition to half a dozen uninhabitable planets. It would take a large number of ships to find her if she didn't want to be found."

He took another gulp of his beer. "Dennis also found evidence of repairs. They had days or weeks to try to fix the damage done to their ship after the fight. What they didn't have was air."

"Excuse me?"

"*Athena* recycles her air, but there is a limited supply. We have three different tankage areas. *Courageous* had six. The fighting breached five of those. The last is empty."

"Did the rebels intentionally do that to her?" Kelsey shuddered. "I'm glad the rebels are dead."

"I hope they are. One of Fleet's biggest fears is that we'll encounter their descendants. We don't have anything like what the Old Empire had in warships. We'd go down fighting, but we'd go down. That's why we can wipe the critical computer systems on *Athena* and *Best Deal*. Just in case."

"That's morbid. Let's change the subject. Now that *Courageous* is safer, when can I go see her for myself?"

He looked like his preferred answer would be "never," but he didn't say that. "If we can restore environmental controls, I'll let you go. Until there's an atmosphere, you'll need to do your visiting via vid. The scientists, too."

That wasn't what she wanted to hear, but she knew better than to argue. "Thank you."

"In the meantime, I know there are a lot of things coming over for the scientists to examine. I'm sure they would love to have your help with some of the personal belongings."

Somehow, she doubted they'd want her looking over their shoulders. Not that she'd let that stop her.

Examining the personal belongings of the dead was even more morbid, but she knew he was right to collect everything. Any bit might provide a clue to something important. A dead man's data reader might have tech manuals on something critical. A dead woman's knickknacks might have incredible cultural significance. Nothing was too ordinary or too small for them to collect.

"I'll stay clear of the ship," she said, "but I want you to make me a trade."

"Name it."

"I don't like being blocked by a lack of skills. Can someone train me on going into vacuum in case this comes up again? Like one of the marines?"

He considered that for a moment and then nodded. "Deal."

They finished their last beer in silence. She wondered what they would find when they finished examining *Courageous*. Secrets she couldn't even imagine? Or just more questions?

15

J ared went back over to *Courageous* the next morning. If there were any kind of trouble, he'd have plenty of time to get back to *Athena*. Graves had taken third shift to oversee things on the wreck and to explore. *Athena*'s day watch would wake him if something developed.

There still wasn't any gravity, but without the wicked spin, he was able to make his way to engineering without problems. Baxter was already there overseeing the splice of a thick cable into the power grid.

They'd strapped the cable to the deck and out through the gash ripped into the hull. Jared floated over and held himself in place beside the engineer. "How goes it?"

"Almost ready to divert power. It won't be enough to power the ship, but it should let us turn on some basic systems like life support."

"I thought the life support reservoirs were trashed."

"One holds pressure. A second looks easily reparable. I've had some of the reserves on *Best Deal* shipped over. We can recapture most of it when we're ready to leave, but having a pressurized hull will make recovery operations a lot simpler."

"Do we know if the ship's systems will even work?"

"Nope. We'll be doing an old-fashioned smoke test. If it smokes, it won't work."

Jared shook his head. "You're a mess. If the computer comes back online, will we be able to interface with it?"

"That's a question for the brains. For the time being, we've disconnected it from the grid." He sprayed something on the exposed connections, hiding the bare metal beneath a black, rubbery covering. "Okay. Here we go."

He must've said something on a different frequency, because Jared didn't hear a word. He did see the overhead lights flicker and come on dimly.

Jared hunted around until he found the frequency they were using and heard people chiming in about the lights coming on. From the locations given, the entire ship had lights. Of a sort.

"Are those emergency lights?" he asked after Baxter finished checking in with everyone.

"Probably. They're too dim to be the main overheads. I'll need to find the controls to turn on anything else. The system knows none of the fusion plants is online, and it can tell the amount of power is limited. I think I can override that for specific systems."

"Will the ship give you access?"

"Let's find out." He pushed off the bulkhead and led the way deeper into engineering. Away from the flip drives, the damage was less severe, but it would've been deadly to the men and women working here.

Baxter went to one of the consoles and found the emergency power switch. The display came to life, dim and coated in dust. It brightened almost immediately. "The console found the power bus, and it's not asking for any kind of authentication. That's probably because it still thinks it's in a combat situation. No authentication required when someone is shooting at you." He tapped the screens, hunting for something.

The displays the chief engineer examined made even less sense to Jared than the engineering displays on *Athena*. Baxter eventually found something, though. "Here we go. Let's put the lighting on a higher priority."

The overhead lights brightened enough to illuminate every corner. With the ship still in vacuum, the shadows were knife sharp and deep black.

"That should do it," Baxter said with satisfaction. "I'll add my authentication to the engineering subsystems. Another benefit of having the main computer offline."

"What happens when the computer comes back online?"

"I'll isolate it from the control runs if we decide to power it up. Then the authentication we give the consoles will continue to work. Adding someone to the main computer is another egghead task. It may not even be possible. I'd imagine there's some pretty tight security coding on it."

Empire of Bones

Jared nodded. "One problem at a time. Next, what about the life support systems?"

Baxter navigated through the screens. "The system still shows itself to be functional. It looks like Fleet designed their warships to last a long time. I'm impressed."

Baxter switched to the all-hands channel. "Okay, everyone. If you're near an airtight door, you need to get clear of it. Tell me now if you won't be clear in thirty seconds."

When no one said anything, Baxter waited and then touched the controls. "All airtight doors have sealed and show green. Life support is online. It shows some glitches, but as a critical system, it can manage. Pressure is slowly rising and the heaters are on, except for engineering and a few other areas still open to space. I'd imagine you could take off your helmet in half an hour, but it'll still be brutally cold in there. I wouldn't touch bare metal for at least an hour."

The idea that an old wreck like this could come back to life boggled Jared's mind. "I'll want a ship's status when you can get it. I want to know what systems could be used if we wanted to. That might help a lot in getting an idea how things work."

"Yes, sir."

"Now how do I get to the other side of the pressure doors?"

"They come in pairs so that you can open one at a time and step through like an airlock. The pressure will equalize, and then the other side will open. I'll get someone to checking the primary systems and available repair parts. Those will tell us a lot by themselves, technologically speaking."

"This ship is full of surprises. I'll want someone to check the weapons systems, too. Call Zia to get some of her people to help."

He made his way forward to the first set of pressure doors. They performed exactly as Baxter had indicated. He couldn't see a difference once he went through, but his suit informed him there was a slight increase in pressure.

Jared made his way to the bridge. It looked better with the lights on, but he couldn't see the place without remembering *Courageous*'s long-dead crew strapped in at their stations. No one was up here now, so he had the captain's console all to himself to do a little looking around.

The floor plan appeared similar to the one on *Athena*, only larger. Significantly larger. The captain's console was on a raised dais overlooking the crew stations. Four forward in square formation. Three each on the right and left sides facing the bulkheads. Two consoles at the rear flanked the lift.

He'd identified a dozen stations, not counting the captain's.

Significantly more than on the largest cruiser he'd ever been on. The compartment was also quite roomy, meaning there was no feeling of being crowded here.

One hatch on the left side of the compartment led to the captain's day cabin, complete with conference room. Another opened to a large head for the crew. He'd missed the closed hatches on his first visit. Admiral Yeats's flag bridge on Orbital One was less luxurious.

He strapped himself in to the captain's chair and brought the console to life. It connected to the power grid and glowed brightly under the smeared dust. He'd left the systems on the life support screen, so he could see an array of amber dots all over the ship. A number of red one's told him engineering was still in a vacuum. No surprise there. Most remaining areas had noticeable pressure. The temperature was coming up, too.

The log had the last commands entered on this console. He could see where he'd enabled the safeties on the fusion reactor. The timestamp was wrong, of course. The console had been without power too long to keep any internal chronometer running.

The previous instructions were there, too. He saw where the captain had disabled the safeties. He also saw where he'd entered a complex set of instructions for the reactor. Then he'd vented the ship to space. All within the space of a minute. The first officer had countersigned the orders.

Why the hell did the ship's designers even have a method to vent the atmosphere to space and scuttle the ship? He couldn't do something that crazy on *Athena* even if Graves helped him cut holes all over the ship. What kind of maniac thought the system needed to account for that possibility?

He tried to make sense of the instructions sent to the fusion reactor and failed. He opened a communications link to Baxter. "Dennis, I'm looking at the console logs from the bridge. *Courageous*'s captain sent some commands to the fusion plant that make no sense to me. Hook up to my helmet feed and tell me what they look like to you."

The other man was silent for a moment. "Are you kidding me? That isn't funny. How did you even manage to program that? I'd never have figured you had that kind of engineering theory."

"I'm not pulling anyone's leg. That's what the captain sent from this station. What does it mean?"

"It means that the captain was a suicidal maniac," Baxter said. "Those instructions should've sent the fusion reactor into overload in less than twenty minutes. It would've gone off like a nova. The only guess I can make is that a systems failure on this end disrupted the command."

"It sure looks like they were determined not to fall into the hands of the rebels," Jared said.

"I can see that. He set the fusion plant to explode and vented the atmosphere. Two very thorough deaths. I'm surprised he didn't set any of the ship-to-ship missiles to explode."

Jared's eyes widened, and he switched to the all hands frequency. "All weapons technicians to the ship's missile tubes! I want to be sure that no one has tampered with the warheads. Make it fast."

Baxter whistled. "What the hell is going on here, Jared?"

"Something really disturbing. Does this ship have more than one fusion plant?"

"Yes, but they all went down at some point. They probably deteriorated until the safeties shut them down."

Jared thought furiously. "I want you to go over every system on this ship that might destroy it. Isolate them if you find any evidence of tampering. I don't want the long-dead hand of *Courageous*'s captain to take us with him."

"Aye, sir."

He sat there for a while, thinking. No obvious explanations jumped out at him. After a bit, he shook himself out of his reverie. The command log might tell him a bit more of the final timeline. He brought it up and studied it more closely. Unfortunately, the console only logged commands sent from it.

He wondered why someone activated the distress beacon in the first place. It seemed counterintuitive. Perhaps it activated on its own after some predetermined period without instructions from the main computer.

He made his way around the other stations and brought them online. The tactical console had the times when they'd activated the screens and fired the weapons. It looked like the final battle lasted about an hour. It seemed as though that fight had taken place three weeks before they apparently killed themselves. There was a second battle a week earlier.

Helm indicated two activations of the flip drive between those battles. It also logged the tactical officer's attempts to shift power to reactivate the screens when they failed.

Jared stared at the dead main screen for a while. Too bad the computer was offline. It probably logged both the battles in their entirety.

He needed to get the main computer online.

Or did he? This had happened half a millennium ago. The information locked away wasn't relevant to their current situation. Yes, they needed to know. They just didn't need to know this second. It wasn't as though the rebels would come pouring through the flip point while he feverishly searched for the answers.

Baxter reported in shortly with the all clear. That removed the danger for now. Jared checked the air readings and popped his helmet. The icy atmosphere smelled musty but breathable. He'd let the ship warm up and then send for the brains. Maybe they could shed some light on the situation.

He returned to the captain's console and explored for a while longer. He wanted to find any personal log, but there didn't seem to be one. It was probably on the main computer.

What he did find was an icon on the main screen marked "play me." He tapped it, and the main screen at the front of the compartment flickered and came to life. A chill ran up Jared's spine that had nothing to do with the cold. He was looking at the bridge of this ship as it had been. Only, live men and women filled the crew stations. All wore the strange headsets.

The captain had dark hair with a hint a grey. He looked to be about Jared's age.

"If you're watching this message," the dead man said, "then our attempts to destroy this ship have failed. I beseech you, stranger, to inter our dead as if they were your own brothers in arms. I commend them to you. I couldn't have wished for braver companions in this terrible time."

The dead captain gestured around himself. "*Courageous* has served us well and defended the Empire with honor. We drew off the remaining rebel battlecruisers so that our task force could escape without detection. We disabled one of the enemy ships two systems back and destroyed the other here.

"Unfortunately, the bastards took out our flip drives and most of our life support reserves in the fight, damn the luck. Rather than wait for the air to grow foul and prolong our suffering, we've decided to end things swiftly. I'd prefer to overload one of the fusion plants, but the chief engineer and most of his staff are dead. I'll make an effort to do so, but I have little confidence in my ability. With some justification, since you're seeing this message."

The black humor made Jared shake his head.

Courageous's captain continued. "The backup plan is to vent the ship's atmosphere. It isn't the most desirable way to die, but it will be graciously quick." The man rubbed his eyes tiredly. "I dearly hope you're Fleet yourself, but that seems hard to imagine in these dark times. Whoever you are, if *Courageous* can serve your needs, please take her with my blessing. Treat her like a lady."

Empire of Bones

The horror of the long-ago situation again washed over Jared. This crew had known their end was inescapable. They'd chosen to die by their own hands rather than suffer. Most had gathered in the mess compartments for one last time, to be with their friends at the end. Others like the woman he'd found in her cabin had chosen to die alone.

The captain and his command crew had met their end at their stations.

He'd been through emergency decompression drills, including an actual loss of atmosphere. Unlike the common misconception, you didn't swell up and explode like a balloon. Fleet trained them to open their mouths and let the air rush out so that their lungs survived undamaged. Then you suffocated if you couldn't find any air.

The long-dead captain straightened in his chair. "Well, our time is up. I apologize for leaving our home in such a mess. I again beseech you to take our remains home with you. Bury us with whatever ritual and honor you hold dear and accept my gratitude for your kindness."

The long-dead Fleet officer sat up straighter and brought his right fist to his chest. "I hope you'll forgive the paraphrase, or at least understand it. Go tell the Empire, stranger passing by, that here, obedient to Imperial law, we lie. *Courageous* out."

The screen blinked out, and Jared brought his own fist up to return the salute. Much of Terran history had been lost to the ages, but he knew the story of Sparta and the 300. He couldn't imagine a more fitting epitaph for these heroes.

16

Watching an autopsy wasn't very high on Kelsey's list of things to do, but somehow Doctor Stone convinced her to do exactly that. She promised herself she wouldn't lose her lunch and that she'd get out of there as fast as she could. The very real appointment she had on *Best Deal* to look over some of the artifacts would make an outstanding excuse.

Stone had a man laid out before her on the diagnostic table. He had a sheet pulled up to his chin, but he still looked painfully vulnerable. He also looked like a long-dead corpse. The faint scent of decay hung in the air.

The doctor looked up at Kelsey. "You look a little queasy. If you're afraid I'm going to cut this poor soul up, you can rest easy. My scanners are more than capable of getting me all the data I need without violating him."

The princess relaxed a little. "I suppose I was thinking exactly that."

"I've been present when an old-fashioned autopsy was conducted on a body donated to science, but unless something looks wildly out of place, that won't be necessary. If it were, I wouldn't subject you to that."

"Can you tell what killed him without going inside him?"

"I can tell you what killed him right now. He died from asphyxiation. The burst capillaries in his eyes are a dead giveaway, if you'll pardon the unintended and wholly inappropriate pun. Really, I'm not looking for cause of death. I'm looking to see if there are any oddities."

Kelsey felt herself frowning. "Like what?"

"I don't know, but if we don't scan some people, we won't know for sure. This, by the way, is the commanding officer of *Courageous*. I'd tell you his name, but we don't have any idea what it is. Fleet uniforms didn't have name tags back then, apparently. I can't imagine how that worked."

Kelsey examined the dead man's face. Thankfully, someone had closed his eyes. She didn't want to see any burst blood vessels. Judging his age wasn't easy. With his body mummified as it was, he could've been any age at all. He did have a full head of dark hair that seemed to be only a little grey. Maybe in his late thirties or early forties?

Doctor Stone initialized the diagnostic bed and turned to face the large screen. It lit up with the outline of a human body. It began filling in with bones and internal organs almost immediately. Then the head began flashing yellow.

"What's that?" Kelsey asked.

"An anomaly." Stone tapped the head on the screen. It expanded to show more detail. Kelsey had a vague idea of what a human brain looked like, and she was fairly certain that one didn't usually have a web of filaments running through it and several small discs implanted under the skull.

"Wow," Stone said. "He's got some kind of artificial implant in his brain. Three processors of some kind attached to the skull itself and ultra-thin wires branching throughout the brain matter."

"What do they do? Why would anyone do that to themselves? And how could they do it at all without killing themselves?"

"I have no idea." Stone expanded the view on his head until the filaments loomed large. "It looks like some kind of graphene derivative."

"Graphene?"

Stone nodded. "It's an old material, discovered on prespaceflight Terra. An engineer could tell you more, but it's a crystalline allotrope of carbon that has two-dimensional properties. It's basically an atom-thick lattice of carbon. Conductive and twenty times stronger than steel.

"They used it in all kinds of equipment, and so do we. That's what makes communicator screens so thin and flexible. It's a lot more useful than silicon electronics."

The doctor examined the thin strand on the screen. "I never imagined it could be used inside someone's brain, though. I don't think this is exactly the same material, either. How did they even get it in there?"

She shook her head. "There'll be time enough to research that. The rest of his body looks normal enough. Let's look at a few more people before I call in some of the scientists to help explain this."

Stone had her orderlies take the man's body out, and they brought a woman to replace him. Kelsey saw that the woman had the brain implants, but she also had extensive modification to the rest of her body. Her arms and legs especially. It looked like she had thick bands running through the muscles of her limbs. She had a cylinder behind her lungs and inserts under the lenses in her eyes. There were things inside her ears and nose, too.

The doctor expanded the view on one of the woman's legs. The bones also had a thin coating of something that seemed impermeable to the scanners.

"This is a lot more invasive," Stone said. "These look like artificial muscles woven into her real musculature. Her bones have some kind of coating. Probably to reinforce them. I'll wager she could kick like a grav lifter." Stone checked her notes. "This woman was found wearing an armored body suit. Maybe she was a marine."

Kelsey shuddered. "That's awful. She was like a machine."

"More like a cyborg—part machine, part human. Enhanced. These brain implants might allow for a better interface with something. Maybe each other, if there's some kind of transmitter in there. I'd better call in the science teams before I open one of them up."

"They can come back in the cutter I'm taking over to *Best Deal*, if it's all the same to you. I'd rather not see the inside of someone."

Stone nodded and smiled. "No problem. We'll need to examine more of them to be sure exactly what we're seeing. It's not a pretty sight. Do you want the final report?"

"Please. This might tell us a lot about them. Thanks for the invitation to come down."

Kelsey thought about what the brain implants meant all the way over to *Best Deal*. They almost had to be interfaces of some kind. Why they needed them was something of a mystery, though that probably explained the lack of name tags. They could recognize one another, even if they'd never met. They might even have been able to access some kind of biography on the fly. She'd have to think about the implications of that on a society for a while.

A number of Fleet crewmen got off the cutter with her, and an equal number of scientists waited to board. They chatted enthusiastically about how they were going to look into the brain implants.

Kelsey resisted another shudder and made her way to the labs. She only got lost three times. What she found was a huge room with lots of tables. Each had an assortment of objects covering it, and there were a few dozen lab-coated men and women examining things and making notes on their tablets.

Doctor Cartwright was among them, so she wandered over to his side. "Thanks for inviting me over, Doctor."

The older man looked up and blinked in surprise. Then he smiled. "I'm sorry, Ambassador. The time got away from me. I'd meant to meet you in the docking bay."

"No need to apologize. I came over a little early. I couldn't wait to see what sorts of things you're finding. And call me Kelsey."

He looked as though he didn't think that was a good idea, but he nodded. "As you wish. Please, call me Zephram. What we have here are many ordinary items and a few mysteries. They haven't removed any of the larger artifacts from *Courageous* yet. The half dozen small fighter craft in a bay amidships have the Fleet people quite excited."

The older man gestured to the tables around them. "We have items ranging from tablets to toothbrushes. All appear slightly different from those we use. Oh, and weapons. The vacuum has preserved everything in an almost pristine state."

"What kind of weapons?" The marines had taken her to their shooting range. She wasn't anywhere close to being an expert, but she at least knew the general classes of weapons.

"A number of projectile weapons and some that defy a precise explanation. Come take a look."

He moved to a table across the room, where they'd laid out a number of pistols in neat rows. At a glance, Kelsey could see two models. One had an opening for a projectile and an exceptionally thick barrel. The second had no opening at all. The barrel looked like a thick canister half again longer than the projectile weapons and a little thicker than the weapons themselves.

"Are they safe to pick up?"

"Yes. Both kinds used power packs that have completely discharged over the years. Still, do an old man a favor and don't pull the trigger. Just in case."

She picked up one of the projectile weapons and searched for the release to the magazine. There was no slide on the barrel, so it didn't look like it ejected a casing. That alone made it different from the marine weapons.

Once she had the release identified, she pointed the weapon at the floor and pressed the catch. The magazine resisted but finally came free. The bullets inside weren't bullets at all. They were metallic darts with fins in a clear gel-like blob. The blobs seemed all melted together, but Kelsey wagered they were once separate.

Empire of Bones

"Do you have a knife?"

"There are some on one of the other tables, but I have a plastic pick. That should do." He stepped away and came back with a little tool that would do the job.

"Thanks." She used the pointed end to pry out one of the bullets. Doctor Cartwright had put thin gloves on and held them cupped to catch it.

He held it up after it came free. "Interesting. No propellant. It looks like a tungsten alloy. With a power pack and this thick barrel, the weapon may use electromagnetic propulsion. I'd imagine it discards this gel sabot in flight almost at once. The small fins would provide admirable stabilization for the projectile."

"Wow! That sounds very high tech. How fast do you think it could go?"

He shrugged. "We'll be able to make an educated guess once we disassemble one of these. Certainly fast enough to be effective. Perhaps five times the speed of sound. Maybe more. This metal is almost certainly armor piercing as well."

"You might want to have one of the marines consult. Their armorer has quite an extensive knowledge of projectile weapons."

"An excellent idea." He put the bullet into a small bag and set it on the table. He then picked up one of the other pistols. "This has no way for a projectile to be expelled. The thick barrel suggests some kind of electromagnetic force, but it isn't a laser. We use those in our labs, and this is not the magical hand-held laser pistol. Whatever it does can't be good, though. Otherwise, why make it into a weapon?"

"True enough. Did they have larger weapons?"

"Certainly. We have some on the next table. The projectile weapons look similar to the pistols here, but there is something new."

He led her to the next table and showed her examples of the two rifles. One looked like the projectile pistol, but the other had an exceptionally wide barrel. Almost like a rocket nozzle from the early space program.

She found the magazine and ejected it. The bullets looked more like metal pellets rather than projectiles. There was no way they could be aerodynamic enough to do much damage, especially with a barrel as open as this was.

Cartwright picked the pellet up and examined it closely. "Tritium. We use small pellets of a similar nature to conduct plasma experiments. It's put into a chamber and converted to a high-energy state by lasers."

She wasn't about to stare down the barrel of an unknown weapon, but she looked inside the bell from an angle. "If it converted to plasma, what would happen to the barrel?"

"It would be destroyed. So would anything within a few meters of the unfortunate soul."

Kelsey whistled soundlessly. "Let's assume for the sake of argument that the makers of this weapon wanted to keep the person firing it from being turned into a cinder."

The older man felt the bell. "This might be resistant, but it can't survive direct exposure to plasma." He then made her heart shoot into her throat by staring directly into the barrel. "There are some projectors in here. Half are lasers, and the other half are unknown to me. The interior of the weapon appears coated in iridium. That would help."

"Zephram, could you point the deadly weapon somewhere other than at your face?"

He blinked at her for a moment and then smiled a little. "That wasn't the best choice, eh? I suppose you could say I lost my head." He put the weapon back on the table. "Assuming this is a plasma weapon, perhaps those other emitters are similar to the screens their ships used. Perhaps it focused the expanding plasma toward the target. If so, that would have a devastating effect."

"How devastating?"

"It would probably incinerate an armored man and melt the bulkhead behind him. This would be a most lethal weapon. They tell me there are armored suits, but one has not yet made it over. I'll be able to determine how resistant it would be to this kind of weapon when it arrives."

The sophistication of the weapons, and their raw destructiveness, shocked and amazed her. Men armed with these would be virtual killing machines. Add in the heavy modifications the marines seemed to have, and they would be unstoppable. Except they had been stopped.

Cartwright wandered over to the next table and picked up a combat knife. She'd seen something similar in marine country. They all seemed to have a fetish for sharp objects. "This looks relatively normal, but even it has some improvements."

She took it from him and examined it closely. The blade didn't appear to be steel. It was matte black, even along the edge. Holding it with the white tabletop behind it, she could see it had a wicked edge.

"What kind of metal is this?" she asked.

"I believe it might be similar to what is used on their hull. If so, it would be almost impossible to dull and probably take far more strength than a normal person possessed to break it. I'd imagine a strong man could drive it into the table without damaging the weapon. It might even be capable of harming someone in armor."

She was impressed. "I'm certain some have already made their way back to *Athena*, then. No way would the marines pass up the chance to have something like this."

The old scientist smiled. "I'd imagine not. Luckily, there are many of them left over to study." He gestured at the three or four dozen on the table. "Oh, I can think of one other oddity you'll appreciate."

They walked over to a table piled high with headsets. However, unlike normal headsets, these had no headphones or built-in microphones. Instead, they fit over the top of the head in three places. They had circular pads that pressed against the skull.

She picked one up and pulled the pad back enough to see some kind of plate under it. Kelsey frowned as she considered how they would sit on the head. The spacing seemed just about right for these pads to go over the unknown implants in the dead Fleet personnel. The table had more than fifty headsets. She'd wager there were many more over on *Courageous*. Perhaps enough for everyone on board plus some spares.

"Zephram, I think you'd best send some of these over to Doctor Stone on *Athena*. The Fleet personnel seem to have some implants in their heads that would correspond to these locations at the ends. I also think you'd better bump these up in priority. Captain Mertz is going to want to know about them."

"Implants, you say? How intriguing! I will certainly do so. Perhaps a direct inspection is in order. Meanwhile, we have much more to examine. We still have to study their tablets. We're quite hopeful we can recover data from these units once we decipher how the power cells work."

She followed him, although her mind was preoccupied…thinking about the brain implants they'd discovered. What would the headsets allow them to do? That seemed like one of the most important things they could figure out. No one had mentioned anything like this after the Fall. Perhaps it had been a closely guarded secret.

If so, it was one she was determined to unravel. It might be the key to everything.

17

The news about the implants interested Jared, but it got him no closer to solving the riddle of getting home. The probes had scoured the system and only found the one other flip point. No other weak flip points were present. Perhaps they really were rare.

He'd decided the science teams could continue examining *Courageous* for samples of technology to take home while *Athena* probed the next flip point. If there was trouble on the other side, it was better to go without the freighter. That increased his options somewhat and kept the noncombatants out of danger.

He sent two probes back to the other side of the weak flip point. One would wait for anyone to come into the system, transmitting a distress beacon. It had the full logs for the mission thus far, encrypted of course. They could send other probes back to update it as they learned more, as long as they were close by.

The second probe was on its way back to the Empire. It had to make two flips to get to an occupied system. Its distress signal would draw help from Fleet. If it made it all the way. Baxter wasn't certain it would. Even if it did, it would be over a month before help could arrive.

He reluctantly pulled Kelsey off *Best Deal* to go with them as they explored further. If he'd had his way, she would've stayed where she was, but orders were orders. He did leave a couple of lieutenants to restrain the scientists from doing anything truly foolhardy. He hoped.

They'd also continue the inquiry into Carlo Vega's death. Since the investigating officers didn't know his suspicions about the source of the poison, they'd conducted an exhaustive set of interviews centered on the freighter's galley. As he'd expected, they'd determined there was no reason for the suspect substance to be anywhere near the food preparation area.

Two labs had some of the poisonous substance for experiments, but security was somewhat short of Fleet expectations. They couldn't even be certain any was missing. Jared would bet his salary from the entire exploratory mission they'd never officially identify the source of the poison. Or the poisoner.

Those thoughts occupied his time until Kelsey strapped herself into her unofficial seat on the bridge. She watched the two ships shrink on the screen until they were indistinguishable from the stars behind them. Only then did she turn her attention to him. "It's unbelievable. I never expected to find people like this...just bodies. It puts a completely different light on this kind of mission for me. I feel like a vulture."

"I can understand that point of view, but it's wrong. None of the people who died on *Courageous* would begrudge us taking them home or salvaging what we could. In fact, their captain gave us his explicit permission. In their shoes, I wouldn't mind. Would you?"

She took a deep breath. "I suppose not. What do you think about the implants?"

"Since none of the Fleet or marine personnel survived the battle of Avalon, they could've all had them, and the civilians would've been none the wiser. The survivors had other priorities. I'd wager if we exhumed their bodies, we'd find similar equipment. There's so much we don't know about the Old Empire."

He went over the exploration status with Kelsey for the next four hours. It helped to pass the time in transit and made sure that they were on the same page.

Just short of the flip point, he ordered a probe sent through with a short return time. The probe popped back out as they were slowing to a stop. Zia began pulling the data and transferring it to the screen. One thing was immediately clear. The system on the other side had occupants. Communication sources popped up all over the other system. Hundreds. Perhaps thousands. It was as busy as Avalon.

"This puts a new spin on things," he said. "There aren't any ships in range of the flip point, but we won't be able to move anywhere without someone seeing us."

Kelsey nodded. "It doesn't change the fact we have to go."

"No, I suppose not. It's also probable that they're less advanced than we are, even though they obviously have spaceflight."

"Why is that?"

Empire of Bones

"Because they've never come through to explore *Courageous*. They couldn't have missed the distress beacon. That means no flip drives."

"How do we know that the next system isn't full of Old Empire automated transmitters?"

"No distress beacons. I'm not sure what's transmitting, mind you. We need to process some of the traffic to figure it out. Without knowing the transmission protocols, all we have are signals. Zia, can you get us any of that in a format we can understand?"

The tactical officer nodded. "I'm working on a strong signal now. I don't think it's encrypted, but the formatting is…wait…got it. Going on screen."

A man sitting behind a desk replaced the system schematic. Jared instantly recognized it as a news program. There wasn't any audio, but the images behind the man's back seemed to be of some sporting event.

The man himself was dressed in a colorful tunic shirt with some kind of emblem on his left breast. His hair was dark and tied back in a loose ponytail. Whatever he was saying, he looked cool and confident.

"I think we've tapped into the evening news vid," Kelsey said. "That speaks for a relatively high social and technological standard right there. As opposed to some of the entertainment vids I've seen at home."

He laughed. "True. If the first thing an alien civilization saw about us was the strange reality vids making the rounds, I wouldn't blame them for dismissing us as primitive savages."

"The audio is somehow tied into the video," Zia added. "The signal is complex and redundant. Definitely not primitive. I can probably figure it out with a little more time."

Jared considered his options. At the very least, nothing was near the flip point. Going over was a slight risk, but the more powerful passive scanners on his ship could draw down a lot of data fairly quickly.

"Pasco, move us into the flip point and recover the probe. We're going over."

"Aye, sir."

The ship assumed a position in the center of the flip point, and as soon as they recovered the probe, he ordered the flip.

Thankfully, it was a normal transition and nothing like the terrible flip that brought them into this sector of space. Everyone recovered in a few moments.

Then the alert klaxon went off. "Missiles detected, Captain," Zia said crisply. "Ships in motion on the gravitic scanners. About an hour away at maximum acceleration. No immediate danger to us."

"Put the system diagram on screen."

The basic system layout appeared. The weapons fire was located clockwise around the plane of the ecliptic from *Athena*. The gravitic scanners were getting data on the ships and missiles. They were nowhere near danger.

"Stand down from battle stations, but keep us on alert status. Where are the major communication sources?"

Five flashing yellow dots appeared. One of them was at the point of the battle.

"There were no transmissions from that location earlier, sir," Zia reported. "They must've started as soon as the battle began. There were no indications of ships in motion there earlier. I'm picking up non-Fleet distress beacons. I'm also detecting numerous vessels accelerating at high speed."

Operations had already begun mapping them on the screen. "Do we have any feel for who is shooting who?"

Zia tapped her controls. "There are a large number of missiles being fired from hundreds of ships leaving the general area. I believe there is a flip point, and the fleet of vessels transitioned less than ten minutes ago. Probably just after our probe returned. I've designated them Force Alpha."

"Where are those ships going?"

"Their course suggests they are moving toward the strongest transmission source in the system." Zia highlighted another communications hub in the system. "ETA just over three hours. There is a large fleet of vessels moving from there to intercept them. I have designated them Force Bravo."

"What's happening?" Kelsey asked. "Obviously a battle, but who are the good guys?"

"I doubt we'll be able to figure that out while the shooting is going on. Zia, can you crack any of the transmissions? We could use some audio now."

"Working on it, sir. I'm only detecting encrypted transmissions from the battle scene. Also for Force Bravo. I'm not picking up any transmissions from Force Alpha."

The man they'd been watching earlier replaced the images on the screen. He now showed a video of scores of ships appearing in space and opening fire with missiles. They blasted a huge space station, knocking massive holes in its hull that gushed atmosphere and debris. Intense counterfire wiped out a number of the attacking ships before the feed they were watching died. The battle scene faded back to the man's image.

The audio suddenly kicked in. The man spoke Terran with a strange accent, but his words were clear enough. "That was the scene in the interdiction zone just fifteen minutes ago. This station's observation vessel went off the air, and we must assume it lost with all hands. We salute our brave reporters and mourn with their families.

"Royal sources tell us that a significant invasion force managed to break through but that Royal Fleet Command remains confident that all will be destroyed before they become a danger to the Kingdom. However, we urge all citizens to retreat to their shelters for the duration of this emergency. This station will continue to transmit news of the attack as it comes in."

Zia muted the audio and turned in her seat. "I'm picking up several vessels moving in our direction at high acceleration, sir. They're coming from the area they called the interdiction zone."

"Have they spotted us?"

"I don't think so. It looks like two of the attacking vessels have split off to pursue another ship."

The absolute last thing he needed to do was get involved in a local war. "What can you tell me about those ships? How long do we have to flip back before they could reasonably expect to detect us?"

The officer shrugged. "Without knowing the quality of their scanners, I couldn't say. We wouldn't detect a stationary ship like ours at this range for another forty minutes or so. The first ship has an audio-only transmission. I'm putting it on the overheads."

"...any vessel that can assist," a male voice said in a similar accent to the one on the news report. "We are being pursued by Pale Ones. We are carrying women and children. Any Royal Fleet vessels in range please respond." The message repeated. The man's voice held a note of panic.

Kelsey stepped next to Jared. "We must rescue them."

"Look, I'd love to, but that would be the height of irresponsibility. We don't know anything about these people at all, and we have civilians to protect."

"Wrong," Kelsey said in a hard tone. "We know the attackers have absolutely no problem chasing down a ship full of women and children. We cannot allow that to pass, Captain. The Empire does not stand by while noncombatants are murdered."

She gestured at the system schematic. "Look at that attacking fleet. Do you think they're moving toward an inhabited planet at high speed to wave as they go by? No. Even I know that there will be a bombardment. Tell me you haven't been to the spaceport memorial site. The rebels killed almost a million people from orbit on Avalon. Are we to stand by and let that happen right in front of our eyes? Could you live with doing nothing?"

Jared knew she was right. He didn't want her to be, but she was. Even if they couldn't do anything about the ships attacking that planet, they had to act.

He straightened in his chair. "Thank you, Ambassador. I wasn't thinking of the entire picture. Besides, it would be hard to request help from these people if we don't give some when they need it."

Kelsey inclined her head.

"Zia," Jared said. "I need more information."

"The vessels pursuing the single ship haven't fired, but they're closing range slowly. They must already be inside missile range."

"Can we transmit in the format the locals are using?"

Zia nodded. "It'll take me a few minutes to set things up, but we should be able to."

"How about the angle to that ship? Could we tight-beam a transmission to them without the other ships getting it?"

"Yes, but we can't be certain they'll receive it."

"It's worth a try. Let me know when we're ready. How far are the pursuers from our weapons range?"

Zia examined the readings. "I could make some long-range shots in half an hour if we don't move. Effective range will take ten minutes longer."

"Do they have that long?"

She shook her head. "Not realistically. If we intend to save that ship, we need to boost at max. The closing vectors will bring everyone together a lot faster. We'd be in effective range in less than twenty minutes. I think I'm ready to transmit, Captain."

"Pasco, take us in. Max acceleration. Zia, open a channel." He stared at the screen, knowing his image was going out as though he was staring right into the vid.

"Vessel in distress, this is the Imperial Fleet destroyer *Athena*. Change your course toward our position. We are coming to assist you."

For a few seconds nothing seemed to be happening. Jared imagined that there was a lot of additional consternation over there right now. A strange ship had popped up in their system with no warning at all in the middle of an attack. They'd probably have difficulty accepting that *Athena* wasn't part of the attacking forces.

The screen cleared into an image of a small bridge with three men on it. They wore tunics in light green. The man in the center was balding, and sweat ran down his face. "Whoever you are, we're changing course. Help us. The Pale Ones will take us soon."

"We'll do everything in our power to help you. *Athena* out."

"Why did you cut the transmission?" Kelsey asked.

Empire of Bones

"They have more important things to do besides talking to me. We can chat at length if they make it. Sound general quarters, Zia."

Once again, the alert klaxons sounded from the overheads. Jared touched the communications controls on his console. "All hands, this is the captain. Prepare for combat operations. This is not a drill."

He closed the channel. "When will we be in maximum range, Zia?"

"Fourteen minutes, Captain."

"Open fire on the targets as soon as you can. Get them focused on us."

"Aye, sir."

Kelsey cleared her throat. "Do I need to go somewhere else?"

He shook his head. "You're as safe here as anywhere. Sit back down and make sure your straps are tight."

The smaller civilian ship had changed course to meet them, and the pursuing vessels had matched course. It became a race to see who would get in range first. Time slowed to a crawl.

"Commencing missile launch," Zia finally said.

The tactical plot on the screen lit up with missiles as *Athena* opened fire. The missiles were small and relatively fast. The odds of a hit at this range were very small, but the enemy couldn't afford to ignore them.

Yet that's exactly what they did. They seemed so focused on the smaller ship that they ignored the incoming missiles. *Athena*'s opening salvo of four all missed, but not by much.

"They don't have any countermeasures, Captain," Zia said. "They didn't try to screw with our missile guidance at all. Launching four more missiles with the guidance packages devoted to targeting."

"That's insane," Jared said. "What the hell are they thinking?"

"They may not be human," Kelsey said. "Just because the Old Empire never met an alien species doesn't mean they don't exist. Perhaps their outlook is so different that they don't worry about individuals."

"That kind of matches what video we saw of the invasion," Zia added. "The attackers didn't seem concerned about the losses as they broke through the fortifications. They seemed willing to take any damage in exchange for breaking through. It's a sure bet that the attackers on the way to the planet won't make it back home."

"Salvo two coming on target," Ramirez said. "Multiple hits. One ship has ceased acceleration and seems to have broken up. The other has shifted course to come directly after us. They're going to pass close to the...the civilian vessel just braked hard!"

Jared grinned. "Ballsy. That'll get them clear of the fighting."

"Launching salvo three," Zia said. "The enemy is launching missiles at us. They look large but slow."

"Point defense stand by," Jared snapped. "Evasive maneuvers, Pasco."

Their missiles reached the enemy ship first. It glowed on the display, and then a red circle appeared around it.

"Target destroyed," Zia said. "Missiles incoming. Point defense at maximum!"

Something got through, because *Athena* lurched, and the damage control board on his console lit up. Two compartments were open to space.

"One missile exploded just short of the ship," Zia said. "Some fragments have breached the hull. No impact on combat worthiness. Damage control and medical personnel en route. Internal scanners show five crew in the compartments. Condition unknown."

Jared's heart was racing. This was the first real combat that he or any Fleet officer based out of Avalon had ever experienced. It was both exhilarating and terrible. With the oxygen masks on the battle stations vests, the trapped crewmen might still be alive. He hoped so.

"Zia, get in contact with that other ship. I want their status. Prepare rescue teams." Jared looked at Kelsey. "I want you there when they start coming aboard, Ambassador. It's time to earn your keep."

18

The marines refused to allow Kelsey to accompany them on the rescue mission. While she understood why, it made her anxious. The opportunity for misunderstandings was very high.

She was waiting with Doctor Stone and the medical team in marine country. The overheads came to life, and Jared's voice echoed out. "We've reentered the flip point, and the pinnaces are almost back to the ship. If we need to flip, we'll give you plenty of warning, but let's get the refugees aboard. Mertz out."

Running away with the rescued people probably wasn't the best idea, but neither was getting themselves shot to pieces if more hostile vessels attacked *Athena*. Kelsey was grateful the pinnaces had boarding locks that could mate with almost anything. Otherwise, they couldn't have gotten the people to safety nearly as quickly.

Athena trembled as the pinnaces docked, and the medical teams were opening the hatches as soon as the lights turned green. Civilians spilled into the chamber—men, women, and children. Most wore tunics and leggings, but some wore what looked like colorful sheets wrapped around themselves.

"May I have your attention?" Kelsey shouted. "You're safe now. Please move to the rear of the compartment so that the medical technicians can make sure you aren't hurt. Keep moving so the people behind you can get out of the pinnaces."

The marine assembly room was large enough for all thirty marines in battle armor. It proved inadequate for the flood of people. Thankfully, it looked like most people only had bumps and bruises. A man in a deep blue tunic began ordering the frightened people to do what they were told and quickly restored order. The three men in green she'd seen on the bridge deferred to him.

He turned to Kelsey. "I am Oliver Williams, engineer first of the Royal Fleet of Pentagar. Thank you for saving our lives."

She shook his hand when he offered it. "I'm Ambassador Kelsey Bandar of the Terran Empire. It was our pleasure to help you. Is anyone in your group badly injured?"

"I don't believe so. Our abrupt maneuvers bruised a few people, but nothing serious, I believe. The Terran Empire, you say. Are you the old fables come to life, then?" His voice held a combination of disbelief and hope.

Kelsey shook her head. "No. Our people survived the rebellion and have only recently begun expanding from the world the rebels drove us to. The young emperor was with us, so we believe we have the right to use the name. His line is unbroken." *At least until this generation*, she thought.

The man stared at her with an open mouth for a moment and then snapped it closed abruptly. "What an amazing tale! I hardly know what to say. This is the most important moment for the Kingdom since the destruction of the Empire. The other Empire."

He shook his head as if trying to clear away cobwebs. "No doubt the Kingdom and your people have much to discuss and learn from one another. Might I ask how you got here?"

She had to assume they knew what flip points were, though they might call them something different. "We came through the flip point near where we called you from. We're on an exploratory mission."

"Flip point? You must mean the space-time bridges. We do know of them, but the system on the other side is a dead end. The map of the Empire tells us so."

"You have a map of the Empire? That's wonderful. We lost even that. I'm not certain how to explain it properly, but there's a different kind of flip point that our ship used to get there. The only regular flip point there leads to your system." She didn't mention that they couldn't get back through the weak one. That wasn't helpful.

He scratched his head. "This other space-time bridge leads to your worlds? That is good news, though I'm worried that the Pale Ones might find another way at us through one. Are they easy to detect?"

"I'm told they're not obvious at all. We should step away from the chaos and let the medical teams do their work. We'll find somewhere to

Empire of Bones   125

put your people after we see to their medical needs and get them some food. You're not prisoners here."

Oliver smiled. "That is reassuring indeed. I am the only Royal Fleet officer with our group, so I am automatically the senior leader. If you have some food and chamber facilities, I would appreciate both. We have much to discuss."

"Chamber facilities?"

"Ah…where one takes care of private functions."

She flushed a little. "Of course. Come with me."

Kelsey stepped out into the corridor to lead him to the officers' mess. Two marines followed.

"You don't need to accompany us," she said.

Senior Sergeant Talbot shook his head. "I'm sorry, Princess. The captain has instructed that you and any of our guests be accompanied at all times, for their safety and yours."

She was going to have to have words with Jared about this, but now wasn't the time. She turned back to Oliver. "I apologize."

He bowed slightly. "If our roles were reversed, I have little doubt that Royal Marines would dog your steps. We know one another not. Let us address this deficiency with haste."

Once the Royal Fleet engineer was in the head with one of the marines to show him how things functioned, Kelsey called Jared.

"How are things going?" he asked.

"They'd be better if I didn't have marines watching over us like they expected an assassination attempt." She tried to keep the asperity out of her voice, but she knew she was unsuccessful.

He chuckled. "How well did that work with the Imperial Guards?"

She sighed. "Not very well. Can we at least have a little space in the officers' mess? I need to build rapport quickly."

"Certainly. I'll pass the instructions along to allow you privacy for your diplomatic discussions. They'll only shoot him if he tries to strangle you."

"You're not nearly as funny as you think you are."

"Opinions vary. I'll want a full report when you're done."

"Will do. Bandar out."

The officers' mess was empty. Jared must've ordered the compartment cleared as soon as he found out where she was going. Only one man in a white apron stood near the door.

Oliver returned and took a seat opposite her. The marine guards took up positions against the bulkhead. They couldn't easily overhear the conversation, but they'd be able to respond if needed.

Kelsey summoned the server. "A beer for me and whatever Engineer First Williams wants. Sandwiches would be good, also."

"I shall have what she has," Oliver said. "My thanks."

He turned his attention to Kelsey after the server had departed. "One of your marines referred to you as Princess. Are you of the Blood Royal?"

She cursed Talbot under her breath. That might complicate matters. "I'm acting in a diplomatic capacity, but my father is the emperor of the Terran Empire. My older brother is the heir. It is of no import in our discussion."

Oliver stood abruptly and bowed low. "I must disagree, Princess Kelsey. The king would have my guts for garters if I failed to show proper respect to the high nobility of a foreign nation. You are the first our people have ever met."

The marines took two steps forward at Williams's abrupt movements, but she waved them back. "Please, sit back down. I'm not one for standing on ceremony. For God's sake, we're about to have beer and sandwiches."

The man smiled as he resumed his seat. "That does imply a certain level of informality, does it not? Very well, but only in private. One must always show the proper respect for those of noble blood in public. I can hardly imagine having beer and sandwiches with the king or his family. I might just choke. Such as I have not the manners to dine with such as them."

"I assure you, we eat just the same as you. However, I understand how you feel. Captain Mertz—our captain—is my half brother and has always said he felt very out of place when he came to visit our father." She took a little relish in telling Oliver that. If she was going to be embarrassed, Jared could keep her company.

"Your captain is a prince?" Oliver seemed surprised. "Commanding a warship away from your Empire must be dangerous duty."

She considered how to explain things without making more of a mess. "The captain isn't a prince. His mother wasn't the empress, if you know what I mean. Even if he was a prince, he could serve. My father was a Fleet officer in his time."

The Royal engineer inclined his head. "Honor to him, then. The emperor acknowledges the bond to your captain?"

Kelsey nodded. "Yes."

"The Kingdom has its own share of those born on the wrong side of the sheets. An acknowledged bastard is of the Blood Royal, and the king often appoints them to high positions and important tasks. There is no dishonor in such here."

Empire of Bones

The server delivered the beer and sandwiches. Conversation paused as they ate. Oliver devoured his larger share as though he hadn't eaten in days. He didn't seem impressed by the beer, but he said nothing.

Once they had eaten, he ordered another beer. "That was a repast worthy of a king. My thanks."

"It's my pleasure. Tell me, exactly what does an engineer first do?"

"The title means I am an engineer of the highest order. I supervise others in major repairs or command them on board a ship."

"I think that would be similar to our chief engineer. I'll need to introduce you to Commander Baxter if time permits. So now that we have a meal inside us, can you tell me about these Pale Ones? We're not familiar with them. Are they aliens?"

The man smiled grimly. "If only they were. No. They are ravening human hordes that occasionally sweep out through the space-time bridge and attempt to overwhelm us. If they capture anyone, they whisk those unfortunate souls away. We never see them again. Else they slay any they can lay hands to."

"Why do they do that?"

Oliver shrugged. "No one truly knows. We regained space travel very quickly after the Empire fell but are trapped in this system. When ships came through the bridge a few decades later, we welcomed them with joy. They responded with missiles and incinerated tens of thousands before our ships destroyed them. War was joined, and it continues to this day."

"That's terrible."

"Indeed. They sweep across us every few years like a plague of locusts. They have not reached Pentagar in centuries. The loss of life in this attack will be high but not ruinous. The Royal Fleet knows its duty and the fate we face if we fail. We volunteer to stand between the Kingdom and the Pale Ones." He took a deep breath. "What happens now?"

"That's up to our captain, but I am confident you will be returned to your people as soon as possible."

"He commands even though you are in the line of succession? Is not your position higher?"

"My father entrusted overall command of this mission to him. I am the force of political will. Together we'll figure things out."

"Perhaps while we wait, you can tell me of your Empire."

Kelsey nodded. "Avalon is the capital of the Terran Empire now. It is a beautiful world with tall mountains and clear lakes. Once it was a pristine vacation world far from the bustle of the core of the Old Empire. That changed when the rebels chased Emperor Lucien to our surface. The rebels destroyed the spaceport and the city surrounding it. The only significant city on our planet. The battle in our skies ended with no survivors.

"We lost much of our technology but never our civilization. We regained space travel a hundred years ago and have spread out to a number of systems. We found people on many worlds and helped them recover too. We can finally spare the ships to explore the flip points around the Empire more thoroughly, and here we are."

"It sounds as though you have a wonderful home. I hope to see it with my own eyes one day. While I cannot speak for the Crown, I am certain our peoples will get along well."

She smiled. "I'm very hopeful that we will. I'm sure we each have strengths that we can use to support one another. How long has your world been a monarchy?"

"Since almost the very beginning. Our ruler was an Imperial baron when the Empire collapsed. His family has ruled us since those days, guiding us with wisdom and strength." He raised an eyebrow. "Though I feel I should warn you that I doubt the king will bow to your Empire or your position."

"Of course not. I wouldn't expect him to. We'll form a relationship appropriate to the times."

He seemed to relax a bit. "That is wise."

"How long do you think the battle will rage?"

"The Pale Ones committed to attack Pentagar will be destroyed shortly, I have no doubt. The ships and orbital weapons platforms will stop them. They will not save a reserve force. They will dash themselves against the defenses and die."

"I hope they don't hurt any more people."

He nodded. "As do I. Unfortunately, it is all too likely some weapons will slip past. We dig deep, but many will die today."

"Then perhaps the best we can hope for is to stop them before it happens again."

The engineer first raised his glass. "I can drink to that."

19

Jared maintained battle stations until he was certain that none of the hostile vessels were going to come directly after them. Only then did he let his crew step away from their posts. He made sure that a standing watch was ready to respond and left the bridge in Charlie's hands.

The medical center was still busy when he walked in, though Stone was in her office. He rapped his knuckles on the hatch frame.

She looked up from her screen. "Come in. Are we safe again?"

"For the time being." He stood behind one of the chairs. He'd already been sitting for hours. "What's the crew status?"

"Two dead and three injured. I know it could've been a lot worse, but I hate losing people." She sagged a little in her chair. "How bad will this get before we're done?"

He shrugged. "Bad enough, I'm sure. How are our guests?"

"All alive. A few had some bruises, but nothing to be concerned about. I do have some new information for you though. The marines snagged a body from one of the hostile ships. I've had the time to perform an initial examination, and I've got some unexpected news."

She brought up the screen on her wall. A man lay on the table. His long hair was filthy and wild. His face was gaunt from what looked like malnutrition. He looked like a savage.

"He wore minimal, quite primitive clothing—barely more than animal skins. His nails and teeth showed no signs of care. He looks like he's in his mid-thirties, but I'll wager he's a decade younger than that. Old before his time."

"Was he carrying a club? How do savages pilot flip spaceships?"

"I was wondering that very thing." She replaced the image with one of the internal scans from an Old Empire marine. He recognized the extensive modifications.

"Look familiar?" she asked.

"Yes, those are an Old Empire marine's implants."

"This is the interior scan of the savage."

Jared stood there with his mouth open in shock. "You're not saying this is an Old Empire marine, are you?"

Stone shook her head. "Doubtful. The technology looks identical, though. He has all the modifications the Old Empire marines had. The big difference is this."

She brought up another picture, this time of the side of the man's skull with his hair pulled back. A long, poorly healed scar ran from his temple around the back of his head. "He has scars like this all over his body. There were no attempts at regeneration. My best guess is that this was done about ten years ago."

"Let me get this right. Someone took a savage and ran him through a highly invasive modification? That doesn't make sense."

"It sure looks that way. There are another couple of things. First, they have the same equipment behind the lungs as the Old Empire marines. I found a wide variety of drugs that the unit seems designed to put directly into the bloodstream. At least one is a powerful painkiller, and another seems to be some kind of antiviral med. I think. I'm still working on the rest. Time degraded the drugs in the Old Empire marines, even though they were frozen.

"Second, these implants are still live. We have a few scientists on board, and they're testing one of those fancy headsets to see if they can pull any data off him. Perhaps that will tell us how Mr. Primitive can pilot a spacecraft."

"What about the new people? Do they have implants?"

Stone shook her head. "No. I've looked all of them over very carefully. None of them have any implants."

"That's good, but the other is very disturbing. Are you certain it's the same modifications? With the same level of technical sophistication?"

"As sure as I can be without cutting him open. I'll save that for when the scientists are done. Those implants probably interface with the headset and other equipment. Since they still have power, it may be possible to access their programming."

He nodded. "Keep me informed. I want everything kept on comps that are not connected to the ship's systems just in case." He started to leave but stopped. "And get some sleep."

The doctor smiled wryly. "There's an order I have no problem obeying."

Jared left the medical center and used his communicator to locate Kelsey. To his satisfaction, she was still in the officers' mess. Good. He was hungry.

Both she and her guest rose as he walked in. "Captain Jared Mertz of the Imperial Terran Fleet," Kelsey said, "allow me to introduce Engineer First Oliver Williams of the Royal Fleet of Pentagar."

The engineer first bowed low. "I am honored, Lord Captain. On behalf of the people under my care, thank you for our lives."

"It's my pleasure, Engineer First. The Empire doesn't stand by while innocents are in danger." He gave Kelsey a nod to show his own thanks and respect. "I'm no lord."

The older man straightened. "You may not be in line for your throne, but we of the Kingdom respect the Blood Royal, Lord Captain. Or in your case, the Blood Imperial. The princess was wise to inform me of your status. It will make a difference in how you are received."

Jared narrowed his gaze and spared the smiling Kelsey a mild glare. "Please, call me Jared. Excuse me while I have something to eat. Breakfast was a long time ago."

"Then I am Oliver. I must use the correct titles in public, though. My king would not hear of anything less."

Once they had sat and Jared had ordered food, Oliver continued. "Might I ask the tally of battle?"

"We destroyed the two ships chasing you. No hostile ships seem interested in coming out this way. For the moment, I believe us to be safe."

"A mighty victory indeed. Did you emerge unscathed?"

Jared shook his head. "We stopped most of the missiles, but one made it through. Thankfully, it detonated short of *Athena*. Two of our people were killed and several others wounded."

Oliver's face became somber. "I mourn with you at the loss of your people in a fight not your own. I pledge that they shall be listed on the rolls of our honored dead."

Jared nodded. "On behalf of my emperor, I thank you. Are you and your people receiving everything that you need?"

"We are being housed as well as can be expected on a warship and are truly grateful. Everyone has eaten, and most are sleeping. If I might ask, when will you contact the Royal Fleet to come meet you?"

"As soon as we can be certain we won't be fired on. No offense, but there's still a shooting war going on."

The man nodded. "A wise precaution. I sent a message to Pentagar of our status and your assistance. I believe they will restrain themselves from impulsive actions."

"We'll send a follow-up message, preferably from you, telling them who we are, but I don't want to do it until the battle plays itself out. Does this kind of attack happen often?"

The engineer first nodded. "Every few years. They come flowing in with no regard to their own deaths, striving to kill and capture. The ship I was on had just left the interdiction zone with the families of some of the officers there. We shuttle them out for the occasional visits because the stations are always fully manned."

Jared listened to the short version of the history between them while he ate. "It's as though they build up strength and come back at you. Do you ever try to communicate?"

"Many times, but they never respond at all. If they didn't fly in spaceships, we'd think them completely savage. The mystery of how they can travel between the stars and yet not speak is a great one."

"They don't speak? Via communicator?"

"Nor in person. We have captured some few alive over the years. They truly are savages... ravening, murderous savages with no regard to their own survival. Left alone and not visibly monitored, they eat, defecate, and fight. Since they are enhanced, they make formidable opponents."

Jared shook his head. "We brought one of their bodies back for examination. We noted extensive modifications. What's the story there?"

"I cannot explain why. It is one more mystery about them."

"Why don't you take the fight to them? Since they attack without reason, they might not have a very good defense."

The man held his hands out to his sides. "We cannot. We know the theory of traversing the space-time bridges, but we have no access to several critical elements necessary to construct the drives. We are prisoners in our own system."

Jared glanced at Kelsey. "That explains why you haven't journeyed in the direction we came from."

"We might not go there even had we been able. We believed it to be a cul-de-sac."

"You know?" The admission surprised Jared.

"We do. The rebels destroyed our spaceports and the orbitals, and they used EMP weapons, but some records survived on an asteroid

Empire of Bones

mining outpost. Some of the surviving computers there contained basic maps of the local area."

Jared felt himself sitting up straighter. "Do you know where Terra is?"

"Very generally. We have detailed maps of our sector and general maps for the rest of the Empire. Pentagar was far from the center of the Empire. The knowledge you came into this system through an unknown kind of space-time bridge will both excite our scientists and fill the Royal Fleet with dread. Where you find one, there may be others. What if the Pale Ones find one and pour in on us unannounced?"

"That would be a disaster," Jared admitted. His communicator chirped. He unclipped it from his belt. "Mertz."

"This is Graves, Captain. The last of the hostile vessels was just destroyed short of the planet."

"Did they get any missiles through to the surface?"

"Not that we could see, sir. Even the active scanner readings are vague from this far out. There seem to be a number of orbitals that shot down everything they fired."

Oliver sighed and smiled. "Thank the gods."

Jared returned his smile. "Do we have any ships on the way out here?" he asked.

"About a dozen have changed course toward us. We're looking at them arriving in our area of operations no earlier than five hours from now. Longer if they intend to decelerate."

"Understood. Keep an eye on things, and I'll be back up there before they get too close. Mertz out."

He put the communicator away and smiled at Oliver. "Good news. It appears there isn't a large loss of civilian life. I hope your fleet losses were light."

"They won't be," the engineer said with a deep sigh. "They never are. I saw many of the interdiction stations blown apart. Thousands are dead. No doubt, the losses in the ships engaging the Pale Ones were also heavy. You escaped lightly with only two casualties, Lord Captain."

"Still, you're right that we will celebrate. Once more, we have survived, and another attack will not come for a few years. We have time to repair the damage."

Jared took a sip of his beer. "Are you certain they won't come through again to surprise you?"

Oliver nodded. "We have many years of experience with them. They will lick their wounds and build their strength to try again. Why they only attack with everything at once isn't known to us, but they do."

"Perhaps we could provide the elements you lack to build flip drives. You could then attack them in their home."

The engineer smiled. "That would be wonderful. Such a gesture would be a great boon. The king and his ministers would be willing to negotiate most heavily for such when you meet, I am sure."

"I know we'll talk about many things, but first we need to keep them from shooting at us. Will you tell your people we're not Pale Ones? The very last thing I want to do is fight with your people."

Oliver rose to his feet and bowed deeply. "It will be my greatest pleasure, Lord Captain."

20

Kelsey stood in the main cabin of the Pentagaran ship that they'd saved and tried not to think about the terror she smelled in the air. Not her own but the stench of people expecting death or worse. Oliver stood beside her, and two marines in full combat armor with the full panoply of war covered her from behind.

She'd once again tried to convince Jared to let her proceed without them and failed. He adamantly refused to allow her to meet the representatives from the Royal Fleet without them. That was after he'd tried to block her from being the primary contact at all. Her arguments that the presence of armed men risked a lethal misunderstanding didn't deter him at all. The man was maddening.

If he could've had an armed pinnace with its weapons covering everything, she suspected he would have insisted. Thankfully, she'd negotiated an initial meeting without any armed ships. Three people from the Royal Fleet would come across in an unarmed cutter. Two of those people would be armed marines.

"Princess, the Royal Fleet cutter is about to dock," Talbot said. "I have a vid feed inside the airlock. If anything looks off, I want you in the compartment behind us before the echo of my voice fades."

At Engineer First Williams's insistence, she'd agreed to the use of her honorific. She was surprised at how little she'd missed it.

Kelsey had played cards with the marines so many times she couldn't count them anymore. Talbot's normal easygoing nature was completely absent. She had absolutely no doubt he'd stuff her in the other compartment himself if she hesitated to run on his command. Her orders were to obey his instructions if there was any trouble, much to her annoyance.

"Yes, Senior Sergeant." The tone sounded exactly liked she'd said "Yes, Mother."

The ship jolted a little as the cutter docked. Oliver smiled at her. "Do not worry. They will do exactly as they have agreed. I have the word of Commodore Sanders."

"I'm sure they will," she said.

"Three people have entered the ship," the marine said. "Two heavily armed and one with only a pistol. That's not according to protocol."

"I never said he couldn't be armed."

"He hands his pistol over to one of the marines before he approaches your person or we're done." Talbot's tone brooked no argument.

The hatch in front of them cycled open, and the two marines came in. Apparently they deemed it safe for their officer to enter, because a young man wearing a bright-red tunic trailed in behind them.

Kelsey held her empty hands out at her sides. "I greet you in the name of the Terran Empire. I am Princess Kelsey Bandar. My marine guard insists that you lay aside your pistol before you approach."

The young man bowed slightly. "I am Lieutenant John Fredrick of His Majesty's Royal Marines. We are not allowed to be unarmed during possible combat situations."

"Then this meeting is over. Withdraw."

She suspected this was some kind of test. Perhaps merely male posturing. The two occasionally looked very similar. From the tensing of the marines behind the officer, her Imperial Marines had backed her up with some posturing of their own.

Oliver took one step forward and stood board straight. "Lieutenant, I am Engineer First Oliver Williams. I vouch for these people. I beg you not to allow a rule to come between our people on this important occasion."

The officer looked at Oliver for one long moment and then bowed again. "I meant no offense, Your Highness. I crave your forgiveness." He pulled his pistol from its holster slowly and set it on the deck before kicking it to the wall behind him.

"On behalf of my king and Commodore Walter Sanders, I welcome you to Pentagar. I am instructed to ask what ransom you demand for the return of our people."

"You misunderstand, Lieutenant," Kelsey said. "Your people are not prisoners. You may take them with you as soon as you feel comfortable.

Engineer First Williams may return with you now to make arrangements, if you wish. They can be transported here for you to pick up."

He nodded. "Allowing the engineer first to return to my ship is within the bounds of my instructions. I will accompany you in turn. Commodore Sanders wishes to have at least some examination of your ship before it is allowed deeper into our system."

"That is also within my instructions. Once your marines are gone, I will allow you to take up your arms, as a show of trust in your honorable behavior." She felt it was the right thing to do, no matter how much her marines might disagree.

"You honor me. I give my word in turn that I will not take up arms against you this day, unless I believe my life or mission is threatened."

"Accepted, and I in turn give you my word that you will be given access to all areas of the ship to examine, and you will be allowed to return to your fleet unharmed as soon as you choose to do so."

She turned to Oliver and held out her hand. "It has been my pleasure to meet you, Engineer First. I hope that we meet again soon."

He bowed low over her hand and kissed it. "May that day come speedily, Your Highness. Until then, I bid you a peaceful farewell."

The Royal Marines gave Oliver a thorough search and escorted him out of the compartment. Kelsey said nothing until Talbot spoke. "They've left the ship, Princess."

"Please pick up your pistol, Lieutenant Fredrick. As soon as your cutter departs, ours will come for us. Tell me, what precisely are you looking for on *Athena?*"

Fredrick knelt to retrieve his pistol, stood up slowly, and holstered it. "I'm just to see that nothing looks overtly dangerous to the fleet or the Kingdom. Once I have done so, I will return to the fleet and brief the senior officers. The next steps are up to them."

"Well, it is a warship…and has missiles."

The Royal Marine smiled. "So I've heard. Any destroyer that can take two Pale Ones without suffering grievous damage has my deep respect. However, those are not the kinds of danger I'm to look for. Truly, I suspect my superiors only want to know more about you."

Ten minutes later, they were on their way back to *Athena* and docked without incident. Jared and two marines stood waiting for them. While his guards were not wearing armor, they were armed.

Jared, too, was armed. She'd never seen him wear a pistol, though he now had one strapped on his hip. She wondered if that was to make a point of his own to the Royal officer. On the other hand, perhaps he was sending a message to her.

"Lieutenant Fredrick, I am Commander Jared Mertz, captain of the Imperial Fleet destroyer *Athena*. On behalf of the Terran Empire, I welcome you aboard."

The Royal officer bowed, but not quite as deeply as he had for Kelsey. "Welcome to Pentagar, Lord Captain. My orders are to examine your ship so that I may report fully to my commanders. Will you allow me free access to see all compartments and question your crew?"

Jared nodded. "I will, with the understanding that there may be some classified subjects about which they may not answer."

"Of course. May I first see your bridge?"

They proceeded on a long tour of the ship. Kelsey sent the armored marines on their way and followed Jared and the Pentagaran officer. They visited the bridge, engineering, several weapons rooms that she'd never been in, and then the medical center.

Fredrick asked many questions of the people they encountered, some of a military nature but mostly about Imperial society. He seemed to be looking for an understanding of their culture.

He spent a lot of time talking to Doctor Stone. He didn't ask about *Courageous*. Kelsey couldn't imagine how he'd know about it, but Doctor Stone was smooth. It didn't seem like she was worried about the Old Empire bodies they had aboard at all.

The lieutenant asked to see the people they'd rescued. The number of them determined to tell him about their ordeal and rescue quickly overwhelmed him. They also wanted to know the fate of their loved ones.

He promised them a speedy repatriation and that he would personally convey the status of their families as soon as he knew himself. He seemed nonplussed that most of them didn't seem to feel any rush to go back to his ships. Most seemed content to wait where they were until they could go home.

He smiled lopsidedly when he came back over to Kelsey and Jared. "I can think of no better marker of your character than the fact they seem so disinterested in leaving. Princess, Lord Captain, I am ready to be taken back to the intermediary ship. I will consult with my commanding officers, and I feel confident they will feel more comfortable with your presence."

"Thank you, Lieutenant," Kelsey said. "We look forward to speaking with them at length. Our peoples have much to say and many ways to help one another."

They escorted him back to the cutter, and he declared the marines were the only escort he needed going home. Jared agreed, and they parted there.

Empire of Bones

Once he was gone, Kelsey turned to her half brother. "Don't yell at me about allowing him to keep his pistol."

He smiled. "I think that was an appropriate gesture of trust. I saw the vid of the meeting. You showed a lot a spine telling him to go home when he showed up armed but allowing him to regain his lost face. Well done."

She relaxed a little. "Thanks. You armed yourself because of him being armed?"

"It seemed like the right thing to do." He headed back to the lift and instructed it to go to the conference room. "We need to decide what we can tell them and what matters we need to keep to ourselves. *Courageous* is off limits for now. So is the fact that we're trapped. Our isolation might make them attempt to take undue advantage. We're the only flip-capable ship in the system."

She sat down at the table. "We need to tell them before too long. It would be grossly unfair to let them think we might be able to help them directly with their war effort. Besides, they'll figure it out soon enough. We are stuck here...in *their* territory."

He nodded. "We might eventually tell them about *Courageous*, too. That would provide us a measure of leverage if we share some of the technology. I want to help them, but it has to be contingent on help from them."

"Do we tell them about the Pale Ones' body we recovered?"

"You heard Oliver. They've captured some live ones. They've seen much more than we have. The only bit of information we have that they don't is the link to the old Fleet implants."

Kelsey considered that for a few moments. "Agreed. Has there been any additional news on that front?"

"A little. The science team figured out how to hot-wire a headset to a standalone computer. They've pulled quite a lot of data off the implants, but they really don't know what it means. They have no frame of reference. I'm told it looks like programming code, but they don't know the language."

"Will anything on *Courageous* help with that? Getting her computer back online, perhaps?"

"It's possible, but I'm not sure. It'll probably be more code we don't understand. We might not even be able to access it without implants of our own."

She shuddered. "That sounds horrible. I can't imagine how they could put things like that in their brains. Much less what the marines did. They'd have to be cut open like a fish."

"I agree that it seems horrific. Especially considering what the Pale

One had done to him. There has to be a link between them and the Old Empire Fleet. I just can't imagine what it is. Perhaps some equipment was left on and still running after all this time?"

"That's set up to kidnap people and does this? There's something more to the story. I'm more interested in why these obviously savage people are compelled to fly here and attack. What guides them? How can the implants even make it possible?"

"More questions without an answer. We'll send those people back over to their fleet as soon as we can and flip back to *Courageous*'s system. It won't hurt to let the Royal Fleet know we have people there. It's almost like an insurance policy. We can get a download of data and more scientists. If we're going deeper into the system, I want to have our best people with us."

Jared's communicator chirped. Graves responded when he answered. "Captain, the Royal Fleet commander wants to speak to you."

"On my way."

He stood. "Time to cement our introduction."

21

The next few days went by quickly. The Royal Fleet arranged to take their people off *Athena*, and Jared sent a probe back with a message to have a number of scientists brought to the flip point. They made the flip back the next day to pick them up and ended up spending an unplanned few hours offloading the large cargo shuttle that they'd packed with equipment.

He'd told them to bring only the essentials, but their definition of that word differed from his. He should've known that would happen.

Commodore Sanders, the Royal Fleet commanding officer, invited him over shortly after they returned. Though somewhat concerned about isolating himself, Jared agreed. These people hadn't given him any indication they were likely to behave treacherously, so he'd make the first big step in building trust.

Kelsey wanted to go, but he refused. Trust didn't need to be an act of stupidity. They could take him prisoner if they chose. That wouldn't force *Athena* to do anything. He considered himself expendable if need be. The emperor's daughter was not, no matter how she styled herself.

So he boarded one of his cutters with two unarmored marines. All three wore sidearms but brought no heavy weapons. They approached the Royal flagship a short time later. It looked big in the vid feed. Much larger than the biggest cruiser the Empire boasted.

Of course, the Terran Empire wasn't at war. If that changed, the Imperial shipyards would commence building larger vessels. They'd done the design work, but there was little need to incur the expense with no threats on their borders. With the dangerous universe he'd discovered, that might change.

They didn't need a special docking collar this time. The Royal flagship had a bay large enough for his cutter. The pilot deftly brought them into the massive ship's bay, and the large hatch slid closed behind them.

Jared rose to his feet and checked his uniform one last time. He started to open the lock when it turned green, but the pilot told him their hosts wanted him to wait a few minutes while they prepared to greet him.

When they indicated they were ready, Jared cycled the lock and stepped out onto the cutter's ramp. Two short rows of men in red tunics flanked the ramp, rifles held upright in front of them. Two men stood at the other end of the impromptu corridor. One of them was Lieutenant Fredrick. The older man with three times the ribbons on his gold tunic was probably the commodore.

Jared walked up to the two officers and saluted, right fist to his chest. "Greetings, Commodore Sanders. I am Commander Jared Mertz, commanding officer of the Imperial Fleet destroyer *Athena*. Thank you for inviting me over."

The older man brought his stiff hand to his forehead in a salute with which Jared wasn't familiar. He then extended his hand. "It is my pleasure, Lord Captain. You already know the good lieutenant and, as you so astutely surmised, I am Commodore Walter Sanders, commanding officer of this task force. On behalf of my king, allow me to thank you once more for acting in defense of his subjects in their hour of need."

Jared shook the man's hand and smiled. "It was the right thing to do."

"You took a leap of faith in your decision. My understanding is that you arrived while the attack was in progress. In your position, I might well have decided to proceed more cautiously until I established the lay of the land."

"I considered the data we had at our disposal and the wise counsel of our ambassador. She immediately knew the right course of action. Honorable beings do not attack innocent civilians. Character is important."

"Quite so. I'm disappointed that she couldn't come, but I understand your caution. I hope to set your mind at ease today, because our peoples have much to offer one another. Technology, culture, and much that I'm certain I haven't considered. Come, I insist on giving you the same tour you gave my officer. *Mace* is an old battleship, but I'm proud of her."

Empire of Bones

The Royal Marine guards didn't follow them, so Jared made a decision. "Perhaps my marines could spend some time with yours. That might foster more understanding between our people."

The commodore laughed. "Knowing marines as I do, I shudder to anticipate what trouble they will find together. You can summon them when you're ready to depart."

The marines didn't look happy at leaving his side, but they went off with their counterparts. He hoped they wouldn't get into a fight over gambling debts. Fredrick went with them, perhaps to make certain they didn't.

The number of crewmen in the corridor surprised Jared. There were a lot of people. "What size crew do you have aboard?" he asked.

"Three thousand two hundred and fifty three. *Mace* has many systems to maintain and operate. What of *Athena*?"

"Two hundred and fifty, not counting a detachment of thirty marines."

Sanders stopped, his expression surprised. "That's an incredibly small crew for even a destroyer. Ours have double that number. Your systems must be quite advanced."

"I hadn't considered them overly so, but perhaps. We've only been back in space for a century, but our scientists had been working on the theory long before we had the technology. Once we started making breakthroughs, we built ships quickly. *Athena* isn't the cutting edge of our designs either. She's about fifty years old, though she's been well refitted."

"We need to build ships quickly after every invasion, and innovation has been slow. The continuing raids have taken their toll on progress. We do indeed have much to learn from your people. Let's start with engineering."

The main engineering compartment looked large enough to hold most of *Athena*. He had no trouble recognizing the massive grav drives. They seemed powerful enough to move a planet.

"What are these?" He gestured at the massive power plants. "Fission plants?"

"Yes. Heavily shielded, of course. I'd imagine you've figured out cold fusion?"

Jared laughed. "I'm told that's a mirage. We do have fusion plants, though they take up much less space. My chief engineer could ramble on about them for a few weeks."

The old man smiled. "Engineers are all alike, eh? I'm certain my engineers would be ecstatic to converse with him at length."

"I feel confident we'll come to some kind of understanding.

Ambassador Bandar will need to make the final decision on something like that, but I can envision sharing technical information very soon."

"That would be wonderful. Perhaps we can even barter for some of the exotic elements needed to make space-time drives."

"Those elements are found in most star systems in small quantities. The last system we travelled through may have them in one of its asteroid belts."

"Or the ones beyond it. I'm sure your Empire could have a brisk trade in them. They would be literally worth a king's ransom."

Jared took a deep breath. Here's where he had to lay some of their cards on the table. It wouldn't do to let their new friends think they were misleading them. If this were going to cause problems, it would be best to find out now.

"At this time, bilateral trade with the Empire may be premature." He explained their current difficult situation to the commodore.

The officer listened without interrupting until Jared wound down. His frown deepened. "Indeed, you are in a fix. Thankfully, you'll find the Kingdom a friend in your time of need, just as you were in ours. Unless there is another of these weak flip points in our system, we cannot offer an alternative route back to your Empire, but we can make certain you have other supplies you need. One day your Fleet will come looking for you, and they *will* find you among friends."

"We appreciate that. The Empire doesn't forsake its friends, either. The emperor won't forget those who sheltered his daughter."

The commodore started walking down the corridor slowly. "I've spoken with His Majesty. He has given me leave to speak with his voice in this matter. No matter what agreements we come to, you and your people are welcome here as our friends. His shelter is yours. Frankly, he can't wait to meet you both, Lord Captain. Your timely arrival has fired his imagination."

"I hope we can live up to his expectations." Jared considered their situation. Hiding *Courageous* might come back to bite them if they never got home. If they traded technical information, the Royal Fleet would use the flip point to that system to test their new drives. Its presence would become common knowledge fairly quickly.

"Commodore, might we speak privately?"

"Of course. Let's adjourn to my day cabin. We can have something to eat while we talk."

The commodore's day cabin was twice the size of Jared's office. The older man sent for food and offered Jared a drink. Having no idea what drinks they had here, he told the other man to surprise him.

Empire of Bones

Sanders poured an amber liquid into two small glasses. "Sip this. It's quite smooth, but a gulp would be uncomfortable at best."

Jared sat at a small table beside the senior officer and sipped the drink. It was quite alcoholic and burned nicely as it went down. "This is very good."

"Aged apricot brandy. My family has brewed this for centuries. It's only available for limited consumption. I'll send a few bottles back with you."

A buzzer announced the arrival of food. It looked like a platter of cheese, meats, and bread. The scent made Jared's stomach rumble. The man left the food with them and departed.

Commodore Sanders considered Jared. "What shall we speak of, Lord Captain?"

"My people may be trapped here, and I have knowledge that you should be aware of. Consider it my gesture of trust." He proceeded to tell the full tale of their arrival.

Sanders sat bolt upright when he first mentioned the Old Empire battlecruiser, his drink forgotten in his hand. He listened raptly to the entire story without interrupting. Only when Jared finished did he move.

More precisely, he gulped the entire glass of brandy and went to refill their glasses.

"That is the most amazing tale I've ever heard. I've read adventure stories like that but never imagined that something so...astonishing could happen in real life. Dear gods, an Old Empire Fleet vessel." His tone was reverent. "They were as technologically superior to us as we are to the Pale Ones now."

"I'm confident that Princess Kelsey will negotiate allowing your specialists to join the examination of the ship, but I need to discuss the Pale Ones, as well." He explained about the implants they'd found inside the Fleet personnel.

The commodore frowned deeply. "That *is* troubling, Lord Captain. Are you positive these implants are the same? We knew the bastards had such technology, but this link to the Old Empire is chilling."

"They appear to be the same equipment and implantation method, except the old Fleet personnel had no scars."

"Are you able to compare the contents of these implants to those of the old Fleet personnel?"

Jared shook his head. "The ones in *Courageous*'s crew are as dead as they are. We modified one of the headsets to copy what they think is the programming code from the Pale Ones onto a separate, secured computer. We're examining it now."

The older man nodded. "If you were to find the right power settings, do you think some of the original implants might be brought back online?"

"Perhaps. I don't want to desecrate one of the dead Fleet personnel unless we're sure."

"We would appreciate it if you could try," the commodore said. "I find myself wondering if they are identical inside or if perhaps the programming of the Pale Ones has been overridden somehow."

Jared sipped his brandy. "You mean like a computer virus? That's an interesting theory. I'll discuss it with my people. If it were, wouldn't the Old Empire have fixed it? These savages might be the descendants of people conquered by the rebels. Surely the old Fleet would have captured some of the rebels and reversed the process if they could have."

The commodore shrugged. "It is conceivable that they did. The old stories tell how rapidly the rebellion spread. If it *is* a virus, perhaps correcting it took time. Perchance the same held true for modifying the implants to resist the infection. The vast and mighty Terran Empire fell within two or three years."

"That's an interesting theory," Jared agreed. "Are these Pale Ones a relic of the rebellion where some lingering imperative forces them to continue to seek out unconquered humans to enslave? How could they still have the advanced technology for the implant machinery yet still use such primitive ships? If they had access to the kind of ships found in the Old Empire, we would all be dead or enslaved long ago."

Sanders nodded. "There's the rub. Without going to look in their system, we have no idea what we face. Could we end this cycle of attacks by destroying some facility? Perhaps that is all there is…a single complex modifying people from a slave population."

"We have probes," Jared said. "The attack here is over. What if we sent one through the flip point as a gesture of goodwill? Knowing what awaits us over there is the first piece of information that we all need to formulate a plan."

"And if they have defenses to destroy it?"

"Then that tells us something important, too."

The commodore sat silently for a few minutes, and then he nodded. "We would be in your debt for any intelligence you could gather for us, Lord Captain."

Jared smiled widely. "We'll get started, but I'd like to ask you for a small favor in return."

22

Kelsey sat in her seat on *Athena*'s cutter and fumed. The destroyer was moving toward the flip point leading to the Pale Ones' system to launch a probe, and she was on her way to Pentagar. She knew Jared had to have been behind the commodore's insistence she leave now for Pentagar to begin negotiations. Unfortunately, she couldn't do anything about it.

Kelsey eyed Talbot. "Am I going to get the silent treatment the entire trip?"

"It's nothing personal, Princess, but we're not a barrel full of monkeys while on a combat patrol either. There's time to be serious and there's time to have fun. This is the former."

"This isn't combat."

"No, but what kind of impression would you make if we joked around with you? That might cause the people here to think you don't take them seriously. Or that you're making some kind of subtle insult. We just need to do our jobs, and then we can have a beer when everyone isn't watching your every move."

He was probably right, but she'd never had the chance to be so casually friendly with anyone like the marines before. She found she fit in really well with them and missed doing so.

She sighed and looked out the port at the ship they were approaching. It was much smaller than *Athena*. Two men in light-blue tunics met them when they docked. Both bowed.

"Princess Kelsey," the one on the left said. "I'm Lieutenant Parker, the command pilot of the fast courier *Lance*. This is my engineer, Lieutenant Walker. Welcome aboard."

"Thank you. I appreciate you taking us to Pentagar."

The main compartment of the Royal ship proved to be very small. There were just enough seats for her, the four marines, and the three scientists accompanying them. "We'll be departing at once," Parker said. "With our fast grav drives, we'll be in Pentagaran orbit in just under two hours. There are facilities through that door, and we have some bottled water if you get thirsty. I apologize for the lack of amenities, but we don't normally carry passengers so far."

"Thank you," Kelsey said. "We'll be fine."

They settled in, and Talbot promptly went to sleep while the other marine kept watch. She decided that was a stellar idea and settled back to catch up on some well-deserved rest herself.

She woke when Talbot nudged her. "The pilot says we're about to enter the atmosphere."

Kelsey stretched and wished there were some ports. She took a minute to use the facilities and to drink a bottle of water. They landed fifteen minutes later.

The pilot opened the hatches, and sunlight poured in. Kelsey took a deep breath. It had been over a month since she'd smelled unfiltered air. The breeze had a hint of something sweet but otherwise seemed completely natural. Someone had moved a portable ramp next to the ship, and the pilot gestured for her to go down first.

She stepped out into the open and took everything in. The blue sky was so pale that it almost didn't look like a color at all. Small, fluffy clouds raced above her, but the breeze brushing her face was light. The sunlight was somewhat redder than she'd expected but not overly so.

The ship had landed on a wide field of stone, some kind of poured mix very similar to plascrete. A number of other ships sat at varying distances away. Some were near large buildings and others sat alone. Hers was the only one with a group of people waiting near it.

Two lines of men in white tunics stood at the base of the ramp with weapons held in front of them pointing into the sky. A glance at Talbot showed he wasn't worried, so she walked down the ramp.

Two men and a woman stood waiting for her. Behind them were half a dozen men in colorful tunics. The woman wore a wide headband of gold. She smiled and stepped forward. "Princess Kelsey of the Imperial House of Bandar, I am Crown Princess Elise of the Royal House of Orison. On behalf of my father, I welcome you to Pentagar."

Kelsey bowed slightly. "Thank you for your kind welcome, Highness.

On behalf of my father and Captain Jared Mertz, I bring greetings and well wishes."

"As we are both of high rank, I insist you call me Elise. Allow me to introduce my companions. This is the royal chancellor of Pentagar, Sir Ellery Matcliff, Baron of Windshire." She gestured to the tall man with the distinguished gray hair to her right. "This is Lord Admiral Sebastian Shrike, Deputy Commander of the Royal Fleet."

The last was obviously a reference to the short, bald man of indeterminate age to her left. Kelsey couldn't tell how old he was, but he obviously kept himself in shape. His arms were quite muscular. The two men bowed.

"Thank you," Kelsey said. "Please call me Kelsey as well. I've brought three members of our scientific staff to consult with your people about the Pale Ones."

"Of course. Our scientific and medical delegation will receive them. I know they have much to discuss."

It turned out the people behind the other woman were that delegation. They led the scientists away, jabbering in technospeak as they walked. All but four of the honor guards faded away.

Elise gestured for Kelsey to walk beside her. "We have a grav car to take us to the palace. His Majesty is looking forward to meeting you, but he asked me to make the initial overtures of friendship. He believes that we women might come to a decision more quickly without his official presence."

Kelsey raised an eyebrow. "I see. And who are these gentlemen?"

"My keepers," Elise confided. "They're to make sure I don't sign away the Royal Palace."

The baron smiled. "Actually, Your Highness, the lord admiral and I are here to provide more detailed information if required. Between the two of us, we know where all the figurative bodies are buried."

"And more than a few of the real ones, I'd wager," the bald admiral rumbled in a surprisingly deep voice. "Are you the sole Imperial representative on your mission, Princess Kelsey?"

She nodded, deciding they didn't need to know the sordid details of Carlo Vega's death. 'I am. Tell me, Lord Admiral, does the honorific denote a relationship to your king?"

The short man nodded. "It does. The king did not marry until late and proved to be a lusty youth. We have a good working relationship."

There were two grav limos waiting for them. They climbed into one and the guards into the other. Both sped away together over the city. The view through the windows was quite beautiful. The buildings were lower to the ground than back on Avalon, but they were significantly wider.

After a few moments enjoying the view, Kelsey turned back to Elise. "This is the first time I've been directly involved in negotiating an agreement like this. What are we hoping to settle today?"

"The main goal of the evening is for us to become comfortable with one another. Agreements can come later. No one gains anything by rushing into something with strangers."

"Though if we can come to a few minor understandings quickly, that might make things less tense," Lord Admiral Shrike said. "The very idea of space-time bridges we were unaware of makes my skin crawl. Just because the Pale Ones haven't come through one doesn't mean they won't find one tomorrow. That could spell the end of us."

Kelsey nodded. "I've already spoken to Captain Mertz. We would be happy to scan your system and to pass on the specifications of the scanner without any preconditions. We'll also share what we know about flip drive technology."

Sir Ellery looked a little surprised but pleased. "That's most generous of you. You cannot believe how difficult it is to see savages with interstellar drives but be unable to create our own."

"Two peoples that want to be friends will find a way to help one another," Elise said. "I'm certain that we can offer you support. Then when you manage to find a way back, our help will also not be forgotten."

"True enough," Kelsey said. "Our scientists have probably already handed the data we collected over to your delegation. Unless they forget they have it with them. For being geniuses, they can be awfully absentminded."

The crown princess laughed. "I see that our people are more alike than I'd imagined."

The limo crossed a boundary of some kind. The city became manicured woodlands. Beyond them rose a magnificent castle. Bright pennants flew from the highest towers, and men patrolled the stone walls.

"Welcome to Orison Castle," Elise said. "Home to the Royal Family since before the monarchy was established. Of course, we were only a house of minor nobility before the Empire fell."

"Don't worry," Sir Ellery assured Kelsey. "The plumbing has been updated."

The crown princess smacked him on the arm. "Don't make her think we're backwoods folk with twigs in our hair."

"I think it's beautiful," Kelsey said. "I must take vids back home to show my father. He'll be absolutely green with envy. He would have loved to live in a castle growing up. Me, too."

Empire of Bones

The limos settled onto a landing pad beside the castle. The marines and Royal guards came out and made sure the pad was secure before Talbot gave her the high sign. The lord admiral exited first and held the door for the ladies. The chancellor followed them out.

Elise gestured to the wide entrance. "My father is waiting inside. This is a casual visit, so we're not standing on ceremony. He wants some quiet time to get to know you and to assure you that we're decent people."

"I already knew that," Kelsey said. "I've been watching the news vids. It didn't take long to figure out that what we were seeing wasn't propaganda. The people here seem genuinely happy for the most part. Even those who criticize the Royal house don't seem to feel afraid to do so. That told us a lot."

The crown princess laughed. "I can only imagine what you heard. Some people seem to go out of their way to find something to be unhappy about. Or look for some conspiracy. If so, they're free to do so. Open speech is a cherished right here."

She gestured for Kelsey to precede her. "Come on. Let's have lunch and get to know one another."

23

Jared brought *Athena* to a halt outside the sphere of orbital fortresses surrounding the hostile flip point. He didn't need to be inside it to send the probe, and being under all those missile tubes would make him itchy. Their Royal Fleet escort stopped with him.

The damage to the fortresses was...extensive. Many were little more than floating clouds of debris. The Pale Ones had severely damaged most of the rest. Smaller ships were flitting around, grabbing large chunks of wreckage and moving them toward a collection point. They also towed the remains of the enemy ships, some of which looked surprisingly intact.

He looked down at his console, focusing on the image of Commodore Sanders. The other man sat on *Mace*'s bridge, watching the same scene on his main monitor, Jared presumed. "Commodore, some of those attackers look better than I'd have expected after a missile duel at knife range."

The older man shrugged. "Sometimes they appear too close to one another and their grav drives mesh as they attempt to accelerate. That fries them right quick. Their actual momentum after transition is too small to get the derelicts far."

"Have you pulled any usable intelligence from them?"

"Not in years. We'll casually examine them, but they're not our priority. The space-time drives burn out with the grav units. For whatever reason, they make their drives as a single unit. On rare occasions, they manage to repair a ship and continue on, but no space-time drive has survived one of these burnouts. Or the battle damage required to stop the ship."

Jared frowned as he considered the man's words. "Exactly how does a savage repair a damaged drive unit?"

"Most likely in the same way they can pilot a spaceship. We hypothesize their implants have some automatic way to do some of that work without intelligence. We've seen the manner they fight hand to hand in the ones we've captured. Rote execution of advanced martial arts moves based on the situation. They are quite deadly in a fight."

"Might we have a relatively intact ship to study? Sometimes an outside eye can see something new."

Sanders nodded. "I'll have them shift one of these to your care. What will you do with it?"

"See if I can strap it to a cutter dock and flip it over to the other system. The scientists can disassemble it to their heart's content. If there's anything to be learned, they'll find it."

Zia turned in her seat to face Jared. "We're ready to launch the probes, Captain."

The plan was to launch two probes through the flip point. One would stay just long enough to get a scan of the immediate area and return. The other would remain for fifteen minutes. If it survived that long, they would have an idea of the star system on the other end. They'd also launch a widespread volley of probes set to scan the Pentagar system for any anomalous flip points.

Jared raised an eyebrow at Sanders. "Are we good with launching these? They look like missiles, and we'll be launching a lot of them. I do not want my command fired upon."

The commodore shook his head. "Everyone has been told multiple times. No one will fire on your ship, even if you inadvertently launched a salvo at one of the fortresses."

"I think we can avoid that particular blunder. Zia, launch the probes, starting with the ones going elsewhere in this system. Flip the two going over to the next system as soon as you're ready."

"Aye, sir."

The probes appeared on the plot of local space. A dozen moved quickly out of the general area and began probing. The final two quickly traversed into the flip point and disappeared before they reached the center. Perhaps by going over at the edge of the flip point, one would survive long enough to get back home with a snapshot of the tactical situation in the enemy system.

The probes had been gone less than ten seconds when the first one

Empire of Bones

popped back into existence. An overview of the far side of the flip point began taking shape as Zia added details from the data feed.

"It looks like the immediate area around the flip point is empty," she said. "No defensive installations and no ships detected. There might be some close by, but with only a glimpse, we won't see them."

"Can you give me any details on the system itself?"

"The star is a medium-sized yellow capable of supporting life. We have some images of the stellar background that the computers are crunching to see if they can narrow the location down using the computer records the Kingdom recovered after the Fall."

It took a few minutes before Zia confirmed the stellar location of the target system was the Erorsi system. Old records indicated it was at one time a populous world with several billion citizens.

"The second probe just reappeared," Zia said a few minutes later. "I'm pulling the data feed now."

The diagram on the screen updated. No transmissions showed on any of the scans. No ships or structures detected. That didn't mean there weren't any. No ship or artificial structure would be visible at the kinds of ranges a flip point normally sat from habitable planets. All they could possibly see at that range were radio transmissions or the gravitic signature of a ship moving at high speed.

Sanders shifted his attention from the display *Athena* was forwarding to *Mace*. "Does that say what I think?"

"If you think it says the flip point is completely unguarded, sir, you'd be right. That's insane."

Graves looked up from the console he'd appropriated at the rear of the bridge. "Perhaps not. Those things seem to operate on some preprogramed berserker imperative. Perhaps they aren't designed for defense. From what I've surmised, they overwhelmed the Old Empire with sheer numbers."

"It seems to have worked well enough for them." Jared considered the readouts. "We'll send the probe back over with instructions to return if it detects any enemy activity."

"Well, then," Sanders said. "I suppose I can shift my people into helping with the search-and-rescue operations. I'll want to know at once if you detect anything unusual at all."

Jared gave Graves a lopsided grin. "Just how much trouble would I be in with the princess if I popped over for a detailed scan, Charlie?"

"She will eat you alive," Graves assured him. "Is that what you want to do? They might note the incursion and respond."

"It doesn't look as though they keep a close watch."

"Our scanners are far more sensitive than the ones on these probes.

If we can get a detailed scan of the system, it could prove decisive when the Pentagarans make their own incursion."

He shifted his attention to Sanders. "Can you avoid shooting us when we come back?"

"If we arrange for you to be transmitting something known as you come in, I think that would work." They quickly worked out a signal that Zia could begin transmitting before they came back. That would keep the Royal forces from firing on *Athena*.

Commodore Sanders gave his final approval. "This is quite a risk you're taking for my people, Lord Captain. We appreciate it."

"I might need a place to hide when the princess finds out I didn't bring her along."

The older man laughed. "She won't be pleased, I imagine."

"We'll either be back very quickly or we'll be there a while. It depends on what we find. Don't be alarmed if we're gone for a few hours. We'll send a probe back with our estimated time of return."

"Good luck and Godspeed, Lord Captain."

Once the transmission ended, Jared brought *Athena* to combat readiness. They'd go over with their fingers on the triggers. This time he brought the ship to the center of the flip point and gave the order.

The momentary disorientation faded. Zia scanned her console closely. "No ships in the general vicinity, Captain."

"Stand down from combat stations. Hold station and passively scan the system. Prepare a dozen probes. I want to send them deep into the system to map it for flip points and Pale Ones. Program them to transmit the results to our location via tight beam."

"Aye, sir."

Graves moved over to Jared's console. "You don't think they'll spot them? The scans might be passive, but the probes are moving. Even if they don't, it will take days to cover the entire system."

"We'll leave a probe here to record data until they stop transmitting or ships approach. The reaction will be almost as useful as the data they get."

It took Zia an hour to locate the formerly inhabited main world of the system. Another two passed before the probe was close enough to detect artificial structures orbiting the planet. She detected no transmissions from either the orbitals or the planet's surface. While Zia couldn't be sure, she thought there were three clusters of artificial structures around the planet.

"Zia, how long to get the probe into range for a close look?"

She checked her console. "Another hour. Less if you want to let it shoot past the planet."

Empire of Bones

"If we can keep it there without it being seen, I'd rather have the extra intelligence a stationary probe could get."

He let the crew cycle off for meals and downtime. He'd know if they needed to come back long before trouble could come to them. He took the first break with half the bridge crew and relieved Graves an hour later.

By the time everyone was back, the probe was slowing into position. He waited the final minutes with some impatience. He really wanted to know what they were going to find.

"I'm getting good data from the probe," Zia said. "I'm also detecting three clumps of fusion plants in orbit. They are each roughly a third of the way around the planet from the others. At the orbital distance above the surface they occupy, they don't have line of sight with one another. Our probe is in a position to see the first two now. The third will take a few minutes to come into sight."

The system diagram they had been reviewing vanished, replaced by the breathtaking view of a planet. The greens and blues looked very much like Avalon. A small speck crossed in front of the ocean, and the image swelled as the vid zoomed in.

The orbital it revealed looked deceptively small, but the scale on the bottom of the scan made it apparent it was bigger than all the orbitals around Avalon put together. True, it was mostly an open framework, but that didn't change the scope of it.

"What is that thing?" Graves asked.

"It's a shipyard," Jared said. "I visited a freighter construction dock a few years ago. This is a lot bigger."

"How much bigger?"

"Big enough to construct an invasion fleet," Jared said grimly. "Thankfully it looks empty now. What else do we have?"

The view shifted. The second orbital structure was almost as big as the shipyard, only it was a solid sphere. Jared pursed his lips in a soundless whistle. That crude-looking facility could've housed tens of thousands of people.

The wait for the third set of power sources seemed an eternity but was less than half an hour. To his horror, it was another shipyard.

This one still looked to be under construction. That didn't seem to have slowed down its use, though. It had hundreds of ships in various stages of construction. It looked like they'd been working on this one for a while, and now it was almost ready to launch a new invasion. Not in years like the Pentagarans expected, but in days or weeks. An invasion they had no way of stopping.

24

Meeting the king of Pentagar was a bit anticlimactic. The short, rotund gentleman would've made a great tavern keeper. He welcomed Kelsey warmly and made her feel like a member of his family before a simple and delicious lunch was over. He insisted she use his given name any time she tried to be formal. She now knew what a favorite uncle must be like.

He seemed to have an endless supply of amusing stories, many from segments of society that she wouldn't have guessed he had knowledge of. After a particularly funny story about the construction crew of a building in the capital, she asked him about it. "Raymond, how could you possibly know what a bricklayer does on a construction site?"

His eyes twinkled. "I learned at a young age how to slip out of the castle and get to know the people I was to rule. Just like in an old story. They never suspected I was the crown prince. It drove my father simply mad. He would post guards, but I always managed to slip past them. You see, I'd found the secret passages."

Kelsey's eyes widened. "Secret passages? Seriously?"

"Absolutely," he assured her. "They were built into the castle when it was constructed. They had lain disused until I stumbled upon a secret room. Once I knew something like that existed, I made it my mission to find them all, though I doubt I succeeded. I think I may have, but even now, I'm not completely sure. They are hidden devilishly well."

Kelsey glanced at Elise. "Is he being serious?"

She nodded. "I've seen them. He insisted on showing them to me when I was old enough to appreciate them. You can get from almost any part of the castle to another. A few lead out into the woods. The exits are works of art."

"In any case," the king continued, "I still have my bricklayer's certification framed in my office. I think such knowledge and insight are crucial to being a good monarch. All too many noblemen live in little bubbles where they have no idea who their people truly are."

Elise leaned over toward Kelsey. "I apprenticed under a woodcarver for several years. If you haven't considered doing something like that, you really should. We live such isolated lives. We need to be more like the people we lead if we're to be the best rulers we can be."

"I wish I'd had an opportunity like that. It sounds wonderful."

Raymond Orison laughed jovially. "But you see, Kelsey, you have exactly such an opportunity! Here on this mission, you're one of them. You strive side by side with your fellows. You don't have to live inside a bubble. Socialize. Do what they do. Be one of them. The only thing stopping you is yourself."

"Well, I have been spending quite a bit of time with the marines. They were standoffish at first, but now we drink beer and gamble. I almost feel like one of them."

"Splendid! You've seen how easy it is. You can overcome the boundaries set by protocol. Meet your Fleet comrades in the same way. Dine with them. Find out what they do for recreation and join them. By the time you get back home, you will be one of them. And don't forget the scientists. The quiet ones can be the most fun! Such a golden opportunity shouldn't be squandered."

Elise put her napkin on her plate. "Speaking of opportunities, how would you like to go into the city and meet the man who taught me woodcarving?"

Kelsey smiled. "I'd love that."

"You girls go have fun. Kelsey, we'll have dinner tonight, and we can talk about diplomatic things after you've had a good night's sleep."

"I don't imagine these negotiations will be very difficult." She rose to her feet. "Thank you again for your kind welcome."

"It's my pleasure."

The flight into the city proved to be a long one because Elise kept telling the driver to show Kelsey various parts of the city. Not that Kelsey minded. She even made some side trips of her own to look at some interesting pieces of architecture in the distance.

It was close to three hours later when they arrived at the square. The limos settled into a parking area long enough for the occupants to

Empire of Bones   161

disembark and then took to the air again. Elise led them to a small shop on the corner of a busy street.

A plaque of dark wood hung over the door. Someone had cut an eerily lifelike image of a man walking a dog on it. A second, smaller plaque hung beside the door. Master Alec Vestor, woodcarver.

They went inside once their escort had checked it, and Kelsey gasped. Incredible woodcarvings filled the shop. Stunningly beautiful plaques and intricately detailed statuettes of people and creatures decorated the room. Some were familiar to her, others were not, and still others appeared to be fantastical. "This is amazing!"

She walked over to a shelf holding a collection of tiny figurines. None of the carvings stood more than a few inches tall, but all were so elaborate and lifelike that she half expected them to be moving. At Elise's nod, she picked up one of a small boy holding a bow. Looking closely, she could see the serene expression on his face and his meticulously detailed clothes.

"I cannot tell you how overwhelmed I was the first time I walked in here," Elise confided. "While I'm not nearly so talented, I find myself blessed to study with people like Master Vestor."

"Did I hear my name used in vain?"

They turned to find a tall, thin man in a tunic of turquoise blue standing behind them. Elise squeaked and hugged him. "You scared me!"

The older man laughed. "You were so focused on the carvings that I could've driven a herd of marshbeasts past you. It's so good to see you again, Your Highness." He gave Kelsey a smile. "Who is your friend?"

"Master Vestor, allow me to introduce our esteemed visitor Princess Kelsey Bandar of the Terran Empire. Kelsey, my patron Alec."

Alec Vestor bowed low. "You grace my humble shop, Your Highness." He straightened with a smile. "Allow me to say that I am moved by how you rescued those poor people from a fate far worse than death. Such kindness to strangers does you great credit, and I am honored to make your acquaintance. Welcome to Pentagar."

Kelsey felt herself blushing. "Thank you, Master Vestor, but we only did what anyone else would have done."

"I think you overestimate the risks many people would take for a stranger. So, what has this miscreant been saying about me? Rest assured that her base slanders are the result of the rigorous discipline I had to impose on her during her training."

Elise smacked him on the shoulder. "And there I was telling her how terrific you are. Now I'll tell her the truth. You can barely carve your name."

He laughed. "Some days I feel like that is the very truth indeed! My secret is out!"

"Kelsey, Master Vestor is the premiere woodcarver in the Kingdom. His works grace the halls of the very lucky few to whom he'll agree to sell. Not these wonderful knickknacks, but massive landscapes so amazing they take your breath away."

"I can hardly imagine anything more impressive than what I see here. I never knew people could do such wonderful things with wood. I feel guilty for liking a roaring fire now."

Master Vestor took her by the elbow. "There is no need for guilt. I love a good fire myself. It's not the wood that's special, although there are some fine cuts, but the love and passion that one puts into it. Many talented artists did these miniatures. Come and look at my latest work. I'm almost done with it and would love to hear what you think."

He led them to the back of the shop and into a large studio. The scent of wood was so strong that Kelsey almost sneezed. People stood beside tables covered in wood shavings, working on projects large and small. Most of the artisans didn't even glance up as the strangers walked among them.

The thin woodcarver led them into a separate room at the very back. Kelsey made it only a step inside before the sight of what lay before her stopped her in her tracks. She heard someone gasp and then realized it had been her.

Two large stands held an oval of wood three feet tall and five wide. He'd carved the most amazing forest landscape she'd ever imagined into the pale wood. Mountains loomed in the distance, but the vast forest in the forefront captured her attention.

She walked closer and leaned in. She could see leaves on the trees and birds flitting through the limbs. Small animals of some kind peeked out from behind trunks. It was more intricate than any painting she'd ever seen.

"Amazing, isn't it?" Elise asked. "He puts an incredible amount of time into these works and then virtually gives them away."

"I wouldn't go so far as that," he said dryly. "I make a fine living. Yet I do sometimes give some away. Like this one. It's a gift to cement a friendship."

Kelsey smiled. "It must be quite some friendship."

"I certainly hope so. You see, until today, I had no idea what I would do with it. The arrival of your people and their bravery convinced me it should be a gift from the people of Pentagar to those of the Terran Empire. May our friendship be deep and abiding."

Empire of Bones

Her jaw dropped. "I couldn't accept such a princely gift. I truly appreciate the thought, but it's too much."

Elise shook her head. "My father had the perfect advice when Master Vestor gave me something like this. If the giver believes you worthy of it, you should accept the gift and be grateful someone values you so highly. That is my advice to you as well."

Kelsey swallowed and bowed deeply to the master artist. "Then I accept your most gracious gift in the name of the people of the Terran Empire. I hope to return it home one day so that many can gaze upon it and marvel at your astonishing talent. Thank you."

One of the Royal guards stepped up to Elise and whispered something in her ear. She frowned and turned to face Kelsey. "I'm not quite sure how to broach the subject, but I just received word that your Lord Captain Mertz has used his space-time drive to venture into the Pale Ones' system."

Kelsey turned her head a little, certain she'd misheard the other woman. "He did what?"

"We should return to the palace so we may gather more information," the crown princess said.

Kelsey bit her tongue. Cursing Jared in front of her hosts wouldn't accomplish anything. She bowed again to Master Vestor. "I apologize for my hasty departure, but something has come up that I must attend to. Thank you again. Your work is magnificent."

"Come back anytime, Princess Kelsey. I should have the carving done in the next week. I'll have Elise contact you."

The two women walked back out onto the street. The intense rage Kelsey felt ate at her. Jared knew she was supposed to be with them! He'd ignored her father's orders.

Kelsey tamped her anger down. "May I borrow your ship again?"

"Going there isn't safe," Elise said. "What if there is an armed response to the incursion?"

"I need to be there waiting for them."

The other woman looked unconvinced but nodded. "Please be careful."

"I'll be back as soon as he returns. Which I'm sure will be soon. Until then, thank you for your gracious hospitality. Please convey my regrets to your father about missing dinner."

Kelsey left the bemused woman at the landing pad and climbed into one of the limos. Her marines followed her. The driver looked back at her curiously.

"We need to return to the ship that brought us here. Quickly."

"Right away. I'll have you there in ten minutes."

Kelsey settled back as the limo rose and filled Talbot in. He leaned over and spoke softly in her ear. "Not to tell you your business, Princess, but it might be wiser to remain here. Isn't taking care of diplomatic relations your function? You can't do that and be with the ship all the time."

"I'll wager that Captain Mertz sent a probe over before he went himself. I doubt he would've gone across if he thought there was any real danger."

"Then wait for him to come back so you can tear a strip off him."

"My decision has been made, Senior Sergeant."

He sighed. "Yes, Your Highness."

Their hasty return trip to the spaceport was so abrupt that they arrived before their crew. It took another ten minutes before they rushed onto the plascrete and opened the ship. Someone must've briefed them on the way, because they asked no questions. They brought the ship to life without any delays.

While the crew worked, she sat in the main compartment fuming. How could Jared do this? He'd likely claim he was protecting her. Then again, he'd lock her in a padded room if he thought he could get away with it. She had to put him back in his place. Hard.

"Princess Kelsey?"

She looked up at the pilot. She hadn't heard him approach. "I'm sorry. Yes?"

"We're ready to launch. Would you care to sit up front with me? My copilot isn't close enough to make it back before we launch."

"That would be very interesting. Thank you." It would keep her mind off strangling Jared for a while.

The controls in the ship's cockpit seemed significantly more complex than those on *Athena*'s bridge. It was a spaceship, too. Why were they so different?

Kelsey kept her hands in her lap as the man brought the ship to a hover and spoke into his headset. "Control, this is *Lance*. Requesting emergency departure."

She couldn't hear the response, but it must've been in the affirmative.

"Roger, control. *Lance* out." He put the ship into a steep climb. The blue sky faded quickly to black.

The pilot turned to face her. "We'll be at the interdiction zone in a little less than two hours. If you have any questions about the ship, I'd be happy to answer them."

"I do have one. Why do the controls on your ship seem so much more complicated than those on *Athena*?"

Empire of Bones

The corner of his mouth tugged up. "Not knowing what the controls on your ship look like, I couldn't guess."

She pulled out her communicator. "I took a vid because I wanted to save it for later."

He examined the image. "We're only beginning to start using touch screens like these. I'd imagine your controls are probably significantly more complex than they appear once you look at the submenus."

The pilot launched into a detailed explanation of the controls in front of her and answered her uneducated questions simply enough and with good cheer. That took her mind off her troubles for over an hour and a half.

His console beeped. He checked a monitor beside his leg. "We're less than thirty minutes out. We're starting to encounter some of the debris from the battle."

"Could there be survivors?"

"Possibly, but not very likely. Only a few chunks seem large enough to hold air. I'll scan those. It looks like there is a ship ahead looking through the wreckage. It just began accelerating."

He brought the visual onto the screen in front of them. A bright dot of light quickly expanded into a ship. The pilot cursed. "It's the Pale Ones! We need to get out of here. Go warn your marines while I call for help and evade."

She unbuckled and ran back to the central compartment. "A Pale Ones' ship is coming!"

Talbot said something not suitable for Imperial ears. "We aren't wearing our armor and only have handguns. Get the princess back into the engineering compartment and barricade yourselves in. Find some oxygen masks in case they breach our hull. Hopefully we can hold them off until help arrives."

Kelsey suppressed her terror and did as he ordered. She prayed that the pilot would evade the enemy ship.

The engineer grabbed a heavy wrench. "Shoot her before they take us. Me, too. Then yourselves. We don't want to become like they are. Trust me. Death is much better."

"I'm not killing the princess," the marine sneered.

"Then at least shoot me. Please."

The marine started to respond, but Kelsey would never know what he was going to say. Without warning, their world went black.

25

Jared had Zia begin transmitting the agreed-upon signal and transitioned back to Pentagar space. He expected to see the Royal ships still engaged in search and rescue. Instead, alarms began sounding before the disorientation faded.

Ramirez changed course with such lightning swiftness that it probably saved all their lives. A missile exploded beside them instead of directly impacting them. Jared's console lit up with lurid red warnings of battle damage.

"A Pale Ones' ship just fired on us and transitioned," Zia said. "Royal forces were in pursuit. No other missiles detected."

Ramirez turned from his console. "We took the hit in engineering. Flip and grav drives offline. Damage control reports casualties."

"Incoming signal from Commodore Sanders, Captain," Zia said. "On screen."

"Where the hell did that damned ship come from?" Jared asked.

The older officer grimaced. "It must've been damaged. It couldn't have repaired itself at a worse time. It ambushed Princess Kelsey and her people just before they got here. We tried to disable it, but we don't really have weapons suitable to cripple."

Jared's blood ran cold. "Where is she?"

"I'm sorry. They were captured."

"I'm going after them. *Athena* out." He opened a channel to engineering. "Dennis, we need to transition now."

Baxter shook his head. The scene behind him was organized chaos.

"Drives are down. It will be hours before we can flip again."

"Unacceptable. The Pale Ones have Princess Kelsey. I want this ship moving faster than that."

"Captain, the drives are physically damaged. We're working as fast as we possibly can. We won't waste one precious second. Engineering out." Baxter cut the connection.

Jared felt like banging his head on the console. What had possessed her to come to the interdiction zone? He took a deep breath. "Zia, send a probe after that damned ship. I want to know exactly where it goes, because we're going after it as soon as we can."

"Aye, sir. Launching another probe to follow and send back everything it can."

"Get me Commodore Sanders back as soon as you're done with that."

A minute later, Sanders reappeared on the screen. Jared tried not to shout at the man. The blame for this could go right to the one responsible for her: Jared Mertz.

"Commodore, our drives are damaged. My engineer tells me it will be hours before we can follow that ship."

"I'm so sorry, Lord Captain. The damned thing jumped them just short of the interdiction zone. We tried to fire a near miss, but they made it through."

"I should've kept her closer at hand. I'll get her back or die trying."

He proceeded to tell the commodore what he'd found out in the other system. The old man looked grim by the time Jared was done. "We won't be ready to repulse the next invasion, and we can't take the fight to them in time."

"We might be able to do something to delay them. I'll have to consider the options."

"Can we help in any way?"

"Yes. We only carry thirty marines, but our pinnaces can hold seventy in armor. We have two. If you could scrounge up a hundred volunteers, I could use more combat-trained ground fighters."

"I have that many on my ship. Major Edwards will gather them and their gear. Can my engineering teams help get you ready more quickly?"

Jared shook his head. "I'm afraid not. We'll send the pinnaces to collect your people. Thank you for your help in this."

"You put yourselves in harm's way for my people. How could we do any less? Besides, it's possible we can strike against this invasion fleet before it is ready to depart the shipyard. I'll communicate with Pentagar and see if they can come up with any options."

"Thank you. *Athena* out."

Empire of Bones

He stood. "Zia, get the pinnaces over to *Mace*. Coordinate with the commodore on any plan he devises. If we can strike against those ships, I want to do it while they are under construction. I'm going to see Doctor Stone."

The lift took him to the medical center while he stewed in a dark silence. Doctor Stone was setting a broken arm on a crewwoman who looked more than a little singed around the edges of her engineering jumpsuit. "How bad is it?"

The doctor turned to him, her face a mask of sorrow. "Twelve dead and a lot of walking wounded, Captain."

The news made his stomach churn. The Pale Ones would pay for this. "As soon as you're done, with that we need to talk."

"Vargas, take over for me."

Stone handed over the work to one of the med techs and led Jared to her office. She closed the hatch behind them. "What's wrong?"

"The Pale Ones' ship that shot us took Princess Kelsey. She's in their hands."

The doctor swore. "Can we get her back?"

"Not right away. Baxter needs several hours to get the drives online. That means she might be implanted or at least in the middle of the process by the time we can get on her trail. If they do something to her, can you undo it?"

The chief medical officer shook her head decisively. "Not a chance. I can't even imagine how they implant those things into a human brain. I sure as hell won't be able to remove one without killing her."

Jared looked out the clear wall at the people working on the injured. "We have to do something. I can't let her become one of them. That's a horror I can't begin to imagine. What about overriding the programming on the implants?"

"You'll need to speak with the science team. Doctor Leonard was working on getting power to the implants of the dead Imperial Marine we have on board. I haven't heard anything about their progress. I know they pulled a lot of data off the dead Pale One. He might be able to do something."

"Where did he set up shop?"

"Down in one of the cargo compartments that we converted to a lab. Jared, I'll do absolutely everything I can to help her."

He put his hand on Stone's shoulder. "I know. We'll get her back. You'll need to be ready to go with the rescue team after we flip. Be prepared to restrain her in an augmented state. Take anything you might need. Grab as many people as you need to make it happen."

"We'll be ready."

The cargo areas they'd converted were down in the bowels of the ship near engineering. Jared imagined the scientists had received quite a shakeup. When he walked through the hatch, he saw that he'd been right. They were busily putting equipment back up and recovering various bits of electronics.

Doctor Jerry Leonard saw Jared come in and walked over to meet him. "That was quite the unexpected shock, Captain. It's a good thing we were all strapped in for the flip. Can we assist with damage control?"

Jared shook his head. "You have more important work to do, Doctor. The Pale Ones captured Princess Kelsey. We're going after her as soon as we get the drives back online, but they might implant her. I need to know you can do something about that."

The rail-thin scientist blanched. "Dear God. Of course. We'll do what we can, but the implants are in the brain. We just don't have the technical ability to remove them without turning her into a vegetable or killing her."

"Then tell me you can do something about the programming that controls them. The captain of *Courageous* killed his entire crew to keep some kind of override in the programming from turning them into monsters. Tell me you have the code from the Fleet officers and can reverse what they did."

"The implants are physically the same. Right down to the model numbers. With Doctor Stone's assistance, we were able to access the programming code in the Pale One's corpse. The units are internally powered and not readily accessible to recharge, so they must last far longer than a person's life span. We've disassembled the implants from the marine we brought with us but hadn't gotten to attempting to swap the power supplies."

Jared gave the scientist a steady look. "Then you'd best get busy. We don't have much time for you to find a solution."

The man nodded. "It shouldn't take more than a few minutes to put them back together. We were worried they might be damaged if we attempted to power them on, but we don't have a choice now."

The scientist strode to a worktable. He opened several clear plastic bins. "I hope it doesn't matter that we removed them from the bodies. If it tries to access the brains of the dead Fleet personnel and errors out, there's nothing we can do."

He laid out the odd strands of hair-thin wires and circular units the size of small coins on the table. He put on magnifying goggles and picked up some delicate tools to work on one of the units. "We developed these tools when we saw how the other units had to be disassembled. The method is quite ingenious."

Empire of Bones

Jared couldn't really see anything, but he could determine the man's progress when he removed a thin shell from each of the three units of the implant. The small object he removed from each with a set of tweezers was about the size of the tip on a writing stylus. If that was a power supply, it was incredible. Just like most things the Old Empire had built.

Leonard took the tiny power units from another implant and put them in the first set of implants. Once he had the covers on the units, he grabbed a headset. It had a cable going to a standalone computer. As soon as he taped the last of the three into the headset, the screen started filling with long lines of what looked like gibberish.

"It's attempting to boot," Leonard said. "We don't really need to attach them to the headset. They have effective short-range communication, good for perhaps ten meters, but the transmission speed and data throughput are significantly quicker with the headsets in place. Probably why they wore them. It's online! We wrote a program to access the code, and this looks like it's working."

"Can you tell what the differences are? Perhaps we can find where the alterations were made and correct them."

The scientist nodded. "Possibly. It will take a few minutes to collect all the code. If they are similar, we should be able to compare them. We still don't understand the programming language, though. If the changes to the programming are widespread, I wouldn't want to go mucking around with it in a living being. I can only imagine what that could do to them."

"Can you make changes?"

"That remains to be seen. One would imagine there is a mechanism for updates. It probably isn't something that could happen by accident or perhaps even easily. If I were designing something like this, the access codes to make changes would be hardware specific. Only authorized units could write to these. That authentication would need to be very complex. That said, it might not be impossible to read it directly off the hardware itself."

"Would recovering installation hardware be helpful?"

The man nodded enthusiastically. "Absolutely! It would be optimal if you could recover reference material, the actual programming, or installation machinery. We should be able to access it and replace whatever malicious code we find. One of my graduate students is my coding expert, and he's the one examining the Pale Ones' programming."

"You brought a graduate student? I thought everyone on that ship was a doctor."

"Carl Owlet is a true genius with computers. I'm surprised that Doctor Cartwright didn't assign him to *Courageous*. He might once they are ready to bring the main computer back online."

The computer beeped, and Leonard examined the screen. "There are some rather significant areas where the code is different. I think we need to let Carl take a look." He brought out his communicator and summoned the other man.

Make that boy. If Carl Owlet were old enough to shave regularly, Jared would eat his beret. The graduate student looked about sixteen standard years old.

Owlet listened intently as Doctor Leonard filled him in on recent developments and then sat at the computer. He typed on the remote keypad so quickly that Jared could barely see his fingers. He typed more quickly than most people spoke.

The screen split into two displays and began scrolling through the code. The computer had highlighted many areas. "This is definitely the same base code as in the Pale Ones, Captain. I can see what looks like version markers buried in the comments. The repetitive pattern of the matches tells me that someone compromised the original code. There also seems to be some extra code in this marine implant."

"Can you tell what the extra code does?"

The boy shook his head. "No, sir. I'll keep working on it."

"Are there too many changes to correct the original code?"

The boy nodded. "Manually correcting the code requires understanding how it interacts with the hardware, and I'm not there yet. I doubt many Old Empire people really knew this in any detail. It would take teams of dedicated programmers working for many years to develop code of this complexity. I know that I wouldn't want to trust my brain to something that hadn't gone through rigorous testing."

"But you think they did update the code in implanted hardware?"

"I've been examining the hardware for the last few days and found a method to make the memory writable. None of the equipment we have could do it, but something must exist. System updates after installation. Security patches, though obviously that didn't work out so well."

Jared considered that. "The old Fleet personnel were captured and their implants were reprogrammed. That makes it possible. Hopefully we can find the equipment in question. I hope we find Kelsey before anything happens, but we can't count on that.

"Doctor, Mister Owlet, I want you both to be ready to assist Doctor Stone when we recover the princess. Start thinking about how we update the programming, because we may have to try."

26

Reality slowly intruded on Kelsey's oblivion. The first thing she recognized was cold metal pressed against her cheek. Painfully cold. It actually felt good compared to the throbbing in her head. She'd had bad headaches before, but this one threatened to crush her brain. Every pulse of her heart sent fresh agony through her skull.

She started to move but stopped when she heard grunting. That didn't sound like one of the marines. She doubted the Royal Fleet officers communicated that way, either. That only left the Pale Ones.

That meant she was in very, very deep trouble.

Kelsey cracked an eyelid and tried not to moan when a shaft of intense brightness burned her retina. Okay, the light only seemed bright because of her headache, but the pain made her eyes water.

Clarity came after a minute of focusing. A man's arm lay in front of her face. The color of the uniform told her it was one of her marines, and he wasn't moving.

Definitely not good.

She looked over him and saw two men facing one another. Pale Ones, presumably. Both wore what amounted to filthy loincloths. Why they weren't just naked she had no idea. Hideous scars covered their bodies. Red, puckered lines trailed down each of their limbs. Even their fingers had horrible scarring.

Both had long, matted hair that hung below their waists. If either of them saw a comb, she'd be willing to bet he tried to eat it. They were as filthy as their clothes. She could smell their stench from across the room.

They faced one another and communicated by snarls and grunts. At least she assumed they were communicating. Or they might be posturing for dominance. Maybe both.

The marine's arm moved, and he groaned. He rolled over and sat up. That got the attention of the Pale Ones. They both snarled in his direction.

The marine, Corporal Brand, climbed unsteadily to his feet. He reached for his weapon, but his holster was empty. He swore and staggered toward the Pale Ones, obviously intending to take them hand to hand.

That worked out surprisingly poorly for him. The nearly naked men fell into what looked like martial arts stances. One grabbed the marine's fist as he swung it and twisted him around, while the other kicked low and swept the marine off his feet. The one holding Brand's fist kicked him hard in the gut.

The corporal tried to fight, but they simply tossed him back onto the deck beside Kelsey, where he lay moaning.

"Brand? Are you okay?" She sat up but didn't climb to her feet. The two Pale Ones watched her, growling, but didn't attack.

The corporal clutched his stomach. "That guy kicks like an avalanche. They barely look like they can stand. How can they fight like that?"

"Was that some kind of martial art?"

"It sure looked like it, but that makes no sense."

They waited, and the rest of the marines slowly regained consciousness. The Pale Ones had taken their weapons, both pistols and knives. She had no idea how a savage knew what a gun was.

The two Royal Fleet officers sat against the wall, terror clearly etched on their faces. Talbot eyed the Pale Ones for a minute. "We can take them together."

Kelsey had been examining the room. It was obviously a ship's compartment, but there were no furnishings. It was easily as big as the briefing room on *Athena*. They could pile dozens of people in here without too much crowding. The only exit was a single hatch behind the two savages.

One of the Pale Ones howled and beat his chest. That was definitely a challenge.

The hatch opened, and a short woman stepped inside. She was also a Pale One based on her personal hygiene. She wore a loincloth similar to the males'. She wore no top, and it was evident she never had. She looked a decade older than the two males.

The woman shoved the man who'd howled, sending him staggering to the side. He postured at her but didn't counterattack.

The marines rose as a unit and charged the three Pale Ones. Sergeant Talbot actually laid a solid hit on the woman's head.

It barely fazed her. She grinned and caught his second punch in her hand, stopping him dead in his tracks. Kelsey couldn't see what she did, but it was fast. Talbot went flying over the woman's shoulder and into the bulkhead. The bone-jarring impact made her wince.

The rest of the scene looked like a badly done fight vid. In less than twenty seconds, all the marines were on the deck, which only made them easier to kick.

She thought the Pale Ones would kill them and leapt to her feet, screaming, "Leave them alone!"

That stopped the fight, but only so the woman could come over and backhand her. It felt as if someone had hit her with a sledgehammer. Kelsey flew off her feet and skidded on the deck. She didn't try to get up and instead lay there. Moaning was all she could manage.

The woman snarled at her but didn't strike Kelsey again. She stalked back over to the men and tossed the marines back beside Kelsey. All of them were conscious, but Talbot looked like he might have a concussion.

"Well, that could've gone better," he mumbled. "Don't tell anyone that a mostly naked woman kicked my ass."

Kelsey suspected she wasn't going to have the opportunity to tell anyone anything, though she was praying for it. "How can they do that?"

The man shrugged. "It can't be training. It has to be in the implants. It would make sense to have basic combat skills programmed in. I can see the pattern in their fighting. If I had a weapon, I might be able to take one."

"But we don't. How are we going to escape?"

"I don't know. Maybe we're still in Pentagaran space and we'll be rescued."

She looked at her chrono. "I don't think so. We were out almost four hours. Whatever that weapon was, it really took us down. At least my headache is getting better."

They waited a few more minutes and then attacked again. The results were just as one-sided as before. The Pale Ones seemed incredibly tough. Kelsey noted how their reactions seemed so much faster than the marines'.

The pattern of their fighting was plain once she knew to look for it. They only had a few basic moves and seemed to use them by rote. In this case, that was all they needed to do. The woman could've been absent and the two men would've still beaten them all senseless.

Kelsey rose to her feet as soon as the marines engaged the next time and sprinted around the fight toward the hatch. She ducked on general principle, and the punch that one of them threw at her barely brushed the top of her skull.

She ran through the open hatch and found herself in a control room. Two Pale Ones sat at the controls, and their hands moved with robotic smoothness. They didn't react to her presence at all. She fleetingly wondered why they didn't use the Old Empire headsets.

The screen beyond them showed a large space station at extremely close range. A wide hatch opened in front of the ship. Going through it was probably going to be even worse for them. She searched around frantically and saw the marines' pistols tossed onto the deck. She grabbed one, spun, and shot the female Pale One as she leapt through the hatch.

Kelsey shot the woman twice more before she landed on her like a runaway grav car. She tore the weapon from Kelsey's hand with no effort at all. The she-beast nearly beat her unconscious before one of the men dragged Kelsey back into the room by her hair and tossed her on top of the marines.

She watched through the hatch as the woman she'd shot stood and moved around as though she hadn't been shot. At least for a minute. She didn't even try to staunch the flow of blood from her wounds.

Then she staggered a little and fell to her knees. The men watched her eyes glaze over and didn't seem bothered as she collapsed. One of them even kicked her while she bled to death.

Kelsey knew she should feel something. She'd just killed someone. All she felt was physical pain, despair, and anger. They were going to become monsters like those.

The ship bounced like it had hit something. Then the engine noise faded. They were inside the station. The whoosh of a hatch opening filled her with dread.

Half a dozen male and female Pale Ones swarmed in and grabbed them. Talbot tried to struggle, but they kicked him until he stopped. They were clearly satisfied to drag him out of the ship by his legs.

He looked back at her as they took him down an exit ramp. "Good job, Princess. At least you got one. See you on the other side."

The hulking mob dragged them into the bay she'd seen opening. It looked big enough to hold dozens of ships. Instead, it held three that she could see: theirs and two shot-up wrecks. They looked like they'd been sitting there for years.

Empire of Bones

The Pale Ones took them to a lift attached to the landing bay. A large hatch sat next to it. Dust and debris covered the lift floor. Everything stank. The Royal officers whimpered, three of the marines appeared unconscious, and Talbot seemed to be praying.

Not a bad idea.

She whispered one for them all. Not for their lives but that they would die quickly. Whatever came after death would be better than this.

The lift creaked up several decks, and the doors wheezed open. The creatures then pulled them quite a distance and made their way down a number of side corridors. She saw a skeleton in the dust. It wore the scraps of some kind of uniform. The color led her to believe it was a Royal Fleet tunic. The filthy marks on the floor showed where they'd dragged others. Many others.

Kelsey wondered how many of them had seen the dead Royal and wished they could die, too. Perhaps she should've used that pistol on herself.

The corridor continued into the distance, but the tracks through the muck made it obvious that all the prisoners went into one room. Her captor took them into what looked like a medical center. A bed on rollers sat just short of a machine shaped to fit all around it.

The Pale Ones tossed all of the prisoners into what had probably once been an office. The marines talked about rushing their captors, but it would be suicidal. There were just too many of them. So they watched as another Pale One deposited their equipment into a large bin.

Kelsey expected the foul creatures to do something quickly, but the Pale Ones seemed content to watch them for the next four hours. Only when a new Pale One entered the compartment did most of the rest leave. The new one looked like the pilots on the ship. An automaton. He stood beside one of the machines and waited.

Two of the Pale Ones came into the room. One tossed the marines aside while the other grabbed her. He dragged her out and threw her on the bed. Two others held her down while he strapped her in. They cinched the straps brutally tight.

She wanted to scream, but she bit her lip. She didn't know why. Maybe she wanted to meet her end with all the courage she could muster. That was one thing they could never take from her.

The Pale Ones pushed the bed into the machine. Darkness shrouded her, and then a low light came on.

"Do not be alarmed," a soft male voice said with an accent she couldn't place. "This scanning process will not hurt."

She swallowed. "Who are you? What are you doing?"

"This unit is Diagnostic Scanning Workstation Twelve. This unit will scan your brain prior to the implanting process and make the final adjustment to the implant hardware before it is installed."

"You're a Terran Empire machine? You know that the Fleet is long dead and that you're making these devices to implant in people against their will, don't you? I do not consent to this process. Stop this at once!"

The voice took on a tinge of regret. "This unit is unable to comply. Its programming has been modified to remove the consent protocol. This unit regrets the inconvenience."

She laughed in spite of the horror. It regretted the inconvenience. "Who updated your programming?"

"That data is not in this unit's memory. Please remain still for the scanning process."

Little flashes of heat zipped up and down her nerves. It felt like something was crawling in her brain. The sensation lasted a few seconds and then ceased.

"Scan complete. Data sent to the surgical unit. Thank you for your patience."

A tone sounded, and the Pale Ones roughly pulled the bed from the scanning machine. Two Pale Ones unstrapped her while two more held Talbot.

The Pale Ones ripped her clothes from her body and pulled her to a second machine. It looked more like a portable water tank with attached machinery. They threw her in and slammed the lid shut. Her heart raced as she lay there. What happened now?

Unseen clamps snapped around her limbs, and blinding pain ate at her head. She screamed, but it only got worse as the machine cut her open.

27

Baxter eventually got tired of Jared looking over his shoulder at about the three-hour mark and tossed him out of engineering. He told Jared that having the captain breathing down their necks was slowing his people down.

Jared took the hint and left to meet with the Pentagaran marine detachment leader in the conference room instead. He turned out to be a familiar face. Lieutenant John Fredrick.

Lieutenant Reese and he seemed to be getting along well. With his four missing men, that meant *Athena*'s detachment was down to twenty-six effectives, plus their commander. Commander Graves and Doctor Stone joined them a few minutes later. Jared gestured for them to sit at the table.

He brought the screen to life. "The drives will be ready shortly. Is everyone ready to depart at a moment's notice?"

They all nodded.

The young Royal officer put his hand on the table. "I've finished getting our men settled. We have a hundred Royal Marines fully outfitted in combat gear. Lieutenant Reese has seen that our communications gear will interface with yours. We also salvaged two tactical fission missiles from one of the wrecked fortresses. I have four technicians who will rig them to explode. One is sufficient to destroy that station from the inside. We need to use the other to deal with the shipyard. We may not get another chance.

"The other shipyard will be inaccessible from our orbit. Particularly once we stir up the hornet's nest. We'll have to deal with it another time."

Jared nodded. "Excellent. Our missiles simply don't have that kind of power. We're not a capital ship. We'll hit the shipyard at the same time we assault the orbital station. Reese, what's your plan for inserting our forces?"

The Imperial Marine tapped his console. The screen changed to a tactical display of the station's orbital space. "The pinnaces have stealth systems and are coated with material that absorbs some scanner radiation. We'll go in on a ballistic trajectory. If we set our initial course to miss the planet, they might dismiss us as space junk. I don't know what kind of scanners they have, but I'm hopeful that they won't recognize the danger until we begin our attack runs. By then it will be too late to stop us."

Graves considered the marked courses on the tactical display. "We need a distraction for the initial penetration. Rather than splitting our forces to attack both targets, we should rig one of the weapons to an external weapons rack and launch it on a ballistic course for the busy shipyard. The device should be small enough to get close before they react. A fission reaction at close range might not destroy it, but it should cause significant damage. The commotion should make a fabulous distraction for *Athena* to make its run in to retrieve the princess."

Jared liked that plan, but it had its drawbacks. "That will severely restrict how much time we have to find Princess Kelsey and our missing men."

Graves shrugged. "Once the attack starts, they won't have much time anyway. The probe we have on the station logged the hatch they used."

Jared grimaced. "Doctor Stone, what is your plan once we find her?"

The petite doctor grimaced. "It isn't very elaborate. We grab her and whatever equipment that's around her. I've engineered some restraints that will probably hold her. I only hope to God she isn't in the middle of some procedure, or we might as well shoot her ourselves. I have some volunteer medical techs and a team from engineering to take what we can. The pinnaces have the capability to load equipment, though it might mean everyone is piled like logs on the way out."

"Doctor Stone is right," Graves said. "This is a smash and grab. We hit them and grab anyone we can manage. Then we run like hell."

Jared looked at Reese. "That means you'll need atmosphere after we breach the station. How will you manage that?"

"The data from the probe indicates they entered a large bay. We have special charges to breach the hatch. The second pinnace will seal it as soon as we're all in. We'll use marine boarding locks inside to breach

Empire of Bones

the corridors without venting the atmosphere. When we're ready to leave, we have compressed air in special tanks on the pinnace that's not carrying the fission weapon to fill the bay. We can get enough pressure to allow us to get the rescued personnel back through the bay. Then we blow the patch and get the hell out of there."

"What kind of timetable are you looking at?"

"That depends on the situation inside. If there's a lot of resistance, we take longer. I'm hopeful they won't see us coming. These Pale Ones don't seem too big on tactics, so I'd imagine there'll be a lot of running and screaming while they try to kill us individually. Massed weapons fire should allow us to make good progress. I want to be out of there in half an hour if we can."

Graves tapped his console. "That's where *Athena* comes in. When we get the signal that the teams are withdrawing, we come in like a meteor. We'll clear a path for the pinnace to withdraw and take them aboard as quickly as possible. Then we run like hell for the flip point. Based on their speed, it'll be close. We're faster, but they'll have a chance to close in as we pick our people up."

"That's where the Royal Fleet comes in," Fredrick said. "We are moving all available ships to the interdiction zone. We will destroy any ships that come through behind you. With luck, we will blunt the planned invasion forces enough to stop them now."

Jared shook his head ruefully. "Admiral Yeats would have my behind for breakfast if he saw how fast and loose this operation is coming together. If something goes wrong, we're totally screwed. Lieutenant Fredrick, I've sent word via probe to the scientists on *Best Deal*. They'll make certain that you have everything needed to construct flip drives if we don't make it back. I did that because if it looks like we can't escape, we're taking out both of those shipyards.

"We don't really have a choice. If that invasion comes through, we all die. We'll do whatever we must to save this system and the billions of people who call it home now. Whether the rescue attempt succeeds or fails, we stop these bastards today. Questions?"

The men shook their heads.

"To your stations. Charlie, a moment please."

Jared waited for the others to leave before he spoke. "You'll be in command of *Athena* during this fight. I'm going with the marines."

Graves looked mulish. "Sir, you're a Fleet officer. You belong on the bridge of your ship."

"Charlie, let's be honest. The odds of any of us making it home are so slim that no one would ever bet on us. My oath to the emperor means

I bring Princess Kelsey back or die trying. I can't leave her there. She's my sister, for God's sake."

His executive officer didn't look happy, but he nodded. "Best of luck, Jared. Bring her back to us."

Jared let his friend leave and pinched the bridge of his nose between his fingers. It tore at him to abandon his command at a time like this, but it felt like the right move. He took one last calming breath and headed for marine country.

Reese spotted him as soon as he arrived and came over. "Captain."

"I'm going with you. I'll need some armor and weapons. You'll retain tactical command, but I have overall strategic authority."

The marine didn't argue. "We keep several sets of spare armor for emergencies." He called over two other marines, and they efficiently stripped him to his undergarments and strapped him into the armor. It would act as a vacuum suit with superior protection against projectiles. The communicator was more complex than what he normally used, but he quickly figured it out.

The weapons they strapped onto him were a different issue. He knew how to shoot pistols. That was required Fleet training, even if they seldom used it. They took him to the range to run through a few magazines of ammunition with the combat rifle, presumably so that he didn't accidentally shoot one of them.

They loaded him down with ammunition and grenades and then told him he was not to use any of the latter. Apparently, he was carrying extras for the rest of them.

The call to flip came just after they finished getting him ready. It felt odd to hear Charlie's voice in the overheads announcing the transition. It was probably the last one he'd make.

He boarded *Marine One* once everyone was ready and sat beside Reese. His communicator had access to the command channels, so he listened to the countdown. The disorientation came and went. Then they waited for the engineering crew to mount the fission warhead to their pinnace.

Athena accelerated into the system but kept her speed below the detection threshold. They'd go into free-fall once they got too close to chance detection. The pinnaces would detach at that point and increase their velocity even more. Due to their smaller-sized drives, they could build more speed than a full-sized ship. Even so, it would be hours before they reached the planet. So many bad things could happen in that time.

"*Marine One* and *Marine Two*, this is *Athena*," Zia said on the command channel. "Going ballistic. You are free to disengage. Godspeed."

Empire of Bones

183

The pinnace broke free with a clank, and intense acceleration pressed Jared back into the padding. They boosted for half an hour and then shut down their drives.

The waiting was much harder than he'd expected. The marines shared rations and traded jokes and insults. The Royal Marines seemed to fit right in. If things worked out, he expected the Kingdom and the Empire would become excellent allies.

He expected the station to launch ships and weapons when they got close, but it didn't. When the mission timer fell to just a few minutes, he had to bite his lip to keep from giving the go order.

When the counter dropped to zero, Jared keyed his communicator. "All units go. Go! Go! Go!"

The pinnace accelerated savagely. Much more power than had been used earlier. So much that it took his breath away. His pinnace turned toward the active shipyard, which was still on the other side of the planetary curve. *Marine Two* dove for the orbital.

The dot representing the fission warhead broke free, and his pinnace turned abruptly to chase after *Marine Two*.

Jared split his attention between the warhead and *Marine Two*. The shipyard would meet the weapon about the same time the other pinnace breached the orbital. If the Pale Ones' station had any defenses, they'd acted before the weapons could come online.

Marine Two fired something that looked like a big net. It spread all across the hatch and exploded inward. Shaped charges. The hatch disintegrated, and *Marine Two* screamed inside as the air and debris came shooting out.

His pinnace followed just a few seconds later. It clamped to the deck and waited for the compartment to depressurize fully. Then both pinnaces started disgorging marines.

Jared waited for a moment and saw the fission warhead expand on his tactical display. The data said it had detected a missile launch and detonated. While too far away to destroy the shipyard completely, it would undoubtedly cause tremendous damage. They'd met one mission objective. There would be no massive invasion before Pentagar was ready.

He followed Reese out the hatch. The marine officer snapped out orders. "Find a main hatch into the station. Avoid lifts. Shoot anything that moves. Except the prisoners, of course."

"Team Five has a lift and what looks like a corridor hatch beside it. There are signs that something was dragged through here recently."

"Set the boarding lock and go in, Team Five."

The marines pointed their weapons in every direction while they waited. The medical and engineering teams joined him. They weren't wearing armored suits, but they were armed. Even the doctor. Stone knelt beside him. "The clock is ticking. Will we have pressure?"

"They'll patch the ruined hatch once we're gone but leave enough space so the chamber can't be pressurized. That should keep the enemy from rushing them. The pinnaces' guns will deal with any intrusions. Once we're on the way back, they'll pressurize the landing bay. Hopefully, we'll be gone before the Pale Ones get inside here in force."

He didn't hear the breaching charges the marines used to open the hatch, but he felt the deck shake a little. The first team of marines entered the boarding lock and reported the other side clear. The marine strike teams cycled through quickly. They found the emergency stairs before Jared came through with the support teams.

"Team Five has Princess Kelsey's communicator on scanner," one of the marines said. "She's somewhere ahead of and above us."

"Up," Reese ordered.

Some of the marines poured into the stairwell while the rest set up a defensive perimeter. They'd hold the landing bay while the strike teams found the prisoners.

He followed Reese and tried Kelsey's communicator just as someone started shooting upstairs. An unknown voice came on the tactical net. "Enemy contact. Engaging."

The fight was on.

28

Kelsey awoke to indescribable agony. It felt as though they'd filleted her like a fish. Lines of horrible pain seemed to cover her entire body. Her headache from earlier was a fond memory.

The tank slid open, and the Pale Ones pulled her out. They dragged her toward the third piece of equipment in the room. Unlike the previous two, it looked like someone had assembled it from other equipment with no thought about how it looked.

Her eyes wouldn't focus right. Things went from blurry to unnaturally sharp, but not simultaneously in each eye. She tried to resist the Pale Ones holding her, but her arms wouldn't move right either. She had no coordination at all.

Her captors stiffened when a distant thump shook the deck.

They dropped her and ran for the door. The fall bloodied her nose, and she flopped around as she tried to sit up. The prisoners took advantage of the distraction to attack. It took all of them to pin one of the Pale Ones.

Talbot struggled with the other one. The beast grunted and dragged the marine to the tank that had just gutted Kelsey. Having only one captor gave the marine some advantage though. He planted his feet against the tank and shoved.

The tank moved away from them, knocking over some kind of bin behind it. The Pale One staggered backward and tripped over Kelsey. She forced her hand to reach out and grabbed the bastard's throat.

Something crunched under her hand, and the thing turned his attention to her.

He smashed his fist across her face. It hurt, but not nearly as much as what they'd already done to her. In fact, an intense wave of something passed through her. It took her a moment to realize the pain had faded to almost nothing. The world seemed to slow a little, and sound echoed in her head oddly. She wondered if she was about to pass out.

Surprisingly, the Pale One failed to tear free of her grip. Her hand seemed to have locked in the closed position like a vise. He struggled to breathe but finally collapsed on top of her.

Talbot staggered to his feet and came to her side. A cut over his eye bled freely, and he looked almost dazed. "We need to be gone before they come back. Can you walk?"

"I can't even make my fingers open." In fact, they'd dug deeply into the Pale One's throat. His blood ran down her arm. The iron tang of it in the air made her nauseous.

Talbot tried to pry her fingers open and failed. "Damn. That's some grip. Let me find something."

He staggered to his feet and ran to the bin with their equipment. He grabbed a pistol and shot the pinned Pale One in the head. Three times.

One of the marines took the pistol and ducked his head out the hatch. "Clear. I think I hear weapons fire. Could it be a rescue?"

Talbot dug into the bin and found a knife. The rest of the men began arming themselves as he began cutting Kelsey free. It only took a few grisly seconds for him to open the thing's neck. With all the slick blood, he managed to tear her free. This day was just going to be full of horrible memories. If they lived.

The chime of an incoming communication request sounded from the bin. Talbot sprinted back and found the communicator. "Talbot here."

"Thank God," she heard Jared say. "We're on our way up. What is your status?"

The marine looked at her. "The princess is alive, but they've implanted her. She doesn't seem to be under their control. Should we come to you?"

"We're meeting resistance, but expect us in a few minutes. If you feel secure, stay there. Doctor Stone said she needed whatever equipment they used. Can any of it be taken down stairs?"

"There are three units. Two look like they're possibly Old Empire machines. One isn't. They all look semiportable. I think enough people can carry them. At least they'll fit through the hatches I've seen."

"Hold your position. Mertz out."

Empire of Bones

Two marines kept watch while Talbot knelt by her side. She smiled up at him. "Next time I suggest something idiotic, you have my permission to lock me up."

"I'll hold you to that."

One of the marines raised his pistol and fired. "Incoming hostiles."

The marines took turns shooting at the trickle of Pale Ones coming their way. It didn't seem like an attack. Not an organized one anyway. Maybe these were headed for the other, progressively louder fight.

Gunfire and explosions came closer until the marines pulled back from the door. Talbot moved her toward the back of the compartment. "Cavalry's here."

Automatic weapons fire sent a storm of bullets down the hall, and she saw men in body armor moving past while firing. It seemed like dozens of them. More than the total marine complement on *Athena.*

Jared and Doctor Stone ducked into the room with some noncombatants. Stone rushed to Kelsey's side as Jared started directing the removal of the equipment.

"Hey, Princess," Stone said. "How are you feeling?"

"Like someone cut me open."

The diminutive physician took out a portable scanner and ran it up her body. "Without looking closely, it seems like they installed a set of marine enhancements. Are you in control, or is someone else?"

"Me, I think. They didn't get me in the third machine."

"Then it probably overrides the default programming. You might just be the luckiest person I know. The brains weren't looking forward to trying to change your programming."

Jared turned to them. "The Pale Ones are massing so we're leaving. Take her to the pinnaces while we bring the equipment. Kelsey, it's good to see you again."

"Thank you for coming for us." She'd never meant anything so strongly.

"Thank me once we make it out of here. Everyone move."

Talbot threw her over his shoulder and quickly took off down the corridor. Undignified but necessary. All Kelsey could see was Doctor Stone running behind them, but she could hear others cursing as they moved the bulky equipment.

The trip back to the landing bay was a confusing blur. Her head bounced all over the place, and her eyes kept losing focus. They passed another marine force shooting at Pale Ones down another corridor. This marine unit wasn't shy about using grenades to keep them back, either. Her head rang as the fireballs exploded, and then the noise grew curiously soft.

They ran through an open lock and into the same landing bay where the Pale Ones had arrived. The two marine pinnaces had never looked so welcoming. A group of men off to the side was working on an unfamiliar piece of equipment.

The medical team rushed Talbot into one of the pinnaces and directed him to strap her to a mobile med unit. He laid her down but didn't strap her in. "No straps. Never again."

"God no," she agreed.

"Trust me," Stone said. "You'll want to be strapped down for takeoff." She threw a sheet over Kelsey's body and ran two straps across her torso but left the princess's hands free.

The grunting men carried the equipment in one piece at a time and strapped it down. Part of her mind noted they hadn't brought the bin Talbot had knocked over.

Then the marines started pouring in. Jared threw himself into the seat beside Stone. "Button us up and prepare for emergency takeoff. They seem to have figured out we're in the bay."

Reese's voice came out of Stone's helmet, which she'd set in her seat while she worked. "The breaching lock is closed and *Marine Two* is loading. We blow the emergency seal in thirty seconds. *Marine One* exits first. We've locked the fission weapon to the deck and set it for remote detonation and timer. It goes off in sixty seconds whether we're gone or not."

Jared handed Stone her helmet. "That's us in the lead. Get her an oxygen mask in case we lose pressure and strap down."

Stone slid a translucent mask over Kelsey's nose and mouth. The doctor then stuffed her helmet on and strapped down. The pinnace lifted and accelerated so quickly that Kelsey was sure the bed would flip over.

The captain grabbed it just to make sure. "Good work, people," he said through an external speaker. Or more likely, he'd turned the speaker on so those without communications could hear. "Phase one of the operation is complete. Let's blow these bastards to hell and go home."

Time dragged for an eternity. "The orbital is targeting us. Weapon detonation in two...one.... Holy God. Hang on!" The pinnace rocked so heavily that Kelsey thought it might tumble. Loud cheering sounded over the loop.

The captain let them have a moment before he cut them off. "Okay, men, it looks like we pissed them off. We have a lot of ships buzzing around the shipyard we just attacked, so keep your eyes open. We'll rendezvous with *Athena* before they catch up with us, but I don't know if

Empire of Bones

we'll make it to the flip point unmolested. Get unloaded as fast as you can."

"Don't let them get too close," Kelsey said. "They have some kind of knockout beam."

"Only some of their ships have those," the Royal pilot said. "Most have missiles. They never send many ships to capture prisoners. Those are smaller. Take those out first."

Jared gave him a thumbs-up. "We'll do that."

The chaotic trip to *Athena* was full of abrupt course changes. By the time they docked, Kelsey felt like she was going to fall off the bed even with the straps. The docking had absolutely no finesse whatsoever. The hatches opened, and men began streaming back into the ship.

Doctor Stone bulled her way through, pushing the medical unit ahead of her. She rushed Kelsey down the corridor with as much reckless abandon as their flight on the pinnace. The doctor commandeered a lift and took them directly to the medical center.

Full medical teams stood by, ready for anything from fixing a hangnail to apparently cutting Kelsey open again. "Get the regenerator ready," Stone snapped. "If we don't get these incisions healed now, she might have permanent scarring."

"I need to scan her implants first," a kid said. Kelsey eyed the boy in shock. How did a teenager get here?

The medical team prepared some device that looked so much like the tank that it made her nauseous. The boy smiled at her. "I'm Carl Owlet, and I'll be your computer technician today. I'm going to download your implant programming to be sure that nothing untoward is inside it."

"What will you do if there is?"

"Nothing right now, but we might try overwriting it later if we have to. This won't hurt a bit."

The words almost made Kelsey hyperventilate.

He put a headset with lots of cables onto her head. "I'm getting a positive signal, and the code is downloading. Her implants seem to be fully online."

That didn't make her feel very good at all.

The process took several minutes in which Doctor Stone looked ready to toss him and his computer out of the medical center. Carl seemed oblivious.

"Download complete. It's an exact match to the Old Empire marine code. No deviations detected. She is not under any external control."

Stone yanked the headset off and pushed Kelsey into the chamber.

"The regenerator is going to knock you out, Kelsey. I should be able to eliminate all of the scarring. The procedure will take five or six hours."

"Can you remove this stuff?"

The doctor's voice took on a note of regret. "I'm sorry, but no. That's so far beyond my ability that I'm afraid you might have to live with it. Maybe this new equipment will help to eventually remove it, but I wouldn't hold my breath."

Kelsey closed her eyes and tried not to cry. She was going to be a monster. Those things inside her head doing God only knew what.

"Princess?" It was Talbot's voice.

"Yes?" she whispered.

"No matter what happens, I'm here. We never leave one of our own behind. You'll never be alone dealing with this."

"Says the guy who didn't get cut open." She took a deep breath. "I'm sorry. That wasn't right. I brought this on myself."

"It was just bad luck, Princess. No one could know that damned ship was going to jump us. Sometimes life just takes a big old dump on you. You'll come back from this."

"Thank you. Thank you for saving me."

He laughed. "I seem to remember things a little differently. You shot one of them down and strangled the other one pretty much by yourself. It took the rest of us combined to take one out. Maybe you should look into a career in the marines."

"I'm told I'm too short and don't have the killer instinct."

"Whoever told you that was as wrong as a human being can be. I bet with some training, you'll be a real badass. That Pale One took two of us on with whatever the implants had programed in hand-to-hand combat. Think about what you could manage with some real training."

Stone cut him off. "I'm not sure this is the right time for this. Go let them examine you while I work on the princess. Time to start the regenerator. You okay in there, Kelsey?"

"Yes," she lied. She knew that she'd never be okay again. The regenerator plunged her into darkness.

29

Jared raced to the bridge, not bothering to strip off his battle armor...or full complement of grenades. Graves gave up the command console.

"Status?" Jared snapped.

"Three dozen ships came out of the shipyard and are on our ass," Graves said. "Several can cut us off before we can get clear of orbital space."

Jared leaned forward. "Zia, those ships may be of two different classes. Are any of them smaller than the rest?"

The tactical officer checked her readouts. "Five of the enemy ships will be in firing range before we can fully change course. One is somewhat smaller than the rest."

"Target that ship for the first salvo. It may have a weapon capable of knocking us out. I want you to turn it into expanding gas as soon as possible."

"Aye, sir. Firing now."

"Acknowledged." He turned to Graves. "Get to engineering. I want them ready for anything. If we have a systems failure, we're dead. Worse than dead. So that will not happen. Make sure Baxter has a plan to destroy this ship if I give the word."

The executive officer's face paled. "Understood." He ran to the lift.

"Zia, if we lose drives, keep shooting up the small ships as long as you can."

Her opening salvo proved to be overkill. The explosions blotted the ship from the heavens. Its companions opened fire with a pair of missiles each. They were larger and slower than those used by Fleet, but that hardly mattered at this fistfight range. All four enemy ships exploded after two salvos, but *Athena* took some hits. Thankfully, none to engineering.

That wasn't to say they were insignificant. A dozen compartments were open to space. Thankfully, with the Royal Marines on board, they had plenty of emergency responders.

Thirty enemy ships fell in behind them and continued firing. *Athena*'s electronic warfare suite was good enough to send many after false targets. The antimissile railguns mounted aft proved successful at stopping the rest, though a few were close enough to raise his hair.

Their own missiles wouldn't bear on the pursuit force, so they ran for their lives without shooting back. He pushed the engines harder than Baxter preferred, but he needed to open the range. One didn't transit a flip point at high speed, so they'd need to brake hard before they transitioned.

The range slowly opened to the point that the Pale Ones stopped firing. If *Athena* could hold this speed for a few hours, they'd come screaming into the Pentagar system with a few minutes warning that the second invasion was on.

Well, he didn't have to surprise the Royal Fleet. "Zia, record a message for the probe on station at the flip point. Have it send the agreed-upon signal when it transitions and then send the message."

"Aye, sir. Recording on."

Jared looked at the screen. "Commodore Sanders, we've recovered the prisoners and are less than two hours away from the flip point. We have thirty Pale Ones behind us, and I'm certain they're coming through after us. They didn't appreciate those fission weapons you gave us crippling their shipyard and destroying the orbital. We'd appreciate it if you could have a welcoming committee on hand for them. *Athena* out. Zia, append our scanner readings and send it."

The next two hours wracked everyone's nerves. It felt like he waited an hour, but when he checked the chrono, only a few minutes had passed. The damage reports came in. Another dozen of his crew dead and many more wounded.

Just when he started breathing a little easier, the enemy did something unexpected. They had ten minutes to go until flip, and the Pale Ones abruptly added twenty percent to their acceleration. One exploded outright and disabled another. Two more fell out of formation with drive failures. Twenty-six sped after them, closing range at a frightening rate.

Empire of Bones

"Zia, will we make it?"

She shook her head. "They'll be in firing range again with a minute to spare when we decelerate before the flip. They'll be all over us."

He opened a channel to engineering. "Baxter, they just boosted their acceleration. They're going to catch us. How much juice can you give me?"

"We might burn out the grav drives and kill everyone aboard."

"Or they might catch us and we'd only wish the drives had exploded."

"That's a point. I'll give you what I can. Engineering out."

Athena's speed edged up, but not nearly as much as that of their pursuers. Their precious lead eroded with each passing moment. Zia turned and shook her head. "They'll be in firing range before we can flip."

"Then we'd best hope our railguns hold out. Do the best you can to evade. If we transition, we might make it."

Another enemy drive failed before they moved into firing range, but that still meant a lot of missiles to deal with. The railguns and electronic countermeasures worked until they were thirty seconds short of the flip point. Even then, the evasive maneuvers kept the one missile that got through from hitting them in engineering. It struck them amidships.

The explosion ripped into the ship at an angle, spreading destruction from the midpoint of the ship forward. The impact staggered the ship and lit his control panel up with lurid damage and systems failure icons. Almost a quarter of the ship was open to space. One of the auxiliary consoles behind him shorted out with a loud "pop," and the stench of burned electronics filled the bridge.

Ramirez somehow kept them on course, and the countdown timer spiraled down toward zero. "Preparing to flip the ship," he said.

When the counter hit two, the ship took a second hit and main power went offline. The dim emergency lights came on, and Jared's heart flew into his throat. They were dead.

Then the ship flipped.

The transition rivaled the weak flip point experience for disorientation. The ship jerked so badly that it felt almost as if they'd struck something.

The screen still had power and showed them tumbling away from the flip point as Pale Ones flooded out behind them. Zia targeted one and opened fire. Only two missile tubes responded.

The Royal Fleet was waiting, thank God. They sat at just the right spot to intercept the intruders, firing their missiles at a high rate of speed. The few fortresses still online added to the destruction with their larger missiles.

The two fleets fought a missile duel at knife range. *Athena* destroyed three Pale Ones' ships in one salvo. She took a third missile hit and lost the remaining two missile tubes. Zia raked one of the Pale Ones with the antimissile railguns. The high-speed flechettes ripped the other ship open like a can of survival rations.

The fight moved past *Athena*'s dead hulk as the two sides mixed and fought. The Pale Ones knocked out some Royal units, but allied forces had the upper hand. Some Pale Ones broke through, but the Royal Fleet quickly chased them down. *Athena* managed to fend off the few missiles fired at her.

"Zia, get that probe back on the other side," Jared said. "I want to have warning if more ships are coming. If a ship approaches the flip point, we need to know about it."

"Aye, sir."

He keyed the channel to engineering. "Damage report."

"We're totally screwed," Baxter said.

Jared could hear some kind of alarm ringing in the background. "That's not helpful. I need more details."

"Both fusion plants fried just before the transition. Safeties shut them down, and it'll take a while to get them back online. Thank God we had the flip capacitors charged, or we'd still be on the other side. I'm not sure how much use the fusion plants will be even if we get them back up and running. The grav and flip drives are offline again. Oh, and our structural integrity is compromised."

"Compromised how?"

"I think we came into the flip point sideways at high speed. The grav drives failed right before transition, and we slewed. The stress forces warped the ship's spine."

"Can that be fixed?"

"No. *Athena* will never boost again."

Jared covered his eyes with his hand. "Understood. Bridge out."

He didn't bother calling the medical center. They'd be swamped.

Zia turned her seat to face him. "I have Commodore Sanders calling."

"Put him on."

The older man appeared on the screen. "Thank the gods you're alive. I'm launching medical teams and damage-control parties to assist you."

"We need them. Thanks. Did you get all the Pale Ones?"

The commodore nodded with satisfaction. "Every last one of them.

Hopefully that was enough to blunt the invasion, because our defenses are in very bad shape right now. What's your status?"

"Our drives and power systems have failed. We've taken critical structural damage."

"Do you need to abandon ship? We have cutters standing by."

Jared shook his head. "I don't think so, but I doubt *Athena* will ever leave Pentagar. If you could assist us with evacuating all nonessential personnel, that would be helpful. I'm sorry, but I don't have word on your people's status. Most of us made it back from the raid, but we took some major knocks when we transitioned."

"We'll figure that out as soon as we get you the help you need. Sanders out."

* * *

HARD WORK FILLED the next few hours. A lot of the ship was open to space or in danger of becoming uninhabitable without emergency repairs. The extra hands from the Pentagaran ships helped, but the list of things to do seemed endless.

An exhausted Doctor Stone called him with the final battle tally. Miraculously, only eighty-five people died in battle after the Pale Ones captured the princess and her protection detail: thirty Royal Marines, five Imperial Marines, and fifty-eight Fleet personnel. A heartbreaking number of friends and shipmates were gone.

Graves coordinated damage control from the bridge, finally allowing Jared enough time to check on the princess. Wounded filled the corridor outside the medical center. He stopped and spoke with them as he made his way in. He was amazed to find most appeared to be in good spirits.

Kelsey would probably tell him that he should've let her die or be enslaved. She wouldn't see the trade as worthwhile. Seven people saved in exchange for more than ten times that number killed, twice that injured, and *Athena* wrecked beyond repair.

And she'd be wrong.

Fleet didn't abandon their own. They weren't suicidal, but these Pale Ones weren't the kind of enemy you let take prisoners. If they learned of the Empire, Avalon would've been in grave danger.

This fight was going to happen anyway. An enemy invasion would've overrun Pentagar in a month or two. It was better to strike now and trade dozens of people for the billions that would've perished in the invasion.

Royal personnel in white smocks filled the medical center. At this point, they were setting bones and stitching cuts. Most of his medical personnel were probably dead on their feet.

Stone stood beside a regenerator, examining the readouts. She looked up as he approached. Her eyes were black pits of exhaustion. "Captain."

"Lily. How is she?"

"Asleep. The regenerator can repair the incisions, but I don't dare mess with the physical modifications. I'm certain the implantation procedure should've taken place in stages so the patient could recover. The trauma to her body may cause any number of problems going forward."

He looked through the window. She looked so vulnerable. "How long will she be regenerating?"

"At least three more hours. Then she can come out and I can begin a more detailed assessment. We think the Pale Ones could recover physiologically without intervention, but we don't know how many of them died because of the gross insult to their bodies. Princess Kelsey will most likely recover, but she will have to relearn her gross and fine motor skills. Things like walking. Shaking hands."

Stone turned to face Jared. "She has artificial musculature inserted alongside her real muscles, and her bones are reinforced by material stronger than the hull on this ship. Talbot told me she grabbed a Pale One by the throat and strangled him. I'd really hate to lose all the bones in my hand in a handshake gone awry."

Jared could hardly believe the petite woman in the regeneration chamber could break anything. She didn't look like she could resist a bully on a school playground.

The doctor rubbed her eyes. "She's going to recover physically, eventually, but she's going to need a lot of emotional support. She's been raped in every conceivable way except sexually. She's going to be in a very dark place."

"I'll be here for her. We'll all be here for her. We're family."

The doctor gave him an odd look, but he put it down to her exhaustion. He clapped his hand on her shoulder. "Catch some sleep in your office. Today isn't over. We still have a lot left to do."

30

The white ceiling confused Kelsey when she woke. Her cabin's ceiling was grey. Then the events of the day caught up with her and she almost moaned. She clumsily raised her arm and stared at it. There were no scars.

At least on the outside.

She finally realized this room wasn't on *Athena*. The wide windows displayed a bright blue sky. She was on Pentagar.

"Princess Bandar, it's so good to see you awake."

She turned her head toward the jovial man in the white smock coming into her room. She felt like she should say something, but her mind swirled with too many questions. Saying it was good to be awake seemed too much like a lie.

The man patted her arm. "I'm Doctor Trenton Plant. You're at Capital Hospital on Pentagar. You're doing very well."

The unsaid addition "all things considered" hung in the air between them.

"Tell me what happened. Is everyone else okay?" Her voice sounded so weak.

His expression didn't change, but his eyes radiated sympathy. "I'll let Doctor Stone bring you up to speed. She'd give me one of her patented parental looks if I didn't wait for her. She was sleeping, but I've summoned her."

Doctor Lily Stone walked through the door just in time to hear that.

The only sign she'd slept was her mussed hair. "Nonsense. I'd just tap my foot. Kelsey, you're looking better. All things considered."

Kelsey's chuckle earned her some curious looks. "Sorry. I was just thinking that."

Stone shook her head. "You're going to recover. You've already made quite a bit of progress."

"I've been asleep."

"And you've healed. The regeneration was completely successful. There isn't any remaining scar tissue."

"The scars seem like the least of my worries. Tell me what happened."

Stone gave Doctor Plant a glance, and the man graciously headed for the door. "I'll check on a few other patients and give the two of you time to catch up."

Once he was gone, Stone pulled up a chair and sat. "Some doctors might sugarcoat things, but I believe in putting everything on the table. *Athena* suffered a lot of damage during the escape. We obviously made it back here, but it's not livable. The Kingdom has all of our wounded here in this hospital, and they're providing some excellent care."

A chill passed down Kelsey's spine. "How bad is it? Please tell me no one died."

The haunted flicker across Stone's face told the princess all she needed to know. "How many?"

"Eighty-five."

Kelsey closed her eyes and felt the tears start. "God. You should've left me there."

"Listen to me," Stone said firmly. "The Pale Ones were preparing to invade again within weeks. We used a fission weapon to damage the shipyard and another one to destroy the station they took you to. If we hadn't fought them now, we would've been fighting much more serious odds shortly. Those people would've almost certainly died right along with all the rest of the people in this system. Billions of innocent people. We couldn't allow that to happen."

"That doesn't help so much. Jared wouldn't have come after us if I hadn't been there. He'd have figured out another plan. One that didn't mean rushing in. And he did it for a lie. I'm not even his half sister."

"Blood doesn't make relationships," Lily said softly. "Look, I can't stop you from tearing yourself up over this, but I wish you'd give us all some credit. We came because it was the right thing to do. We all knew that it might result in our deaths. Don't make their sacrifice be for nothing."

Kelsey tried to wipe her tears, but her hands were so clumsy. She was

Empire of Bones

lucky she didn't put her eye out. Stone found a tissue and wiped Kelsey's eyes as the terrible sobs wracked her body.

When she finally cried herself out, Kelsey felt completely spent. This had all happened because of her. It was her fault. She'd insisted they come out and wait for Jared. Her petty anger had killed so many people.

She looked over at Stone. "How long before we can go back to *Athena?*"

"I'm afraid that isn't going to happen. The ship is a complete loss. She'll never fly again."

It took a few moments for the doctor's words to sink in. The sheer scope of the disaster took her breath away. Her throat swelled closed. She'd doomed them. They'd never get home.

"Stop," Stone commanded. "A ship is just a machine. The Pentagarans will help us get home. They've already promised everything we need to convert a ship for our use. You need to stop focusing on what happened and look to your own recovery. Are you ready to talk about what they did to you?"

Kelsey swallowed and nodded.

Stone squeezed her arm. "The good news is that the science teams are pretty sure that no control code was put in your head. They don't understand much of what is there, but it seems to be identical to the Old Empire code. You will not become a Pale One."

"I suppose that's the best that can be hoped for. I thought I was going to die when they cut me open. Then I wished I had."

"Yet here you are. As near as I can tell, your physical modifications are the same as the Old Empire's marines. You're going to have a lot of rehabilitation in your near future."

"I know. I feel like I'm so clumsy. I don't think I could walk if I had to. My eyes still aren't focusing right, though it's a lot better than it was."

"We'll deal with all that in time."

Kelsey sighed. "I suppose I'm lucky. At least I get this second chance. Did Talbot make it?"

Stone nodded. "He did. He'd still be sitting in the chair over there if I hadn't made him get something to eat. I'm sure he'll be back as soon as he hears you're awake."

A rap at the door made Kelsey turn her head. Jared stood in the door smiling at her. "Look who's awake."

Stone stood. "We'll talk later, Kelsey. Just rest for now." She nodded to Jared and walked out.

He took the seat the doctor had just vacated. "You look a lot better than the last time I saw you."

"You should've seen the other guy. Jared, I'm so sorry. I really, really screwed up."

He shook his head. "You had no reason to think something like this would happen. I've given this a lot of thought, and the order of things might have changed if you hadn't come out to the flip point, but the results would've been the same or worse. You know they crippled the ship, right?"

Kelsey nodded. "Doctor Stone told me. What will we do?"

"Make do. Commodore Sanders assures me that the Pentagarans will be starting new ship construction that includes flip drives before the month is out. They'll name one of those ships *Athena* and task her to take us home.

"They believe that our intervention—especially the trip to rescue you—saved their planet. Now, instead of an overwhelming invasion in a few months, they'll likely be able to knock out the shipyards before the Pale Ones get back on a war footing. I'm inclined to agree, though the public adulation freaks me out a little."

"I'm pretty sure that adulation won't be the first thing that comes to mind when they see me."

He shook his head and smiled a little. "You couldn't tell that from the number of people who've tried to come see you. I think every single man and woman from *Athena* has come by at one time or another. There's been so many flowers delivered that I hear they had to stop putting them in the chapels. There wasn't room for them and people. I know that many Pentagarans have sent their own well wishes. You'll be reading get-well and thank-you notes until the end of time."

The idea that people she didn't even know were writing her made her head spin. "Why would they do that? They don't even know me."

"You've captured their hearts and imaginations. You're the mysterious beautiful foreign princess who arrived just in time to save their world."

"Thank you for the compliment, but you saved them. I've been more a hindrance than a help on this trip. My coming was the worst idea ever."

"I disagree. You are the soul of our expedition. We fight for what's right, and you embody that for so many of us. People would and did give their lives for you. Not because you're royalty, but because you're you."

She wanted to scream. "I'm not the person everyone seems to think I am! I'm such a colossal screw-up. I'm a fraud."

"Everyone is a fraud," he said calmly. "People make us out to be things we're not and then we have to work hard not to disappoint them.

Empire of Bones

You can't sit around blaming yourself and feeling sorry. You have to pick yourself up. For them. For all those people who need you. For all the people who gave everything for you."

Her voice was almost a whisper. "I don't know how you do it."

"One day at a time." He rose to his feet. "I have to go meet with the Royal Family. They've also sent their well wishes, and I'm sure they'll come to visit soon. Focus on getting better, Kelsey. We all need you."

He gave her arm one last squeeze and walked out.

She lay there trying to understand what had just happened. Why weren't they blaming her for all the terrible things that had happened? It was obscene how many people had died because of her petulant anger. Her entitled arrogance.

She wasn't blind to the fact that Jared had just masterfully manipulated her. Even so, she couldn't discount his words. She had to change. She wouldn't let all those people down. She'd work hard to recover and then do everything in her power to be who they needed her to be. To be worthy of them.

Not that she had any idea how to do that. She'd work with Jared. They had to be a team if they were going to get home. The future would take care of itself.

Kelsey found the call button and pressed it. She had a lot of work to do.

MAILING LIST

Want the next book in the series? Grab *Veil of Shadows*
today or any of Terry's other books below.

Want Terry to email you when he publishes a new book in any format or when one goes on sale? Go to TerryMixon.com/Mailing-List and sign up. Those are the only times he'll contact you.
No spam.

Did you enjoy the book? Please leave a review on Amazon or
Goodreads. It only takes a minute to dash off a few sentences and
that kind of thing helps more than you can imagine.

You can always find the most up to date listing of Terry's titles on
his Amazon Author Page.

The Empire of Bones Saga
Empire of Bones
Veil of Shadows
Command Decisions
Ghosts of Empire
Paying the Price
Reconnaissance in Force
Behind Enemy Lines
The Terran Gambit

The Empire of Bones Saga Volume 1

The Humanity Unlimited Saga
Liberty Station
Freedom Express
Tree of Liberty

The Fractured Republic Saga
Storm Divers

The Scorched Earth Saga
Scorched Earth

The Vigilante Duology with Glynn Stewart
Heart of Vengeance
Oath of Vengeance

ABOUT TERRY

#1 Bestselling Military Science Fiction author Terry Mixon served as a non-commissioned officer in the United States Army 101st Airborne Division. He later worked alongside the flight controllers in the Mission Control Center at the NASA Johnson Space Center supporting the Space Shuttle, the International Space Station, and other human spaceflight projects.

He now writes full time while living in Texas with his lovely wife and a pounce of cats.

www.TerryMixon.com
Terry@terrymixon.com

http://www.facebook.com/TerryLMixon

https://www.amazon.com/Terry-Mixon/e/B00J15TJFM